RAVEN MOON

Raven Chronicles
Book 5

Deborah Cannon

ISBN-13: 978-1979965767
ISBN-10: 1979965765

Also by Deborah Cannon:

The Raven Chronicles Series:
Raven Dawn
The Raven's Pool
White Raven
Ravenstone
Raven's Blood

Close Encounters of the Cryptid Kind (Kindle)
Crowd Demon
Lightning Snake
The Hooded Bird
Water Wolf
The Bigfoot Murder
The Loch Monster
Tunnel Terror

Short Story Collections:
Wolfbird and other Stories
Tales of the Raven

For Aubrey

PROLOGUE

The Giant's Dance stands on the south end of a broad plain about eight miles north of the city of Salisbury and two miles west of Amesbury. It is the high spot of the densest concentration of open-air temples anywhere in Europe and it was why the archaeologist of ancient religions stood on the grassy downs at its midpoint, spinning her web. She was actually twirling her body, childlike, with her arms outstretched in ecstasy.

People drew attention to her by whispering and staring, and pointing to the sign:

No Visitors Beyond This Point

She danced for fifteen minutes before anyone bothered to stop her, and when she defied the tour operators and security guards, they summoned the area police.

Blue uniformed officers sprinted across the grass while rope barriers held the crowds back. A man with a nightstick fingered it warningly. "Come dear. No folks are permitted inside the barriers."

She hurriedly added the finishing touches where she had scratched the sacred emblem. *Quick now*. The time of the Handfast approached.

"I'm warning you. I don't want any violence. Don't make me use force."

In the background she heard the tourists gossiping about her. "She must be crazy," they said, tapping their heads. "Looney."

"All right. That's enough. What are you doing? You're defacing a national monument!" The young officer climbed over the barrier, another crawled under it to assist him. They lunged at her, and missed.

Oh, how they missed!

Facing the wide-open vista, the wind whined in her ears and beat on her skin. The crowds and the Giant's Dance vanished. In their place was a completely different scene. The swelling hill and plain of the high chalk downs ran westward. A great earthwork and several interlocking stone circles shaped the landscape. The arc of the outer pillars was so great that it hemmed in part of the village, and the houses and roads obscured its original plan. At the town core a winding lane led from a car park to a charming thatch-roofed inn. As her eyes revolved to take in the vastness she perceived an enormous moat with a bank at its rim. Here stood the remains of a ring of standing stones—originally one hundred in total and the largest of its kind. That was why she had chosen the ruins of this temple.

Parts of two smaller features survived, each containing their own configuration of stones. And there—there was the remnants of what they called the Cove. It was in this spot that the transformation must take place.

To the north was the first of four entrances to the sacred site. From the south and west entrances avenues of megaliths coursed for miles. One of these was the entrance to the Great Stones Way.

Excitement rippled through her body as she inhaled the view.

It works! The ancient magic still exists!

Swiftly, before the spell broke, she scored the same symbol she had left on one of the massive sarsens at the Giant's Dance. Then she flung her gaze to the sky. Moaning an incantation, she spoke with her mind's eye.

A murder of black birds appeared from nowhere and settled on the peaks above her head. She watched them, and they glared back.

She focused her attention to the temple, concentrating as though the stones themselves had ears.

Find him. Bring him to me.

With that she found herself back at the Giant's Dance, in the arms of the law. They were astounded as she landed in their midst beside a bulging stone. This time they did not hesitate to seize her, handcuff her and take her down to the station.

She wasn't there long. She laughed, a short, ringing laugh. When she told the police at the station what she had done, they conveyed her to exactly where she wanted to be.

"How are you feeling?" a quiet but authoritative voice asked her.

"A little tired," she answered. "But otherwise quite well."

She was propped up in bed, supported by thick pillows. Her head felt a bit woozy and a bitter taste lingered on her tongue.

"Do you know where you are?"

"Yes," she said. "I'm in hospital."

The official-looking man who she assumed was a psychiatrist nodded. "Do you know why you're here?"

She dipped her chin in the affirmative. "Because of what I told the nice policeman."

"Do you believe what you told him?"

"Yes."

He paused. "I'm afraid we will have to keep you a few more days for observation. Do you have any next of kin? Anyone close to you?"

A woman in nurse's uniform walked into the room at that moment with a tray carrying a hypodermic needle. She paused, startled. "Who are you?" she asked the stranger disguised as a doctor. He was no one she even remotely recognized. "What are you doing in this room?" She glanced quickly from him to the bed, then back again. "Doctor will be in to see you shortly. But you, sir, will have to leave. Visiting Hours are over."

"Not just yet." The official-looking man removed the white lab coat he had borrowed to reveal a smartly cut suit, and fetched a badge from his breast pocket. "MOD," he said. "Military Intelligence. I have orders to remove this woman to a secure location."

PART 1: THE HANGING STONES

<u>CHAPTER ONE</u>

Jake Lalonde, archaeologist and expert in raven iconography, lobbed a jacket and a couple of shirts onto the quaint, handmade country-style quilt now shoved to one side of the bed from a night of restless sleep. He was jetlagged by the flight from Seattle to London. To save a few bucks he had caught a train directly from Heathrow Airport and made his way to Cambridge, then to Swindon. From there he had rented a car to convey him to Avebury, and hence to Mrs. Dixon's Bed and Breakfast. It was a long journey, but he had better things to do with his meagre professor's salary than to squander it on cabs and lavish hotels.

So you've come.

The voice had appeared in his mind unexpectedly, and he waited a moment to savour her presence before he replied:

I'm always here, no matter where you are.

For as long as he could recall her companionship had been near. Was this some kind of telepathy? Or was he bordering on insane?

He only knew that her presence was like a piece of a puzzle. She belonged with him. She made him whole. And although her face was a mystery to him he no longer pursued her identity. She was female and she spoke inside his head. That was enough.

His stomach grumbled; his mouth watered. The savoury

aromas of sausages and eggs percolated up from the kitchen and almost persuaded him to change his mind about skipping breakfast.

Only thirty-five minutes to shower and dress. Socks, underwear, blue jeans. Where were the breakfast bars? The corner of something rectangular jutted up from between his extra pair of shoes. He ripped open the box of granola snacks and tore open the wrapper of one. He shoved honey-coated oatmeal and nuts down his throat with one hand while extricating his shaving kit with the other. He rose to head for the shower and was stopped at the sight of something now exposed inside the crowded suitcase.

Where had that come from? He swallowed the last lump of crunchy granola, crumpling the wrapper into a ball and discarding it onto the floor. He disengaged the strange plastic bag and shook it. Was this a lock of somebody's hair? Black hair with a lovely bluish sheen, it was long and carefully coiled to fit snugly inside the plastic bag.

When he opened it a subtle fragrance sent a shockwave throughout his system.

Is this yours?

Silence. He closed his eyes. She was fickle with her conversation. Often she would appear just to let him know she was close, and then she would vanish for days. Whenever he asked her specific questions, she resisted answering them.

Who was she?

The therapist he had sought help from was no help at all. Imagination, he had insisted. Or was it hallucination? He was lucky they had not locked him away.

Jake's gaze dropped to the hair once more. It was not Serena's. She had gone from redhead to brunette to raven-haired several times over—although what her current shade was drew a blank. All he knew was that they were together and they were... happy? He once asked her (long before they became engaged) whether or not she suspected she possessed telepathic abilities. After all, she was familiar with his facility to commune with his ancestors…. well it was best not to think about that. The memories of visits to therapists and psychological tests were unpleasant. Serena warned that it could mean his job if he persisted. However this wasn't the same, and when he asked, she sniggered and said, "Of course I can read your mind, darling. You and I, we are simpatico."

Widening the plastic bag's opening, he spilled the hair onto his left hand.

He was due to marry Serena Dunnel, the marine archaeologist from California, in two weeks. They had met at a conference in Vancouver years ago, and he believed this voice, this female presence that comforted him in his hour of need must be her. Because—although she was evasive when he spoke of the mind link—who else could it be?

The irony struck him. If the voice belonged to her, she would already know.

Fine, soft and silky, he sensed without question that the contents of this plastic bag did not belong to her—and yet, sending him off with a lock of her hair was exactly the type of narcissistic thing she might do.

He zipped the bag closed, and tucked it into a side pouch of his suitcase. He struggled to his feet, recovered his bathrobe from the tumbled clothes on the bed, and went out into the quiet hallway in search of the guest bathroom.

CHAPTER TWO

He should have phoned Serena before leaving, but he hadn't. Now there was no time. The ground darkened under his training shoes from a crowd of black huddling in the tree above of his head. Every few minutes he heard a throaty *quorking* sound, which made him look up. A warning shuddered up his spine.

Ravens were not a sign of impending doom—contrary to superstition.

The stench of guano invaded his nostrils mingled with wet grass, cow dung and herby wildflowers. The terrain was bleak, adding to the ominous feel. He hurried under the cluster of birds. Three hundred ravens were roosting in that tree. The wind blustered across the meadow, biting his face. It lashed at his hair and clothes as he batted grit from his eyes. The scenery had a watercolor quality about it. Wet and windswept the vast meadowland sank below a heavy slate sky. The dampness reached his bones and he ached for a glimpse of the sun.

He had lost his way a few times on his way up from Swindon, never having driven on this side of 'the great pond' before. His cellphone had died and the Scion he had rented contained a broken GPS. Perhaps he had abandoned the rental prematurely, but he felt more confident trusting his feet and his eyes—than a piece of technology.

The village sat on the edge of the chalky high country, furrowed with hedgerows that rolled into flat downs. Scattered stone and thatched cottages lined the base of the hills and the fields were fenced with barbed wire. Through rockroses, harebells and trefoils, he trudged, passing some twisted trees along the way. The ancient barrows—mounds that once interred the Bronze Age dead—formed a ghostly background against the skyline, and further on was the misty outline of Silbury Hill.

A strange figure moved in the near distance. It was a man, and either he was dressed in a medieval costume of wool tunic, leggings and wooden clogs, with a pouch-like satchel on his shoulder or he was some homeless guy who had cobbled together whatever he could find to serve as clothing. As they approached one another, the man's appearance grew clearer, and Jake could see how grimy he was although he oddly complemented the landscape. A few minutes later a mysterious welling of fog rose from the ground burying them both.

"Hi there, you look lost. Can I help you?"

Jake rotated on his heel to catch the most beautiful woman he had ever seen materialize out of the floating miasma. She was medium height, slender. Her face glowed in the fuzzy morning light, cheeks slightly flushed and eyes radiant. Her legs were clad in tight jeans with a loose white blouse beneath a tailored tweed jacket, and her dark hair fell soft and heavy on slightly padded shoulders.

"Hey," he said. From her accent he could tell she was not British. To make up for his awkwardness he pointed a finger downhill at the billowing fog where every now and then a massive greyish block appeared like a fairytale troll turned to stone. "That's Avebury?"

"Yes."

"And the Alexander Keiller Museum…?"

"You're almost there. I'm headed that way myself. I'll show you."

By now he had composed himself and followed her in the direction she indicated. They saw no one else as they continued to walk.

"You're from out of town," she said.

"I'm an archaeologist from Seattle, USA."

"I know where Seattle is," she said, and grinned.

"You're not from around here either?" he asked.

"No, I'm not."

Her answers were curiously brief. Was she going to tell him where she was from? She was delightfully reserved unlike most Americans, who couldn't wait to tell a stranger their entire life story. Was she Canadian?

When she failed to enlighten him, he asked, "Are you a tourist?"

"I wish."

He chuckled. "I can only conclude by that response that you are married to some very lucky Brit." His eye caught the glint of a diamond ring on her left hand. Excellent call. Well, maybe not married, but certainly engaged.

From where they were they could see more of the stones of Avebury peeking out of the moving fog. "Surreal, isn't it?" she said. "No matter how many times I see it, the stones never fail to leave me breathless."

They stood at the edge of a circle so large that the eye could not capture it entirely. Jake made out the crest of the ditch, and the shapes of the standing stones. The ancient temple surrounded much of the entire town, and that was what made it so unique, she explained. It also consisted of more than one feature. In the center of the humungous ring were two smaller ones—the North Circle and the South Circle. Pathways, originally lined with parallel stones, but now marked by white wooden posts, crisscrossed the diameter. An earthwork in the form of a ditch and a high, chalk rubble bank surrounded the whole.

"You know a lot about this stone circle," he said, impressed.

"It's sort of my job to know," she answered. "Over the centuries the site was the focus of mysterious activities, which included a frenzy of religious paranoia causing villagers in the fourteenth century to bury many of the pagan stones."

He had heard this story. How four hundred years later,

most of the remaining stones were toppled, heated by open fires, doused with cold water until they fragmented, and then were broken up into building blocks for houses and farm buildings. What they were seeing now were the labors of recent excavations. What stones could be found were dug up and re-erected in their original positions.

"They're spectacular," Jake commented.

"In shear size, they are so much larger than those at Stonehenge. In fact, to really appreciate the size of this circle, it must be seen from the air. If you have time while you're visiting you should take a helicopter tour."

"I will," Jake said. He paused then asked, "How much do one of those blocks weigh?"

"Between ten and a hundred tons." She smiled. "You don't seem to know too much about this heritage site for someone who purports to be interested in the area."

"Did I purport that?" Jake asked.

"You said you were an archaeologist."

"Yeah, but not an archaeologist of everything." He chuckled good-naturedly. "I study Northwest Coast archaeology and Raven iconography."

"Ah."

The way she said that single syllable was a little disturbing. Why should his interest in the prehistory of America's Northwest Coast disturb her? Or was it the Raven?

She suddenly changed the subject. "Have you been in England long?"

"Actually, I just arrived last night."

"So you missed the good weather. It was so nice the past few days, sunny and warm, and now this. We're not usually socked in this time of year."

No matter how he tried to steer the conversation back to the Raven, she insisted on chatting about the uncompromising local weather. Ravens she said always knew when it was going to rain. They gathered in clusters.

Jake sent a backwards glance at the flock of ravens he

had passed earlier; then looked up at the hurrying clouds. It was going to rain? And yet, by the time they left the downs the fog had cleared.

A patch of sunlight drenched the grass, sparkling the dew. The young woman raised her hands to the warmth. They were both damp but the climate Jake decided agreed with her. Only English girls had skin like that. Then he remembered that her accent was not English, and her features had a delicate Asian cast about them.

She was a good listener and he found himself telling her all about his trip up from London. Her presence made him forget about everything except basking in her company. It was proving to be a pleasant morning and he wished the museum were miles away. He was enjoying his time with her so much that he wanted to stretch it out as long as possible. Unfortunately, they were closer to town than he had thought. They had spent less than fifteen minutes together.

"I have to leave you here, but it's not far. Just follow that path. I have an errand to run for the museum. We're expecting a guest speaker." Her lips curled compellingly, and he felt the strangest flutter in his chest. "Maybe I'll see you again?"

For the first time in his life Jake Lalonde was at a loss for words. After a few seconds of silence she sent him her sparkling smile, and left him in the laneway. He stood mesmerized, before he realized he had forgotten to ask her name. But at least he knew she had something to do with the museum.

***

A dirty brick cottage with a rusty lean-to shed and a **No Parking** sign in front of a church appeared as he entered the village. To his left and right were souvenir shops, public lavatories and car parks.

The road led around some dark-tiled brick houses with plain dormers over the windows to a row of terraced cottages creeping with lavender. The scent of the herb was a welcome reprieve after the smell back on the downs. The museum was further along the lane and beyond it he caught the glimpse of a manor with a flagstone pathway and manicured topiary. The limestone and sarsen walls were studded with lead-glazed windows thick with hanging vines.

The door to the museum was propped open, and he walked in and up to the front desk. Someone dressed like a custodian lifted his head. Before Jake could speak, the man said, "Dr. Lalonde? Mrs. Pickerton is expecting you. She asked me to escort you outside to the circle."

Jake's eyes flitted to a stack of half unwrapped, brown paper parcels on the desk and gave the custodian an accommodating smile. "I can see you're busy. Just point me in the right direction. I'm sure I can find her."

Standing once again in the laneway, Jake's immediate impression was of awe. The stones stood like soldiers all around the field. His mysterious guide across the downs had told him that no one knew their purpose, although some believed they related to the worship of a Celtic deity. Human hands had not shaped the stones, but had erected them; and they were chosen for their natural forms. The tall rectangular shapes she had said represented the male, and the squatter more diamond-like forms were representative of the female. In fact, in the South Circle, there was originally an obelisk that represented a male phallus, and in the North Circle was a group of three female stones called, by local myth, the Cove. Apparently they were aligned with the northerly rise of the moon.

Someone stood on the landscape. Jake had been expecting to see throngs of tourists, but this person worked alone. She was dressed in a white blouse, sleeves three-quarters rolled, and black pants. He fumbled in his pocket for the computer printout the museum curator had sent him, and glanced briefly at it before refolding and shoving it back into his jeans. A harrowing shadow descended and he realized that the ravens had followed his trek over the downs. He refrained from inhaling too deeply. Frankly, the air stank, and he knew what was causing it.

Jake waved a hand in front of his nose as the curator greeted him. She had phoned his B&B last night to welcome him and to provide directions. He smiled. "I see what you meant about the birds."

"Frightful nuisance," she replied, returning his smile from under straight-cut bangs. She gave his appearance a once over. Denim jacket, black T-shirt, faded blue jeans—the universal uniform of the archaeologist—and identified him instantly. "So glad to finally meet you, Dr. Lalonde. I'm Maia Pickerton."

She dropped the rag she had been using to clean the stone's surface.

"It's really strange," she said, plucking off her surgical gloves and adding them to a growing mound of rags. "We have never experienced wildlife activity of this nature before. Ravens are mostly found in Scotland and Wales; God knows what they're doing in Wiltshire. It's not like this is lambing season or anything. It has really become a nuisance. All that guano has ruined the start of the tourist season. But not to worry, I have a specialist arriving any minute to help us figure out the whole mess." She offered her right hand, apologizing for being caught in the act of such an unpleasant task, and Jake clasped it in a warm handshake.

She was concerned about the absence of tourists, she explained. The National Trust lacked funds to upgrade and rebuild the site to its original splendor as had been done at Stonehenge. Stonehenge was not accessible to the public in the same way as Avebury's ancient temple. Here, visitors were free to wander at will, while at Stonehenge they must view the site from behind rope barriers. So while the latter was certainly picturesque, it looked exactly the way one would see it in a book. Avebury on the other hand was a total physical experience limited only by the visitor's endurance and imagination.

Her enthusiasm and loyalty to Avebury's stone circle

was contagious. The new reconstructive work at Stonehenge had drawn away most of the foreign and even many of the local visitors. They were no longer bothering with the side trip north, and she wondered whether the flocking ravens would further frighten them away.

Jake found himself hoping he could help but how she thought he could help remained to be seen. She had lured him away from his job of Associate Professor at the University of Washington when she stumbled upon his work in the Pacific Northwest. She had read his thesis on the Raven icon, how the mythical figure might have once been a shaman. He was the first archaeologist to extensively investigate and record the Raven's migration and, so far, he had documented its movement from Siberia down the west coast of North America and across the South Pacific to the Tongan Islands. Last year he had even recorded a new historical link, which had led him to Italy.

Now he was in England, and he was skeptical as to why his expertise was relevant. It was uncanny that he had found himself here.

It began with a nightmare of a spinning megalith much like the giant stone the curator was showing him now (only, of course, this one wasn't spinning). A face had emerged from it, shocking him awake—a face that was familiar and yet was not. It was a man's face, someone he thought he should know, but for the life of him he could not place. The next day Maia Pickerton had emailed him and sent him the photograph.

CHAPTER THREE

Jake turned as a man wandered up to them. The 'specialist,' he presumed. The specialist was tall and oddly dressed for an excursion into the countryside. Under a beige trench coat he wore a navy blue suit and yellow tie, and slung over his shoulder was a nylon satchel just large enough to fit a computer tablet.

"Mr. Chancellor," Maia Pickerton said. "I'm glad you're here. Did you have any trouble finding us?"

"Not too much. I used the GPS on the rental." He thumbed toward the town center where he had parked near the Red Lion Pub. Then he raised his head to the group of ravens that had stirred on his arrival. "Quite a spectacle, I see. Read about it in the *Daily Mail*." He refocused his attention on the curator. "So how can I be of service?"

The man was a foreigner. In contrast to the curator's prim and proper upper crust accent, he sounded like an American news anchorman.

"Dr. Lalonde, this is Thomas Chancellor, an authority on the paranormal. He is in the capital for the World Congress on Paranormal Sightings, and has kindly taken time out from his schedule to help me."

Whoa, he thought. *This is not exactly Armageddon. It's a perfectly normal behavior quite explainable by science.* Still, what was the big deal? The birds were doing nothing but perching in the thousands on the megaliths, offending visitors with their guano, and creating a stench to beat all stenches.

"Now that you're both here, there's something I want to show you," Maia said. "The reason why I asked you both to join me in the first place."

Jake breathed shallowly, attempting not to be distracted by the odor surrounding them. He was confused as to which object the curator's vision was fixed. She seemed to be spellbound by the stone perched in front of them, but she had stepped back and was indicating with her hands that they should do so, too. He back-peddled a few paces, but noticed nothing. Was her gaze fastened to the view beyond the stone, rather than the stone itself?

The huge sarsen stood at the north entrance, at the head of the avenue leading away from the town of Swindon. Filling in the landscape were grassy fields and thatched-roof cottages where sheep and cows grazed on the early summer grass.

"I was really hoping Ms. Lune could join us, too, for this excursion."

Jake perked up at the name Maia had just mentioned. While the local archaeology was interesting, Jake's primary reason for accepting Maia Pickerton's invitation was not the archaeology, or the strange appearance of thousands of ravens in the stone circle, or even the photograph she had emailed him. The reason he was here was to confront the woman Diana Lune, a self-admitted adventurer and antiquarian who had written a series of outlandish books, twisting archaeological theories in the most nonsensical ways. Her latest release, entitled *Sacred Stones of Raven,* proposed that Native Americans crossed the Atlantic Ocean sometime in prehistory and built the megalithic monument of Avebury.

It was all a bunch of crock of course, except that this wasn't the first time such a theory had been postulated. In 1883 an amateur named W.S. Blacket proposed that Appalachian Indians and their priests erected the temple of Stonehenge. It was published in his treatise *Researches into the Lost Histories of America,* which naturally no scholar took seriously. Jake would have left it alone if it wasn't for the fact that this modern amateur was impinging on his turf and tainting his research. He was an expert in the field of Raven iconography and migration theory, and had shown, scientifically, links between cultures that exhibited the icon in prehistoric as well as historic art and religion. It was a field where one trod lightly and cautiously, and made certain to back up one's arguments before presenting evidence to the academic world. Ridicule was always just around the corner. And he didn't need this Diana Lune, who could well *be* a loon (he would reserve judgment until he had heard what she had to say) to tarnish his credibility.

He would soon have a chance to confront her. She was delivering a talk at the museum tonight. As soon as he could free himself from the curator and her 'paranormal bird behaviorist" he was out of here to prepare his response.

"Her train might have been delayed," Chancellor said. "As I was driving up I heard on the radio that there were some delays due to an electrical problem."

"Train delays? Well, that's unfortunate. I was hoping she could meet you both to consult on this matter before the lecture. As you know"—Maia glanced over in the direction of the museum—"she is coming down from Glasgow to present a special talk this evening. "But I did wish to obtain your opinions before tonight's events, so as to make it a more lively discussion after her presentation. I can't stress enough how important it is to make a success of tonight."

Jake could well understand how important it was to her. The village thrived on tourism and in this bad economy the absence of visitors was having an impact. But despite his desire to help the museum, he refused to turn the event into a circus for some amateur's eccentric theories. The media were calling Diana Lune the 21st century's answer to Erich Von Daniken. He was pretty certain Diana Lune could never attain the cult status of the 1968 bestseller *Chariots of the Gods?* A book which touted (among other things) the idea that the Egyptian and Mayan pyramids, Stonehenge, the Easter Island heads and other ancient monuments were erected by aliens. But she was getting pretty close to it. She was on all the talk shows.

Odd thing was, he had watched an interview with her and found her dramatic looks and edgy confidence—what some might call arrogance—compelling. He was actually looking forward to hearing her theory of how Native Americans could possibly have canoed to England, trekked inland to Wiltshire and erected a massive stone temple. That would be a trick. But he squashed his cynicism and ridicule.

Most of all he wanted to know why. Why would anyone break their backs dragging those humungous sarsens from the surrounding downs, and hoist them with nothing more than man or ox power into a gigantic ring, given that they could somehow have reached these chalky shores from America in the first place?

"Have you read her book?" Maia asked, looking hopefully from him to Chancellor.

Chancellor nodded. "So very interesting." He sounded quite noncommittal.

"Not yet," Jake said, hoping he didn't seem dismissive. "Haven't had a chance to get a copy."

"Too bad. This megalith figures strongly in her theory." She spread her arms to direct their vision at the massive standing stone in front of them. Then took another step to the rear and so did Jake and Thomas Chancellor. "Now, tell me what you see."

CHAPTER FOUR

Jake gasped at what appeared to be the face of a raven.

One thing was certain; the image on the rock's surface was not a petroglyph. The megalith before them was an enormous boulder tipped upright to stand like a sentry at a postern, and unmistakably natural. What was happening was a trick of perception and he told her so. In reality there was no image carved into the rock face. There only *appeared* to be one. But any way one looked at it, it seemed there was.

"It's not unusual for the human eye to piece together different elements in large surfaces that are heavily featured like this megalith—and combine them into what looks like faces or animals," Jake said, disguising the annoyance in his voice. After all, he had come to examine a petroglyph or some kind of carving, not a figment of the imagination. "That's where the whole idea of The Man in the Moon comes from. There really isn't a face in the moon, but I'm sure I don't need to tell *you* that. This is a natural phenomenon."

Although to be honest, he wasn't sure what she *did* need to know. This whole venture was beginning to look a bit dubious, and a waste of his time. He hoped he had not flown all this way just to see *that*.

"So what about it? Why are we looking at it? I could probably see a bird silhouette in just about anything I looked at, if I tried hard enough." He raised his head to the passing clouds and, sure enough, he did. "I can't stress strongly enough, Mrs. Pickerton. This is not an archaeological carving."

To his surprise, Maia inclined her chin in agreement. She

stooped and lifted a carryall onto her left shoulder. "Yes, quite. Now follow me."

Past the megalith, several other sarsens perched in a curve above the ditch near some elms towards the west. The bank was level and on it sat a barn with a house on the other side. Maia led them along the ridge following a well-worn track. From here other tracks were visible; visitors had crossed directly to the inner circles following the remnants of old hedgerows and walls to where more megaliths stood on their peripheries.

The remains of the two inner circles were difficult to make out because most of the original sarsens were missing, and small concrete markers had been put in their place. In the northeast quadrant two unbelievably large megaliths sat at right angles to one another. But this was not what she wanted to show them. She headed south to where some cattle grazed. Here was an almost perfect arc of sarsens, the survivors of the south inner ring.

She stopped and shot a high glance at the wide towering stone, notched at the top. "Do you see it?"

A short exhalation came from Chancellor. Jake sucked in a tight breath.

"And that's not the only one," she said.

She led them further across the grass to a third megalith, again similarly shaped but minus the notch. The next one they came to was the same. And the next. When they arrived at the sixth stone, there was no doubt in Jake's mind. They couldn't all be hallucinating.

"Do you see it?" she asked. "When I first read about this—let's call it a phenomenon—I was skeptical. After all, I've worked here for twelve years and I never noticed this before. Ms. Lune came to study the monuments two years ago—while I was on vacation—so I never actually met her in person. But can you believe it? All six project images of ravens. And there are photographs of them right here in her book."

She pulled out a soft cover version from the cloth

carryall on her shoulder, and flipped to the centerfold.

These images were perceptions, not actual sculptures. They looked exactly as they looked in the book. This was sincerely weird and Jake found it difficult to believe that the three of them had seen the same thing. These were natural rocks. They were not carved. They had sat in this field, been defaced, abused, buried and re-erected over several millennia, and in all the time they had been studied no one had ever recorded the strange effect they had on the human perception.

"But what is really disturbing is this. Not until I saw the photographs did I have any suspicion. It was then that I went to check the stones, and I could not believe my eyes. I have never seen these 'faces in stone' until I saw them in her book. I immediately contacted her and invited her to do a presentation. Simultaneously, I contacted you and Mr. Chancellor." Maia Pickerton's gaze darted wildly out across the field past the earthwork. "And then, a couple of days ago, this—" She threw up her hands. A cloud of ravens had risen over their heads and now circled, before roosting on another row of stones. "They're getting worse."

By now Jake had the volume in his hand and was flipping through more pages. Thus far, Tom Chancellor had not commented on the coincidence. His very silence gave Jake a feeling of unease.

He looked up and caught Chancellor staring at the back cover. Jake flipped it over to see an author photo. This time he had an awareness, almost of déjà vu. Wow, was that ever odd. He did not know Diana Lune and yet her image triggered something. She was no academic, so he couldn't have gone to school with her. Other than seeing her on TV and hearing her on the radio, there was nothing else to explain this impression of familiarity.

But it was more than that. When he looked at her face, he recognized her the same way one might recognize an old friend. He remembered having that sensation the first time he watched her interviewed. How could he feel that with someone he had never seen before?

At that moment, the custodian, the one he'd met inside the museum earlier, and who did the afternoon rounds of the ancient site, came up to the curator with an armful of pamphlets.

"Sorry to intrude, Mrs. Pickerton," he said in a hoarse, rasping voice. The walk across the field had been an effort. "But these just came in and I thought you would want to see them."

The custodian had a worried look on his pale, wrinkled face and Maia quickly took up one of the pamphlets to see what they were. "Ms. Lune telephoned to say that she has arrived, and is booked at the Inn, and she sent these pamphlets ahead to be passed out to the audience." He swept his comb-over in the opposite direction from the wind as he explained. "Thought you would want to see them before I posted any around town."

Maia inspected the front of the pamphlet. Then passed one to Jake and one to Chancellor. The lead photo was of the upcoming guest speaker posing in front of the Swindon Stone and, well over her head, on the outward surface was a clear image of a raven. Hunched on top was a row of the living birds.

Six to be exact.

Was this some sort of publicity stunt? How could Diana Lune possibly know there were going to be ravens flocking in Avebury on the day of her lecture? The curator looked to be at her wits end. "Oh dear, what am I going to do? I...this can't be happening. Why would she do this?"

"There is no evidence that she's done anything," Chancellor said. "The ravens, the faces in stone: it's all a coincidence. She's probably just taking advantage of it."

"Well, I must call her. Now, where did I put my cellphone?" She searched her pockets. "It's no good, I am going to have to return to the museum. I am so sorry, gentlemen. Can you find your way back? I'll see you tonight at the lecture? Eight o'clock, sharp." With that she hurried away, her white blouse and black trousers slapping in the wind, followed by the custodian.

Jake was left holding the pamphlet and the curator's copy of Diana Lune's bestseller. Chancellor was now studying the author's photograph.

"Do you know her?" Jake asked.

Chancellor glanced up. "I was about to ask you the same question. You look as though you recognized her."

"Well, in a way I suppose I do. She's plastered all over television and the Internet. Quite a celebrity these days. Never met her in person though."

Chancellor's face suddenly took on a queer expression.

"Do you recognize *me*?" he asked.

Jake made a closer inspection of the man's features. Shrugged again. "Should I? Are you famous?"

"Not exactly, I'm an Interpol agent who specializes in paranormal phenomena."

His eyes widened. "Has a crime been committed?" He stared at the megalith in front of them. "These stones haven't exactly been defaced. That raven face that we think we see is just a trick of the imagination."

"That's not exactly true," Chancellor said. "For one thing, we aren't imagining it. I can see it. You can see it. And Maia Pickerton saw it. As did Diana Lune, who, as is evidenced in that book you're holding, managed to actually capture the images. A photograph is not imagination."

Yes, but an expert could easily manipulate the image on a computer so that people saw what she wanted them to see. What was he getting at? Surely Chancellor knew what he meant. The stones, valuable monuments of history that they were, had not been vandalized, knocked down or stolen. Then he realized that his own argument concerning digital manipulation with Photoshop was nullified by the fact that he had observed the images with his own eyes.

He decided to avoid an altercation. "So, what's Interpol doing here? I don't believe Maia Pickerton knows you're from Interpol, does she?"

"No, I'm not on official business. Not yet anyway. I really am here just in the capacity of an expert on the paranormal." He waved a hand at the megalith and then to the roosting figures on its top.

Mr. Chancellor was being cagey, but Jake wasn't interested in his reasons for visiting Avebury. When Maia had emailed the photograph of one of the 'faces in stone', she had not indicated that it was such. And when he had asked for clarification, she had evaded his questions and instead had asked *him* questions. Such was the beauty of email. You could latch on to what interested you and ignore what made you uncomfortable, and the recipient on the other end could do nothing because there was no face-to-face interaction. You could email the same question repeatedly, but if the recipient chose to avoid it, there was nothing you could do about it.

The photograph was unclear—but it was sharply delineated enough to be convincing. She had allowed him to jump to the conclusion that it was a raven carved into the rock. And so, of course, he would be interested. He had studied rock carvings the world over. To have a link to the British Isles had been an exciting anomaly. His mind had scrambled to numerous theories of why the bird would be carved onto rocks in the vicinity, and how it might link back to the mythical Haida Raven of the Pacific Northwest.

But now it was looking to be a hoax, and she had enticed him here under false pretenses. He was ready to pull the plug on this stunt. Had everything she told him been a ruse just to get him to come to Avebury? And if so, why?

He almost returned to his B&B to pack his bags and change his return flight. But the oddity of the whole affair, the fact that regardless of why the curator had misled him into travelling here in the middle of his field season to look at some rock images that were blatantly not archaeological, had him curious.

CHAPTER FIVE

Evening arrived quicker than he had anticipated. Jake had returned the curator's book to the museum and bought a copy of his own. At the lecture tonight he might ask the author to autograph it. However, after an afternoon of catching up on his sleep and skim-reading the outrageous tome he decided to leave the book in his room.

He had dinner in the pub at the Red Lion Inn, since Mrs. Dixon's did not provide evening meals, only breakfast. He quickly paid the bill and followed the road to the museum, which was behind the church in the village. He had changed into light wool slacks and a shirt with a collar, and a lightweight leather jacket.

The Interpol agent was in the lobby when he entered. The lecture had not yet started, but from the sound of the buzzing conversation, he knew something was amiss. A flustered young woman was speaking to Chancellor and he was listening to her intently. Jake recognized her on the instant. She was not a person he could ever forget. It was the woman he had met on the downs.

He ambled over to Chancellor who looked up. "Lalonde, glad to see you made it."

"What's going on?" Jake asked trying to appear nonchalant.

"This is Angeline Lisbon." Chancellor glanced at him like he should recognize the name. "She's a grad student at Cambridge University, studying ancient religious practices associated with stone circles."

"We've met," Jake said.

"Of course. You must be Dr. Lalonde. I do recognize you from this morning," she said.

He decided she was Canadian. What made him think she was Canadian was her clean speech and politeness. She gave him that smile that made his knees go weak. He made a conscious effort to still his heart and to breathe. Why was this woman having such an effect on him? And why did her voice send pleasant shivers over his spine; he met attractive women all the time.

He realized now that she had green-gold eyes, and that her hair, brushed to a glossy sheen was the shade and iridescence of a raven's wing. That sounded cliché, but it was the first thing that came to mind. If he had thought she was beautiful this morning in jeans and tweed jacket, she was stunning tonight in a salmon-colored sheath dress, with a black silk cardigan overtop, and toeless high heels.

And if it weren't for the fact that her face was contorted with worry, he would have turned on the charm. But something had her frazzled, and it wasn't something small.

"What's wrong," he repeated. "Where's Maia?"

"That's the problem," Angeline said. "She hasn't shown up. Nigel"—she pointed to the elderly custodian—"says she left around half past five to change clothes and grab a bite. She called to say she'd be back by seven, but she never made it. It's just not like her to be an hour late. Not for an event as important as this was to her."

"Angeline has been helping with the organization and promotion of the talk," Chancellor explained. "She's wondering whether we should go ahead with it if Maia doesn't show up in the next few minutes. I think she should. It's what Maia would want I'm sure. From what Angeline and Nigel have told me, everything has been paid for, the caterer has set up canapés and wine, and there's a tremendous turnout. The lecture hall is full, with standing room at the back."

Diana Lune came out of the lecture hall with a trail of admirers at her rear.

"Angeline, is everything all right?"

Her supporters gathered around her scantily clad body to cling to every word she said. Diana Lune was a Las Vegas gal, so it came as no surprise to see her dressed in black strappy stilettoes, a tight spaghetti-strap black gown, with a chunky gold necklace at her throat and matching crescent-shaped earrings that hung below her jawline. Her blue-black hair was highlighted with copper, bronze and burgundy, and flowed over one shoulder with side-swept bangs. Her teeth were kitchen-appliance white and her large eyes with their dark manicured brows were startling to say the least. One could not help but stare at her.

"Everything is fine, Ms. Lune," Angeline said. "Please, go back inside. I'll sound the bell for things to start."

Jake said, "Anything I can do to help?"

"Maybe in a minute."

He introduced himself to the event's celebrity and she gushed all over him. She had heard about his work and was so excited that he'd come to her talk. Angeline rang a silver bell and announced that the talk would begin in fifteen minutes. "Please," she said. "Everyone take your seats inside the theatre."

When everyone was seated, Angeline introduced the celebrated guest and her topic, *Sacred Stones of the Raven and the Serpent Temple of Avebury.* The distinguished speaker rose to the podium as Angeline relinquished it, and boomed into lecture mode, while a technician juggled her PowerPoint. The megalith of the Swindon Stone flashed onto the screen, replete with raven simulacrum. "I propose," she said, "that ancient Native Americans from America crossed the Atlantic Ocean sometime in prehistory and built the megalithic stone monument of Avebury."

Jake knew from her first line that she was a quack. Native Americans from America? Sometimes he repeated himself in a lecture, but never in the first line.

He was seated at the back of the theatre, had retreated there after seeing Diana to the stage. He had wanted to have access to the exit because he had glimpsed something just as he was coming in the door. And now that he was pretty certain the speaker had nothing of great import to say, he slipped through the exit.

***

Thomas Chancellor circled the Swindon Stone. The birds had returned and made a mess of it. He looked up and saw in the fading twilight the silhouettes of thousands roosting on the stones on the far curvature of the bank. He knew he should be inside listening to the lecture, but something told him that he would only find the answers out here.

There were strange grooves in the ground, long grooves filled in with grass. He followed them throughout the great circle, feeling somehow that they formed a pattern he should know. The moon rose into the night sky illuminating the grounds and casting creeping shadows. He pulled out his mini iPad and activated the Draw Feature.

In the center of the North Circle at the locale of the remaining stones from the Cove, moonlight washed the landscape in silver. There seemed to be a groove forming a circle where the stones used to be. This groove could be seen best at nightfall with the shadows just right. To the left and right of the circle more flowed in an easterly and westerly course, and if his instincts were correct, they were identical in each direction. He traced the geometric patterns on foot, and then replicated them on his iPad.

He shuddered, fearing what he suspected. There was only one way to know for certain. Tomorrow he would have to hire a helicopter to fly him over the site so that he could see if what he surmised was true. For the time being he would have to be content that he was almost one hundred percent certain.

It was a strange and lonely world he lived in now. Sometimes he thought he was going insane. All those people he thought he knew did not exist. Names without addresses, faces without bodies. It wasn't until Maia Pickerton emailed him that he realized that he wasn't dead. He was in an Italian hospital with a story that had later thrown him into the psychiatric ward in England. But they couldn't keep him there. It would cost them too much. Even now his thoughts weren't always coherent. But he had to hide it. The things he remembered were frightful, surreal. He remembered being buried alive. He remembered his soul being parted from his body as they left him in a tunnel to die, trapped beneath the earth.

And he remembered the one who had abandoned him. But the doctors told him it was all delirium when they discovered him naked and half dead inside the catacomb. He had tried to explain about the Black Goddess after they resuscitated him, but they said he was hallucinating from lack of oxygen. The brain did strange things when deprived of air. They were surprised he had a brain left at all. He was dead for at least fifteen minutes, they said. That was long enough to cause permanent damage and even a vegetative state. Logically, he should have been brain-dead.

And then he *did* die. And yet here he was. He wasn't delusional; he had one purpose to this existence. To find out what had happened to him and to the one who had done this to him. Because he knew she *did* exist. He tried to find the reporter who had been with him at the time, but she swore she didn't know him, and she was so freaked out by his persistence that she had obtained a court order which prevented him from talking to her or being anywhere in her presence. That was a dead end, and he had almost despaired until Maia Pickerton sent him that email…

He had lied to Jake Lalonde. He was no longer an Interpol agent. Interpol had fired him when they learned he was undergoing psychiatric treatment in the UK. His insistence that he was a kind of walking dead was enough for them to give him his walking papers. So what? They had no idea what really happened. They had no idea what he had become.

Now all he wanted to do was convince Lalonde that he wasn't crazy. If anyone would believe him it would be the archaeologist. Yet, he had not recognized him, any more than Angeline Lisbon had.

Ever since he had come to the realization that he wasn't crazy, and that he was probably dead, he had searched for Jake Lalonde and Angeline Lisbon.

Why? He wasn't sure. This was not a dream, not a memory. He was dead. But not the way the doctors defined death. And only those two people could corroborate what he knew was true.

He ran his hands over the stone's rough surface. The route between the sarsens seemed familiar even though he had no light, other than his iPad.

Avebury was a maze of natural pillars. It was familiar because he had travelled here once before—on a case. *She* had eluded him then. But he had found her in the Mithraic temples of Rome. Eluded once more. Again she was gone. And this was the legacy she had left him—tunnels, black tunnels and lights burning at the end of every passage. But he was trapped, unable to fully return to the living or escape to the dead.

While on the other side, he had not seen anyone he knew. All of the tales of grand reunions with dead friends and relatives were lies. The After World was not open to just anyone. The newly arrived were required to find their way through the maze first.

His chest heaved. Blackness engulfed him. The souls could not be seen—only felt. He could feel their presence, but not see or touch their physical embodiments. Oddly, he could hear them. Even now, he could hear them in his chest, punching in and out, screaming, and attempting to use his body as a pathway back to life. For the time being, he *wasn't* dead or he wouldn't be able to feel this. He knew because he had experienced it before. *He* had been the soul punching his way back through the body of the living. Someone in the operating room, a face obscured to him now. Dark hair streaked with highlights of grey. The OR swirling in shades of red, white and black.

For the longest time, her name had eluded him, while everything else had slowly returned. Jake Lalonde, Angeline Lisbon. And *her*, the elusive one… He doubled over in agony as something tried to pound its way out of his chest. He caught his breath, tucked in his abdominal muscles and straightened his spine. Vertigo assailed him, a sensation of falling. Then anger, despair and sorrow. Not *his* emotions. He had long since lost any emotion. They were trying to get him to return—because they were trapped between dimensions. He had no desire to re-enter that world just yet. He possessed the power to walk the two planes, and he must use this ability for however long it lasted.

CHAPTER SIX

Aha, he was right. Someone *had* vandalized it. Moonlight filtered down and landed squarely on its surface. As he was hurrying down the road from the car park earlier, Jake had passed this megalith and caught what he had thought was another figment of his imagination, i.e. a 'face' in the rock. Across the surface of it, freshly etched, was a circle with two half crescents on either side. What did this remind him of? For the life of him, he couldn't place it. He would have to report this to Maia when she showed up, and she in turn would have to report it to the police. He wondered if the Interpol cop was interested in anything like this.

Vandalism was a minor offense, but when perpetrated on an historic monument it became serious. If this were a new trend, visitors would see their access to the site limited by rope barriers, as it was at Stonehenge, and that could mean the end of tourism for Avebury.

He looked out at the twinkling lights of the village, dug out his smartphone from his breast pocket and snapped a picture of the symbol. He was just starting to look it up on the Internet when a voice spoke from behind him. "So, you saw it too."

Jake turned his head. "Why aren't you inside listening to the lecture?"

"Heard it before," Chancellor said. "What about you? Thought you were interested in her theory?"

He didn't know what to make of this man. Why was he really here? He had shown very little interest in the multitude of roosting ravens besieging the village, and had barely blinked at the discovery of the 'faces' in the sarsens. But he was interested in *this*. Jake glanced down at the page that he had loaded onto his phone.

"Kids, you think?" Jake asked, looking up to see Chancellor's reaction.

The man barely reacted. "Maybe."

"You recognize it?"

"A pagan symbol," he said. "More likely the local cult."

"Moon Goddess?" Jake asked.

Chancellor nodded.

"I hear the Wicca have some sort of celebration associated with the solstice. You here to investigate cult activity?"

"Not officially."

Silence dropped like a blanket between them. "Don't talk much, do you?"

"Not much."

The fellow was rather irritating. Jake wished to get away from him. He shrugged and started to head south along the path. Many of the stones were missing along this curve of the main circle. The megalith at the western entrance where he had encountered Chancellor was an original. But then a huge gap was filled in with a number of concrete markers, leaving most of the field where they stood vast and dark by night. A sharp wind cut through the open paths, then stilled. A chill pierced him although it was a mild June night. If ghosts were real, this was where they would walk.

He exhaled, rubbed his rapidly chilling hands together and proceeded at a swifter pace. The place had an unnerving quality at night that transformed into a mysterious serenity during the day. He passed a standing stone, then the low concrete marker of a missing pillar, then another original stone, then another marker, and then one more—each taller than the one before. Just prior to reaching the entrance to the West Kennet Avenue, he stopped and stared. The evening light whitened the stones against the deep shadows giving them an ethereal appearance, especially the one that now rose against the velvet black surroundings. It was common knowledge among the locals that this one had killed a man. The thirteen-ton block, now re-erected, and delicately balanced on its tapering base, was the Barber Stone. In1938 it was excavated and beneath it sprawled a man's skeleton. The man had been accidentally killed while helping to topple the massive thing in the 14th century during the Christian frenzy. It had fallen when a support gave way, fracturing the poor man's pelvis and snapping his neck. His right foot was wedged so that it had been impossible to remove his corpse.

"Amazes me how they perch like that."

Jake spun around. "You still here? You walk like a ghost. I didn't even hear you."

Chancellor smiled. He sized up the object in front of him and said, "You familiar with the legend?"

Jake nodded. Thanks to his serendipitous encounter with Angeline Lisbon on the downs this morning, he was.

Inside the skeleton's rotted pouch archaeologists had found three silver coins dated to 1320, helping them determine the period of stone-burying. Iron scissors, and a lance or probe, were also among his possessions, suggesting the skeleton belonged to some kind of itinerant barber or surgeon. Unfortunately, his journey to the county's market fairs with his knives and leeches was cut short in Avebury. It was guessed that he had offered to help with the stone-felling, but ironically was crushed, and his body buried in the back rubble.

A flash of lightening forked across the starry night. Jake flinched involuntarily, the image of blue bolts temporarily impressed upon his eyes. But the event did nothing to faze Chancellor. Above, the sky hung like crushed velvet, sprinkled with dust, each speck a bright star, and every cloud that had worried them all morning and afternoon had vanished. A crescent moon shrouded by a strange pink halo frowned down on them. Strange, Jake thought. No sign of rain. Where had that flash come from?

"That poor old barber isn't the only one that died here,"

Chancellor said. "Over the centuries people have been known to vanish when near this stone—for no reason at all."

Jake could almost see those small, surly peasants of past ages muttering how it was ill fortune to disturb the stones. Their ghosts walked here.

He stole a glance at his watch and saw that it was almost nine o'clock. "Better get back to the lecture. She'll be expecting us to ask questions."

A hand suddenly darted out and grabbed him by the shoulder. Jake jerked back, startled. "What the—"

He stopped mid-question. He had taken three steps back and as he pivoted, the Interpol agent dropped his hand and pointed.

Holy shit, Jake thought. "This can't be. I can't be seeing what I think I'm seeing. Can I?"

"That depends," Chancellor said. "What do you see?"

Jake hesitated. He'd only had a half-pint of ale with his steak and kidney pie at the pub, and was not in the slightest inebriated. "What do *you* see?"

After a second's hesitation, Chancellor spoke. "A woman's face. A woman whom we both know."

He didn't have to name her for he had seen the same face.

Jake moved closer and studied the rough surface. Up close it had the usual appearance of weathered rock with the expected grooves and cleavages, pocks and ridges. Two feet back and her face was clearly alive. Same wide-set eyes, same sharp cut bangs. It was a perfect likeness of Maia Pickerton even though no human hands had touched the stone. There were no fresh chisel or knife marks, not like the triple moon symbol he had seen on the stone at the west entrance. That one had been clearly vandalized.

"We'll have to report this," he said. "Along with the vandalism."

"I've already taken note."

"Thought you weren't here on official business?"

"Mysterious disappearances and defacement of heritage

property are within my jurisdiction." Chancellor raised his tablet to the megalith, stepped back several paces and snapped three different shots. "Okay, let's go. Nothing we can do here until morning. These are not matter-of-life-and-death crimes. Let's see what Ms. Lune has to say about all of this. We may be worrying for nothing, and Maia is, as we speak, waiting for us in the lecture hall."

***

When they returned the curator was still a no show. Jake refused to believe that that megalith had something to do with it. Angeline Lisbon was poised on the sidelines ready to take the podium when he and Chancellor slid against the back wall to watch, standing.

The presentation was winding down. The final photo was of an aerial view of the Great Circle. It looked strangely elongated from the angle in which the picture had been taken. The avenues were defined as the serpent's tail and the Great Circle its head. The inner circles formed the figure of a raven with the obelisk representing the beak and the stones of the cove, an eye. Like Native Haida art, the two figures entwined. The closing argument was delivered via a Celtic folktale passed down for generations about the Snake and the Raven. A hungry raven goes in search of food and finds a she-snake sleeping in the sun. When the raven seizes the snake, the snake kills the raven with her venomous bite. Raven returns from the dead.

The story was ripe with symbolism analogous to North American Native folktales. Raven had a rapacious appetite and was always searching for something to eat, hence the eating of the snake, only to be killed and resurrected. The pathway of the Avebury serpent passes through the temple of the sun. The Sun in Haida tales is associated with the Raven.

Jake groaned when he heard this theory. Chancellor gave him a quick look, but refrained from comment. *Avebury as a Serpent Temple erected by the People of the Raven?* It was all Jake could do not to laugh.

He was glad he had not remained for the entire talk. Already his blood was up just hearing the outlandish conclusions. Unfortunately, he had missed the part on how Native Americans could have navigated the seas from the west coast of North America to the White Cliffs of Dover. Had they employed some variant of the Panama Canal? Yes, he was being facetious. It was a long way from the Pacific Ocean to the Atlantic Ocean. And even had they crossed overland from west coast to eastern seaboard, that trip on foot would have taken several lifetimes to cross over mountains and prairie before they even reached the sea. Oh, how he wished he had stayed to hear that theory.

A great round of applause rose from the audience and a few people even gave a standing ovation. She was popular indeed.

"Thank you all for attending this very exciting event," Angeline Lisbon said, taking the podium. "And I'd like to thank Diana Lune very much for engaging us with such an informative and imaginative talk."

Jake decided he liked Angeline Lisbon very much. Just for using the term imaginative—because Diana was certainly that. She had managed to sound complimentary without actually complimenting her. *Kudos for not describing the talk as inspired*, he thought.

"Before we end for refreshments, Ms. Lune has kindly agreed to answer any questions about her talk."

Twenty hands instantly shot up from the audience. Angeline strained to see through the glaring lights and nodded. "Yes, you there, did you have a question?"

A longhaired, redheaded college girl with a skintight turquoise sweater, tucked into discolored khaki's jumped up. "My name is Drey McFee. I'm a grad student at the Institute of Metaphysical Humanistic Sciences in Cambridge. Those raven faces you introduced at the beginning," she said, addressing her comments to Diana. "Have you tried testing any metaphysical theories to explain their appearance? I mean you say those aren't carvings, but natural faces in stone. What makes you think they're ravens? They are massive birds, I'll give you that, but why ravens? As a cryptozoologist I could suggest any number of creatures that they might represent."

Diana chuckled. "Well, that is actually two questions. To answer the first, we are in the process of testing the stones for paranormal activity." Jake audibly groaned, then clamped his lips shut, avoiding eye contact with the speaker. The college girl, who by her accent was either Canadian or American, turned toward him briefly, and then gave Diana her undivided attention.

"In fact we have an expert in the crowd. Mr. Chancellor, would you like to answer this question?" Diana asked.

The Interpol agent showed no visible reaction. He nodded, flashed the minutest semblance of a smile and said, "I have not had a chance to study the birdlike faces in the standing stones. However, it is my opinion that they appeared because the time was right for them to be seen."

An audible gasp came from the audience. Jake forced himself not to roll his eyes. He could see that, on the stage, Angeline was beginning to panic.

The college girl in the turquoise sweater raised her hand again. Diana Lune nodded. "Yes, you have a comment?"

"Another question, actually. You said in your lecture that the simulacra may have always been there, only no one ever saw them or recognized them for what they were until *you* documented them. They may appear and disappear for reasons we don't understand, and *that*, of course, we have no way of knowing. We don't know whether people in history also noticed these faces in the stone because they were never mentioned in historic records—not even by the first investigators like John Aubrey or William Stukeley. But if these simulacra were always present as suggested by Mr. Chancellor, does that mean the ancient builders selected them for that reason, because they all exhibited these 'Raven faces'?"

"That is an excellent question, Ms. McFee. And I wholeheartedly agree with you. I didn't have time to touch on this subject fully in my talk this evening, but it is one of the reasons why I believe that Native Americans built the temple of Avebury. If you've read my book, or care to purchase a copy at my signing later this evening, I would be pleased to discuss this issue further with you."

The woman was not subtle, Jake thought. She was blatantly plugging her book and inviting people to buy it. Angeline glanced at her watch and moved to the podium to take the microphone from her guest.

"Thank you so much Ms. Lune for this very enlightening talk." Diana stepped aside while Angeline thanked the audience for attending and invited them to the book signing and refreshments.

Jake and Chancellor, being at the back of the theatre, led the way into the lobby where food and wine were available, and a table had been set up for the author. Jake's phone vibrated inside his pocket and he dug it out and raised it to his ear. It was Serena demanding why he hadn't called her when he had promised. "Sorry, got caught up in things. Can't talk now. I'm at the lecture."

"You emailed that the whole thing looked to be a hoax. Why not just ditch it and come home?"

"Things are starting to get interesting," he said, trying to keep his eye from wandering over to where Angeline in the salmon-colored dress was entertaining some of the guests.

"I'm leaving with the guys tomorrow, Jake. You should join us. I'm going to win this prize. Nobody is going to beat me. My theory of early human migrations is *the* best yet, and I'm going to prove it. You want some publicity? Here's your chance. I don't know how good the signals will be for our cellphones when we're out at sea, so I'll give you the number to the radiophone on the *Fisher King*. The wedding is in two weeks. I'll expect you back long before then."

His fiancée was blunt as always. It was one of the traits that had attracted him to her, *that* and her stunning California good looks. But did he really want to marry her?

The Interpol agent came up to him with two plastic glasses of red wine. "Trouble in paradise?" he asked, when Jake shut off his phone with a scowl.

Serena could be pushy as hell. That was one thing that had him concerned about their impending marriage. That and the fact that he was almost certain she wasn't his telepathic companion. True at times she could be vulnerable and tender. Sweet even. Which was why he couldn't quite make up his mind. At the moment they only lived together on and off. Her job was in Santa Barbara; his was in Seattle. If she truly were the empathic voice in his head, then the long distance thing would not be a problem. They could communicate with their thoughts. In the back of his mind he hoped she would admit to this secret. But so far she refused and gave no reason. It was true she had ambition; they even joked that she might stoop to murder to get what she wanted.

"You really think she's the one?" Chancellor asked.

He glared, startled out of his thoughts.

"I'm no expert," Chancellor said, but it seems to me if she was the right woman, it wouldn't be so difficult."

"You're right, it's none of your business," he said. *And how do you know who that call was from anyway?* He didn't recall telling the man about Serena.

Chancellor shrugged. "Frankly, I don't give a hoot about your love life, Lalonde. But for some inexplicable reason you and I, and those damned stones outside, are tied up in some great adventure. I don't know what it is. And I don't even want to be here. But what you want and what I want can't be got unless we work together."

Jake shoved away the glass that the Interpol agent was holding out to him, irritably, almost spilling the wine on the floor. "You make no sense," he said, then almost added: *you're also beginning to spook me.*

Chancellor pointed to Angeline. "See that cutie over there? Well, I noticed her too. I noted the way your eyes nearly popped out of your head when you saw her. You feel like you should know her, but you don't. Until today, you never laid eyes on her. At least that's what *you* think…" A long pause followed where Jake said nothing. The young woman was chatting with some members of the audience. She looked poised and quite lovely as her hand reached up to coil a lock of hair around her finger. That action had him fascinated, more than anything else she was doing.

"You want to talk some more, I'll be outside," Chancellor said.

Jake slowly drew his gaze away, and watched the Interpol agent weave through the crowd to the front doors. Seriously. Who the hell was this guy? And why was he goading him like this? But he did have one thing right. He was inexplicably drawn to Angeline Lisbon, and that *wasn't* right. He was engaged to Serena—bossy, ambitious, deliberate, manipulative, brilliant and beautiful, Serena. Serena, who now come to think of it, reminded him of Diana. Or was it vice versa? Was that why he'd had such a sense of déjà vu with the woman? Diana was Serena in black cocktail dress and stilettoes. Oh God, he thought.

Speak of the devil. She rose from her book signing to take a break and partake of a glass of wine. Her eye caught his and she swaggered over. As she neared, his gaze caught the chunky gold necklace at her throat.

Triple moons.

The shape, the form…it was exactly the same as the symbol defacing the stone outside.

CHAPTER SEVEN

Chancellor walked past the stone at the west entrance, and turned to his right. The defacement of the monument did not concern him overly much. It was probably just childish hijinks on the part of some teenaged kids. He was not interested in delinquency or the local cults. He could honestly say that he wasn't sure why he was even here. He only knew that he had to stay close to the archaeologist, and possibly Angeline Lisbon.

The archaeologist would lead him to the answers. He could help him get out of this fix he was in now. When people spoke of walking the line, of straddling the two worlds or different planes of existence, he hadn't thought it would be like this. This was not an existence. He was trapped.

Lalonde's memories seemed to be completely out of kilter with his own. He had his own theories of what had happened to them, but he needed corroboration with the individuals who had experienced the same events as he. He couldn't approach Angeline, not yet. He didn't want to frighten her. The archaeologist, on the other hand, would be easier to convince. After all, Lalonde possessed inherited memories, an ability that had never been proven or disproven by science, but not something people regularly advertised. Not if you wanted to be taken seriously. That was why he was surprised at the eye rolling and skepticism when it came to Diana Lune's theories. If anyone should have an open mind, it should be him.

He continued past the row of concrete markers

interspersed with the odd giant standing stone until he arrived at the Barber Stone. He stepped back and stared at the face of it. The image of Maia Pickerton was gone.

"There's something not quite right with you," a voice said from beside him. He turned to see who spoke. She placed a hand on his sleeve, a smooth, long-fingered hand. He still wore the navy blue suit and yellow tie that he had worn that morning, with beige trench coat overtop. "Expensive duds."

Yeah, when he bought them, in what seemed a lifetime ago, they were pricy. "Ah, Ms. McFee, I believe?"

"You believe correctly, sir. But call me Drey. Everyone does."

"Okay, Drey. And you call me Tom. What brings you out on this fine night? I would think you'd want to pick Diana Lune's brains a little more."

"She hasn't said anything I don't already know. Her theories are hardly original. She's just better at publicizing them than other people."

"And do you agree with her?"

"About Native Americans trekking over here and building these massive stone circles? No."

"So what's your take on it?"

"I'm not really interested in who built them, though I assume they were some local prehistoric folk. No, I'm interested in the images of the birds. The faces in the stones. If you look carefully at the images, you'll see something odd about them. I mean sure they have the perfect silhouette of a raven, but there's something more."

He nodded.

She glanced up quickly. "You noticed it too?"

"Very subtle, and only visible at certain angles and in certain lights. I spent all afternoon studying these faces. The archaeologist Jake Lalonde believes they are images of ravens."

"And they are," McFee said. "If you don't see... But I'm not here to study that. I'm here—" Her voice dropped to a low drawl. "I'm here to study that—"

Chancellor turned to look. A shadowy figure stood by the third stone leading to the West Kennet Avenue. It looked like a large bird, at least six feet tall with wings broad enough to fold over its body. Drey raised her cellphone, and slowly moved forward. Chancellor froze in disbelief.

He had experienced eerier and weirder things than this, so why was he paralyzed? The moment passed, and he fetched his iPad and zoomed in. The creature had wide, dark red eyes attached to a gray, blank face. Its head was bald with a six-inch long beak, and it made a loud shrilling call. The sound came from the creature's throat, which pulsated as it made the call and its beak never moved. He snapped the picture, and then it was gone.

Drey started running to where the creature was seen last. He followed. When they reached the stone where it had been standing, nothing remained. She looked down at the ground and shone the light of her phone to the trampled grass. There were dry patches that showed soil and when he crouched lower to get a better view, he saw a pair of three-toed tracks, sunk an inch and a half into the ground. That was all. He placed his foot near the track and saw that it was larger than his shoe. That meant the track was at least a foot long.

"It only comes out at night," she said. "And until now, it's only been seen in the rolling wooded hills of the Cotswolds. This is a first."

"Best not to tell Maia Pickerton about this. The last thing she needs is a mysterious winged beast to send the tourists packing for good."

"Are you kidding? This would bring them in by the droves. But that's not my business. I'm just here to get my doctorate in cryptozoology, and then I'm outta here to set up a business in cryptozoological investigations."

Chancellor nodded but already he was losing interest. The sighting was probably just a prank and if he added two and two together he would soon learn that the creepy Big Bird sighting was related to the defacement of the megalith.

While most of the Wicca were decent folk and would never mar a stone on a temple they revered, or pull a prank like that, he suspected there was always the odd individual who either wanted to discredit the cult or who were cult members gone rogue. Besides, his mention of the curator reminded him that she was still a no show.

"So what were you doing out here, Mr. Chancellor?" she asked.

"Getting a breath of air. And it's Tom, remember?"

"Hmmm." Clearly she didn't buy it. She touched his sleeve again. This time it was more of a poke.

"Do you always go around poking strangers? Could lead to severe consequences."

"Like what? You gonna haunt me in my dreams?"

Chancellor let his lip hang for a second, before he shut his mouth. Strange girl this one; was it possible that she knew something? What did they teach them in that Institute of Metaphysics?

She grinned. "I hear you're an expert in the paranormal."

"Apparently, you are too."

"I don't study paranormal phenomena. Well, not normally anyway. I'm mostly interested in sightings of mythical creatures, like that bird shadow we just saw. Was it a giant prehistoric bird or was it just a trick of light and shadow? I'll have to study the photographs I took to be sure. I'm pretty certain I saw a face. Did you? The phenoms I investigate are like that—more or less real."

"Everything is real. It just depends on how you look at it."

She shrugged. "Whatever." She gave a big yawn. "Think I'll hit the sack. I'm pretty exhausted. Been chasing Big Bird for days now. Lucky break. I actually got a glimpse of it."

"Aren't you afraid to be walking around in the dark with a thing like that lurking around?"

"Every sighting of Big Bird so far has led to nada. Most of these sightings are unverifiable. Doesn't mean they're not true, but ninety percent of the cases have been proven to be hoaxes. I take my work seriously, Mr. Chancellor. I mean Tom. If Big Bird is real, he won't let me catch another glimpse of him."

"Suit yourself," he said. "But if I were you, I'd keep to the lighted side of the road."

She grinned. "Hope to see you again, Tom. We can compare notes."

Chancellor did not grin. He watched her red hair and turquoise clad body cross the road and disappear into the shadows.

CHAPTER EIGHT

Jake watched the cryptozoologist leave the Interpol agent on the path. It took only a few moments to catch up with him.

"Who is Angeline Lisbon?" he asked. "Stop giving me that stupid look like you don't know what I'm talking about. You've been goading me all evening, dropping hints. Making insinuations. If you've got something to say, just say it."

Chancellor gave him a mild look. "So, you sense there is something wrong too. How about if you tell me what's on *your* mind."

Where could he even begin? He looked back at the lighted museum thinking he should return. This was a bad idea. Who was this Chancellor guy anyway? An Interpol agent and quack scientist who believed in the supernatural.

"I know about your inherited memories," Chancellor said.

Jake's eyes widened.

"Was it one of those? Or was it something else."

It was definitely something else, he thought. More like a dream or a vision, because how could it be a memory? Until today he had not known Angeline Lisbon. And yet the vision was strong in his mind.

He decided to describe the vision—which was more like a nightmare—to Chancellor. The vision made no sense. Maybe it would make sense to Chancellor. The Interpol agent seemed to think he had the answers. Well, let him try this one on for size. He darted one last backward glance at the museum where he could see Diana Lune through the window signing books, and then related his story.

He was inside a dimly lit cavernous space, like a shrine. He was on the ground, leaning over a beautiful dark-haired woman, possibly the most beautiful woman he had ever seen in his life. No—'seen' wasn't the right word. He didn't actually recognize her face. It was just a sense that she gave him, a feeling deep in his heart. And so even though he couldn't describe her appearance in any detail at all, he had felt she was the most exquisite creature he had ever known. But he was frantic. She wasn't moving. Her head was turned to the side and when he raised her slightly, he detected blood.

He had then raced down the aisle to a concealed cavity behind an altar where for some reason he knew there was an ewer of water. He unravelled his bowtie (yes, he was wearing a bowtie, though lord knows why) from around his throat and soaked it well, then returned to bathe the wound.

The abrasion was on her right temple, near the hairline. He washed it and saw that the injury was superficial. The odd thing, though, was its shape. If she lived, if it healed, it would leave a slight scar shaped like a raven.

Then he had turned his eyes to see something else. It was a neo-shamanic symbol. The years of knowing that his inherited memories were a doorway into the metaphysical had not prepared him for the reality of what was happening at that moment. He had no idea what to do.

He remembered a vague thought: *So, the will of the Black Goddess will come to pass.*

Who or what was the Black Goddess? He then saw himself tear a diamond ring out of his trouser pocket, and shove it onto the prostrate woman's third, left-hand finger.

"I love you," he had whispered. "More than life itself." He had taken the sickle that sat on the ground and cut a lock of her hair and shoved it into his pocket.

Suddenly, he looked up at Chancellor, breaking the spell.

"The Black Goddess." Chancellor said. "Do you know who the Black Goddess is?" He answered the question himself when Jake merely stared blankly at him. For some reason, words refused to form on his lips. "She was a Middle Eastern deity of motherhood and fertility sometimes known as Astarte or Asherah." He paused and studied Jake's inert expression. "Does she mean anything to you?"

Jake roused himself enough to reply. "I'm asking *you*. What has she got to do with me, and Angeline Lisbon? Because I'm pretty certain that Angeline was the dead woman in my nightmare."

"What makes you think she was dead?"

"She was lying on the ground and there was blood. I'm not exactly sure why. It was a dream, a nightmare. It wasn't real."

"When did you experience it? Last night?"

He nodded. "I think so. I had forgotten all about it until…."

"Until what?"

"Until tonight…."

He was surprised at Chancellor's concern and interest. He wanted to know everything about the nightmare and the lock of hair and his feelings for Angeline.

And then Chancellor told him a story that Jake refused to believe. But there was no other explanation. He made him promise to keep it to himself, and not to approach Angeline. He promised. He went back inside the museum as though nothing had transpired between them—and wondered what Chancellor was going to do.

CHAPTER NINE

Things were wrapping up. Half the audience had left and the lingerers continued to gather around the celebrity author. Angeline noticed that she seemed to pay an awful lot of attention to the handsome cowboy professor. Well, maybe 'cowboy' was a misnomer. Dr. Jake Lalonde was obviously part Native American, and when she had asked someone familiar with his work, they had said they had read somewhere that he was half-Haida. His height would belie that. He must be at least six feet tall, probably taller. He was built like a strong horse.

She hadn't had a chance to talk to him much, but he had offered to help earlier before the lecture had started. She had wanted to ask him to go to Maia's house to ensure nothing had happened to her but in all the activity had forgotten. It was just as well. How could she ask him to do something so personal without raising suspicion? She had phoned Maia's number repeatedly, but got no answer. Maia lived alone. Her divorce was finalized last month. Nigel, who did not drive, had finally taken the bus to the curator's house and found no one home. What could have happened?

Still, their hands were tied. Maia was a grown woman and they could not report a missing person to the police for at least twenty-four hours.

Angeline was starting to get a headache and wanted to return to the Red Lion Inn where she was sharing a room with Drey McFee. Drey was already gone, and so was that Chancellor fellow she had been talking to earlier. He was nice; she hoped to see him again. Right now she wished she could get everyone to leave so that she could close up. All of the food and drink were consumed. Nigel had returned to help her. The only people left were Diana Lune and Jake Lalonde and a few stragglers.

The archaeologist's eyes consumed her, as though he wished to consult her on something important, but then thought better of it and simply smiled. She bit her lip and returned the sentiment. He uttered something to Diana and she went to locate her purse and coat from behind the table where she had been signing books. They were sold out and she'd had to take orders.

He was coming over to say goodbye. Angeline offered her hand in a breathless handshake. "So nice to see you again."

The look on his face reflected her own feelings. He seemed restless. Why?

"I've heard about your work," she said, politely.

"Really?" He focused his gaze. His confidence returned and he relaxed. "I meet very few people interested in the more academic aspects of my work. They seem to like Diana's theories better." He laughed. She could detect a hint of cheerful sarcasm or mockery in his words. He dipped his head and said in a conspiratorial voice. "You look like you're dying to get out of here. I'll escort our celebrity to the inn so you can close shop."

"Thanks."

He raised his hand to shake hers again, but this time they both stopped before their fingers met. His eyes had locked onto the small diamond on her finger. Did he want to know if she was engaged? The answer was No. He lifted his head, met her eyes. The hesitation couldn't have lasted for more than three seconds, but it felt like three minutes, before his firm grip covered her hand in exhilarating silence. She tucked the ring out of sight and watched him meet Diana as she approached. They said their goodbyes, and everyone followed the celebrity author out the door. Angeline raised a hand as he threw her a final backward glance. Diana turned a split second later and waved. She returned the gesture before swiveling to evaluate the disarray in the museum's foyer. Nigel was thrusting paper plates, plastic glasses, and crumpled serviettes into a black plastic garbage bag. She instructed him to go home, they could finish cleaning tomorrow. Tomorrow would be a big day, especially if Maia failed to show up for work.

She watched Nigel leave, shut off the lights. Turned them back on. Why did Jake Lalonde get under her skin? She felt wildly euphoric in his presence. She went into the theatre for one last look and noticed that Diana had forgotten her PowerPoint.

The screen remained illuminated and she wandered down to the podium to shut it off. When she touched the key a strange image appeared on the screen. It resembled a giant shadow with wings flattened against its body. And the eyes were red. The colors were unnatural and misty, and the figure seemed to undulate in and out of focus. In the background was one of the megaliths that she recognized from the South Circle. It stood an imposing thirteen feet tall and was called the Devil's Chair. That meant the shadow was roughly the height of a man. This was not one of the photographs that Diana had presented.

Then she did a double take. What was that round disk above the ledge, the seat, on the Devil's Chair?

She had never seen that before. What she meant was she had never noticed a disk embedded in the stone, although she imagined she recognized the symbol on the disk, and perhaps even the disk itself. She tried to enlarge the image but was ignorant as to how, and the greater her attempts, the fainter the image became until the disk that she thought she had seen was no longer visible. *Oh boy,* she thought, *I am tired. I must be seeing things. Or else I drank too much wine.* But the shady figure remained. When she focused her attention on it the image seemed to shimmer, oscillate in and out of focus as though it stood behind the lens of a faulty telescope.

She glanced around the theatre. The stone and its

shadowy companion had stopped their preternatural transfigurations when she readjusted her focus to the screen. What was happening to her? Maybe she really had drunk too much wine, and exhaustion was taking its toll.

The shadow seemed to step out of the screen and she almost screamed. It was no longer a shadow, but a man. He had a strange look on his face, a face that clung precariously to the edge of memory.

She clasped her hands to her mouth and slowly breathed. *I know you*, she thought and yet she could not give him a name.

The experience was frighteningly perplexing. He was familiar and yet he was not. His presence, his demeanour filled her with warmth and hope. Excitement. But his face was that of a stranger. He took her by both hands—actually touched her—and she thrilled to his touch, crumpling to the floor. He lifted her as though she weighed nothing, and stood her before him.

His expression was indescribable. His voice was unmistakably sad. Why couldn't she register his face or his name? And yet she knew this man meant more to her than life itself. She stood powerless as she watched herself succumb to him. He lifted her hand, the one with the ring on it. Angeline gasped, almost screamed. She was on the verge of remembering. The screen went black; the lights went out. When they returned, her mind snapped back to the theatre.

CHAPTER TEN

She was in awe of Jake Lalonde. Maybe 'in awe' wasn't quite the appropriate phrase. Strange gripping sensations consumed her in his presence, and since last night when that bizarre incident occurred following the audience's departure from the lecture, she had experienced a terrifying dream. Her surroundings were black and she was lost in a tunnel. Then people appeared and voices, blood and death. It was not the first time she had experienced the dream. Over the course of the last two months it had haunted her sleep. But last night, she awakened in a sweat, frightening her roommate, when she had screamed aloud. She had informed Drey it was nothing, only a nightmare. But it had seemed so real.

The voice came into her head.

Are you okay?
I tried to reach you last night when I felt your terror.

Angeline sent all her thought out to him.

I'm sorry; I wasn't alone.

For as long as she could remember, this voice had accompanied her heart. His identity was a puzzle to her. And to be honest, she was afraid to know. She had revealed his existence to no one, this voice in her head. She was certain people would label her crazy. In fact, there were times when she suspected she *was* crazy. *Is this what schizophrenia is like?* And yet she could hear him, feel him, as though he stood beside her, so she was fairly certain she was not schizophrenic. But normal people did not hear voices, nor did their voices answer them in such a tender and intimate way. No, she was not crazy. And yet, when he had asked her who she was, she could never bring herself to give him her name. He had never offered his either. It was as though he thought she knew who he was. But she didn't.

Her roommate was already up, babbling about breakfast, and tugging on a rust-coloured sweater that matched her coppery hair. They were not really friends, had only just met a couple of weeks ago at Cambridge in the library and had casually chatted, and somehow the topic of the Avebury lecture had arisen. It was such a coincidence that they were both attending that Drey, who was more outgoing than Angeline, had suggested they share a room to cut down on expenses since they were both grad students and cash-strapped.

The cryptozoologist was now chatting about Thomas Chancellor, how she had met him outside amid the standing stones and how they had both sighted a cryptid of the 'Big Bird' variety. Angeline was sceptical of Drey's research but out of politeness remained mute on the subject. The mention of Chancellor however piqued her curiosity. Then she remembered that her boss was still missing. The shrill, nerve-jangling ring of the British telephone in their room interrupted her thoughts and Drey lifted the receiver. "Hello?" she said. "Yes, she's here. Did you wish to speak to her? I see. Yes, all right, we'll both be there as soon as we can."

Angeline was combing out her wet hair. She'd had a shower shortly after Drey, so her roommate's hair was drier than hers. "What is it?"

"The police," Drey said. "They want to meet with us at the museum. It's about your boss."

"Then no one's heard a word from her?"

"'Fraid not. But apparently there's been a development."

The Red Lion Inn was not far from the museum. They

had a quick bite in the pub downstairs, and then hurried outside. As they neared, Angeline recognized Thomas Chancellor speaking to someone dressed similarly to him, although the stranger's trench coat was a little more worn. Instinctively, she knew he was a detective, probably from Scotland Yard. They turned from where they waited just outside the front doors, as she and Drey arrived.

"Ladies," Chancellor said, squinting into the sun. "This is Superintendent Simon Pettigrew from New Scotland Yard."

Angeline swallowed. So, it *was* serious.

The superintendent removed his sunglasses. He was a tall, thin man with a pasty complexion and intelligent blue eyes. He did not waste much time on the niceties but came straight to the point. "When was the last time you saw Maia Pickerton?" he asked.

Angeline told him everything she knew, which wasn't much. The curator had gone home to eat and change for last night's event and had not returned. No one had seen her since.

"Well, that's not exactly true," the superintendent said. And when Angeline raised her brows in query, he suggested they go for a walk in the stone circle.

They crossed the car park and turned south along the path of the arc of standing stones. Many were missing along this curve of the main circle. The one at the western entrance was an original, but a huge gap was filled in with a number of concrete markers. Superintendent Pettigrew followed a familiar path, past several megaliths interspersed with low concrete markers to indicate missing stones—until just prior to the West Kennet Avenue entrance. There he stopped.

A long shadow stretched from the base of the stone where they now stood. She knew its history. It had killed a man.

"This one has an interesting story behind it." She gathered her brows in a frown, wondering what it was he expected of her.

Pettigrew nodded.

A stray cloud passed across the blue morning sky and she continued to observe the superintendent, not quite understanding why the Barber Stone was pertinent to his investigation. She glanced at Drey who shrugged before restoring her attention to the superintendent.

"Don't you see it?" he demanded.

She glanced in the direction of his gaze.

He took three steps away and pointed. She followed.

Her jaw dropped.

A woman's face peered out at her from the stone, a woman whom she knew. No one had to speak her name. The visage stared at her as though she were actually present. Both Angeline and Drey moved closer to the monument to examine and test the illusion. Up close it had the appearance of weathered rock, and yet one needed only to step back a few feet and her face sprang alive. Her stern expression with sharp cut bangs fringed a wide-set stare, a startlingly perfect likeness.

"Is this some sort of a joke?" Angeline demanded.

"A simulacrum," Chancellor answered. "A trick of the eye or really the brain."

"I am well aware of that. But…but it looks like…Maia!"

"So, you also see it." The superintendent looked to Drey for further confirmation.

She nodded. "That's the spitting image of Maia Pickerton."

"The question now is why?" Chancellor said.

"And how?" Pettigrew opened a small notebook and returned his attention to Angeline. "You're studying ancient art, aren't you, miss? Can you tell if there's been any meddling with the stone?"

Angeline inspected it carefully. Her expertise was not in sculpture but in natural stones, archaeological monuments. "As far as I can see, there are no chisel or sanding marks, so I'd say there has been no recent tampering, but perhaps you should call in an expert."

"Your boss was our expert," the superintendent said.

"What about Diana Lune?" Drey asked.

"*She* is not exactly a scientist." Angeline turned to survey their surroundings. "Where is the American archaeologist? He might know something about these things."

"Dr. Lalonde is not answering his cellphone. The proprietress at his B & B says he did not return to his room last night. We have an APW out on him."

"You can't possibly think *he* has anything to do with this?" She didn't know Jake Lalonde at all, but suddenly she felt unexpectedly protective. An All Ports Warning was excessive if he wasn't a criminal.

"Oh, no," Superintendent Pettigrew said. "But you, Miss Lisbon, Mr. Chancellor here and Dr. Lalonde were three of the last people to see your boss before she disappeared. Do you have any idea where he may have gone?"

The last time she had seen him he was escorting the guest lecturer out of the museum and back to the Red Lion Inn.

She hesitated and sent her gaze across the field to the village core. The Red Lion was smallish as far as accommodations went, with a thatched roof and exposed timbers on the exterior. The bedrooms were narrow but comfortable and many of the windows looked out onto the stone circle, a pleasing view to wake up to in the morning.

The inn had a reputation for being haunted by the local ghosts. Had Jake stayed overnight with Diana? She flushed, wished she hadn't because she had no idea why she was blushing, and why she was thinking about him on a first name basis. She tried to hide her high colour by turning her head toward the stone face as though she were examining it for clues. If they should put out an APW on anyone, it should be Diana.

Chancellor was watching her expression, and Drey's lips twitched sympathetically.

Then the cryptozoologist suggested, "Have you tried

Diana Lune? I think I saw them leaving together last night."

The superintendent closed his notebook. "She's next on my list. Well, please leave your contact information with my sergeant. He pointed to a young woman dressed in official uniform. We'll be in touch when we get any leads."

Superintendent Pettigrew departed shortly, accompanied by Chancellor, and after Drey and Angeline had supplied addresses and phone numbers to the Sergeant, Drey told Angeline that she was off to conduct some fieldwork.

Angeline did not pry into Drey's research. She knew it involved strange sightings of mythical animals or some *not* so mythical—alleged prehistoric throwbacks, which were possibly even more unbelievable—but it was not her business.

She returned to the Barber Stone to examine it once more. Why was the image of her boss on this rock and what did it mean? One of the police officers that were left to scour the so-called crime scene asked her to move. He wanted to take some photographs. She obliged and returned to the museum to finish tidying up and to set things in order. She did not know how long she would be staying in town, now that Maia was missing. It wasn't her responsibility, and yet someone had to take charge.

"Nigel," she said when she returned. "Have you heard anything from Mrs. Pickerton's family?"

"No, miss," he said. "I am worried."

"We all are," she said, gently. Her eyes moved to the window in the direction of the suspicious stone. There was no logical explanation for the 'face' that she had seen on its surface. She gazed across the field towards the South Circle and the Devil's Chair. Her eyes lingered there for quite a while before she noticed Nigel watching her curiously. "Will you man the front desk for me, Nigel? I just have a few things to do in the back."

Actually, she had something she wanted to investigate in the basement. Something about her experience last night after everyone had left the museum had triggered a memory.

Solstice was impending and the local Wicca and druids were preparing for their annual celebrations. Late June was the time of the Handfast. A local girl would play the role of Branwen the central deity, and a symbolic marriage would be performed with a young follower. They had drawn a massive symbol on the grounds of Avebury, which could only be seen by air, and within which the ceremony would take place. They had permission from the local authorities and the museum to do this as part of their festivities, but that wasn't the issue.

The point was: the symbol was a circle representative of the full moon with two opposing crescent moons facing outward on either side. That was the design on Diana Lune's necklace, the one she was wearing last night. That symbol was also on the disk she had imagined seeing in the image on the screen. It reminded her of an artefact that was stored in the vaults of the museum. She turned to head for the basement when she caught movement at the closed door.

CHAPTER ELEVEN

"Mr. Chancellor? Were you looking for me? This is a private area. No visitors are allowed back here."

"Terribly sorry," Chancellor replied. "I must have taken a wrong turn. I was looking for the public restrooms."

"Out front," she directed.

He nodded, smiled. "Mysterious business about Mrs. Pickerton. But I'm sure the police will get some leads soon."

"Yes," Angeline said. "I'm sure they will. Was there anything else I can help you with?"

He shook his head. "I'd better not keep you from your work. Good day, Ms. Lisbon."

She watched him go. He was acting rather awkward and overly polite, almost as though he were hiding something or had done something wrong. What on earth could he have been doing back here? She returned to the foyer at a run, tempted to knock on the washroom door, but saw that it was slightly ajar, so he hadn't gone there after all.

"Nigel," she said. "Did you see where that man, Mr. Chancellor, went to?"

"He left, miss."

"What was he doing back there?" She indicated the employee's area with her thumb.

"So sorry, miss. I didn't see him go back there. Honestly, I didn't."

"It's all right, Nigel. No harm done."

Angeline returned to the rear of the museum and fumbled with some keys in her pocket. She started to insert the key, but then on a hunch simply turned the knob to the basement door. It was unlocked. Who had left it unlocked? Maia insisted that the door to the underground vaults be locked at all times. She stared back in the direction of the foyer. What a ridiculous notion she told herself. Why would Thomas Chancellor go down there?

A familiar thrill crept over her from scalp to nape. She released her grip on the doorknob and paused at the top of the stairs. She switched on the light, but it barely made any difference to the gloom. Her heart was pattering. She forced herself to recall what she had learned in group therapy. It was common for people to have fears, but hers were affecting her everyday life. It had all begun because of those stupid dreams, a dream where she was lost in the darkness somewhere underground. There were times when she couldn't get home if the sun was down. She would waste money on expensive taxis to avoid having to walk to the bus stop in the dark.

When finally she had decided to do something about it and completed a 'worst fears' clinic last month, she discovered that her worst fear could not really harm her. "What do you think will happen to you?" the group leader had asked.

She didn't know. All she knew was that whenever she faced the blackness of night she was wracked with irrational fear. Nightfall meant darkness and darkness brought on the terror. But the real reason for her anxiety was buried even deeper. Ironically, the cure was to face her fear.

Okay, deep breath, she told herself, and plunged down the steps.

An eerie feeling followed her although she tried desperately to outrun it. She paused halfway down, and listened. Why hadn't she thought to bring Drey with her? Or even Nigel. This place was not only dark it was creepy. *But I'm still alive.* And that was the main thing. Under these kinds of circumstances her body always reacted as though she were in mortal danger. *It's only adrenalin. Nothing more.*

Even so, no matter how often she told herself she had

nothing to dread, if it wasn't for the sense of urgency driving her, she would have stayed upstairs. She didn't even know why she felt this way. But something compelled her to search the basement, something stronger than her fear. "The dark cannot hurt me," she repeated to herself aloud. "The dark is only a physical state. Everything else is my imagination and the reactions of my adrenal system." *I am not afraid of the dark.*

She found herself on a landing and stopped to get her bearings. She descended a few more steps and turned. Why did museums always have such convoluted passageways? She wandered blindly, her second thoughts becoming third thoughts. Maybe she should forget the whole idea. She didn't even know where she had seen that artefact with the symbol engraved on it. It could be anywhere among these ancient shelves and boxes. Was it worth fumbling around down here in the dust and damp—and risking getting lost?

The lighting from cobwebbed light bulbs was dim at best. The smell that invaded her nostrils was of wet stone, the air frigid after the warmth upstairs, and the walls perspired. Black mould and slimy mildew seemed to creep about the cracks and crevices of wall and floor. They almost seemed to move and slither like snakes. The ground was uneven and in some parts the concrete was broken. A set of uneven steps appeared out of the gloom. Where did this go to again? To a subbasement? She had carefully avoided any reason for visiting the basement. Only once or twice had she been forced to come downstairs to fetch an artefact or box of records for Maia.

She gingerly negotiated the crumbling stone stairs, reached level ground and ducked under the low, arched stone ceiling over the underground corridors. There was a locked door to her right at the end of the grey stone passageway. At her feet was a wooden boardwalk covering a dirt floor. A whisper of moving air crossed the planks and she stepped back, every hair on her body raised.

She glanced up; she was alone.

A creeping sense of unease continued to prickle along her spine. She looked to pinpoint the source of the motion. There was no source. The passageway where she had stopped was dead silent. When she looked back, all was quiet.

She hurried through the corridor and entered an unlocked vault. There were footprints in the dust but no sign of any person. No motion either. Her eyes took in the vault from wall to wall and ceiling to floor. There was still no sign of anyone nearby. Angeline took a deep breath of the musty air and coughed. Her nerves were raw and if she didn't complete her mission she would race out of this room, screaming. She turned her attention to her immediate surroundings. Inside the vault were crates and boxes, stacked one on top of the other. Some were opened and objects were scattered any which way. Someone had been down here recently and hadn't bothered to return the items. What were they looking for? She searched and searched but could not find the artefact—a flat bronze disk, the size of a dinner plate, with the triple moon symbol engraved upon it.

CHAPTER TWELVE

It was with great relief, although empty-handed, that Angeline returned to the Red Lion Inn. She asked at the reception desk if the Interpol agent Thomas Chancellor had returned. He had just checked out, the receptionist told her. Did he leave a forwarding address? In fact, he had. It was the swanky Hotel Savoy in the Strand, London.

Paranormal investigations must be a very lucrative business, Angeline thought. From what Drey had told her, he worked freelance for criminal cases involving supernatural events.

Upstairs in her room Angeline observed through the window the green fields and standing stones that encompassed the village in the sunshine. It was a lovely day, a fine day for travelling. The sky was a sharp, deep blue and any clouds were quickly hurrying away. Too bad she could not linger here. It wouldn't matter anyway. The peaceful serenity of the village was already broken by the presence of the police. She had come to work at the Alexander Keiller Museum in the hopes of gaining experience in cultural management, and instead she was trapped in the middle of a mystery. That mystery had at its center Jake Lalonde.

Why did she feel that way?

She was also perplexed as to how Thomas Chancellor figured in the affair. But she was almost certain that if she located the Interpol agent she would find the missing archaeologist.

She unpacked her computer tablet to search the events calendar of the Savoy on the Internet. It highlighted a meeting of the International Congress on Paranormal Studies. So, that was why he was booked there. And if that was where he would be, then it looked like she would be taking a trip to London. She dragged her suitcase from the floor and flung it onto the bed.

"Where are you going?" Drey asked as she returned from her morning's excursions. Drey was fresh-faced and windblown from being outdoors.

"Any luck sighting Big Bird?"

Her roommate shook her head. "Last night was a fluke. Glad I wasn't the only one to see it. Always helps to have witnesses."

Angeline nodded as Drey sent her a look of inquiry. "I have to take a quick trip to London." Angeline paused from packing and glanced at her roommate. "Hey, I know this sounds weird, but you said Thomas Chancellor was with you when you caught that sighting. What do you know about him?"

She shrugged. "He's a bit of an oddball." Then grinned. "But so am I. I don't really know him. We merely had a short chat beside the Barber Stone. He told me to keep to the lighted side of the road." She laughed.

Drey McFee took life a lot more casually than Angeline, and furthermore she was certain that the cryptozoologist had no fear of the dark.

Drey dragged her carryall from the desk and said, "I'm headed that way myself. Want some company? I have a convention to attend. I would have cancelled if the cops had wanted us to stay here, but I don't recall anyone insisting that we remain in town."

***

The Strand flanked the river Thames and once counted as one of the most prestigious neighbourhoods where one might live in London. Stately mansions, no longer standing but demolished by the 19th century, gave way to office towers and cheap restaurants and quirky gift shops. But the famous Savoy remained, as did the Somerset House and Twinings at no. 216, the teashop of the notorious Thomas Twining, the oldest commercial company in the city. Never a day went by when Angeline did not have a cup of earl grey to start her morning.

It took a couple of hours by train to get to London via Swindon. The familiar station smells of soot and garbage greeted them. They took the Underground to the Strand lugging one suitcase each, and easily located the ritzy hotel. "I don't have enough money to stay here," Angeline said.

"Don't worry, I have a room booked in the east end of town. You can bunk with me." Drey stared at the multileveled opulent glass and concrete hotel with its multiple doormen and permanent taxi rank. "Let's see if we can just leave our luggage at Reception for the time being."

Reception was uncooperative, so being resourceful Drey located an empty broom closet and tucked their bags under some shelves. Angeline was hesitant to leave her belongings but her accomplice insisted they were safe. What did they own that couldn't be replaced at the local pharmacy anyway?

They sauntered into the lobby and Drey pointed to a sandwich board in front of the wide opened doors of a ballroom.

WELCOME TO THE 59TH ANNUAL
INTERNATIONAL CONGRESS ON
PARANORMAL STUDIES
Registration in progress

Inside was a reception area where people were signing up or retrieving registration packages. Angeline borrowed a booklet from an unattended table. Apparently there was a Ghost Hunter University operating concurrently with a three-day seminar series. Participants, it claimed, would gain a better understanding of the paranormal and learn how to conduct investigations of their own. No doubt there were queer things happening in Avebury (did her boss's disappearance and the sudden appearance of her image in the Barber Stone qualify as ghostly?) and Wiltshire had a reputation for local hauntings. But signing up for a three-day ghost-hunting seminar? She hoped it would not come to that.

She turned to look for Drey, thinking out loud. "So, Chancellor is here for the ICOPS convention."

Angeline wasn't registered for the event but Drey was. Now, she was glad she had brought the cryptozoologist with her because they could take turns using her nametag.

The convention hall was stifling. Drey tapped Angeline on the shoulder, and together they slipped into a session entitled, *Poltergeists and Pareidolia.* They settled in next to each other in the packed ballroom and studied the program.

> *Pareidolia is an illusionary stimulus in which vague sounds or images (simulacra) seem clear and significant. It can trigger a series of unpleasant neural reactions in the brain leading to anxiety, fear and panic. The effect is so realistic that people swear they see or hear something that is not supposed to be there. Poltergeists can occur simultaneously or develop out of an episode of pareidolia.*

At the front near the podium sat a familiar-looking man. The view was only of his back, so all she noticed of his clothing was a black leather jacket beneath thick hair that touched his broad shoulders. She squinted. Could it be…? Yes. It *was* the archaeologist, Jake Lalonde, the visiting professor from the University of Washington who was supposedly missing.

And there was Chancellor—right next to him. Did her eyes deceive her or was it true that they were together? A flash—a memory or something—sent a prickle across her scalp. That weird dream or whatever it was she had experienced after everyone had left the talk last night. She was experiencing the same crawling sensation now. Did the dream have something to do with them?

The two men left the theatre together when the session was over, without realizing they had been recognized. Drey said nothing so Angeline assumed she had not noticed them. She asked if she knew whether or not Diana Lune had checked out of the Red Lion Inn.

"I believe she did," Drey replied. "Why? You think she might be here? The cops said they didn't want us to leave the country. They never said anything about leaving Avebury. They could hardly expect any of us to stay in that tiny town. It's got very few facilities. Besides, we have lives. And until they can prove that your boss was abducted or murdered, they can't hold any of us there."

She shifted her glance to the doorway. "Well, at least now we know that Lalonde didn't disappear in the same way as Maia. I wonder why the police haven't looked for him here?"

"So, you *did* notice them. Well, clearly, that Interpol agent found him. That was the man himself who left with Jake."

Drey nudged Angeline toward the hotel exit. "Come on, I want to play Sherlock. Something weird is going on and those two are involved. Let's follow before they get too far away."

***

It seemed the fugitives were in the mood for a sightseeing tour. They boarded a shuttle heading for the Tower of London. Angeline thought this was odd but she was determined to speak to the elusive archaeologist. She would have been happier if he had been alone. It would be a trick to separate the two.

The shuttle pulled out before they could board and she and Drey caught the next one, which left shortly after to weave into the dense London traffic. What seemed like an hour later but could only have been fifteen or twenty minutes, their shuttle pulled in behind the first one.

"Why on earth are they sightseeing?" Drey asked. "With all that's going on their behavior does not make sense."

Angeline was sitting on something lumpy, and shifted over to pull out a folded newspaper that was wedged into the back of the seat. She unrolled it, and started at the headlines. On the front page of *The Guardian* was a picture of the Tower of London with its Yeoman Ravenmaster in the foreground. The caption read:

London To Be Invaded?

Legend had it that if anything happened to the six resident ravens at the Tower, the British capital would be invaded. Historically, ravens guarded the London Tower. Today's headlines stated that the six birds were unlawfully released or abducted. The question was: why would anyone do that?

"Coincidence," Drey's voice sounded over her shoulder. "I know what you're thinking. Why would the Tower ravens go missing the same time those ravens appeared in Avebury? The two events have nothing to do with each other." She flicked the edge of the newspaper. "I *am* curious about that raven face in the megalith though. And clearly so was Superintendent Pettigrew. You say you never noticed it before?"

"No," Angeline said. "And I've been to Avebury dozens of times."

Drey's head jerked up to look outside the bus window where the first shuttle had parked and had already unloaded its passengers. "Look, they aren't going into the London Tower at all. They've gone over there, across that green space, and inside that other tower where those guards in traditional uniforms are standing. I believe that's the Wakefield Tower where the ravens are kept in cold weather."

Angeline tucked the newspaper back where she had found it, and exited the parked bus behind Drey. They strolled in the direction of the raven's outdoor accommodations. She cast a backward glance at the shuttle where the newspaper lay. So the story was true. Nobody was home.

She glanced into the clear blue sky. Her companion did likewise before removing a pamphlet from a metal holder attached to the front of the cage.

"The birds won't be up there. Says here in this pamphlet that the ravens all have their wings clipped so that they can't fly away." Drey turned her gaze this way and that. "So, where are they? If they can't fly away that means they were stolen."

Angeline had her own suspicions and longed to test them out on Drey. How much did she or Maia Pickerton know about Diana Lune? Angeline had heard all kinds of stories involving the notorious adventurer and antiquarian, and had generally laughed it off as the jealousy of colleagues. And yet what was happening with the stone faces and the thousands of flocking ravens was too much to be coincidence. Still, how could Diana Lune possibly have known that they would descend on Avebury like that? The London Tower incident occurred just yesterday and was only featured in this morning's newspaper. The front cover image of Diana's bestseller flashed in her mind. How could she know that the six famous ravens were going to escape?

Unless... *Did she have something to do with it?* Angeline had heard of publicity stunts before, but this was going way overboard. And involving the museum and the village in a possible crime would either attract a flock of tourists or give the historic site a bad name. Was there really a way to have faked those raven faces in the megaliths?

A man dressed like a Yeoman Warder stood at the other side of the cages. This she assumed must be the Ravenmaster. Angeline approached to ask about the legend of the ravens.

"If the ravens are lost or fly away, the Crown will fall and Britain with it," the elderly man said in answer to her query, and proceeded to enlighten them on the legendary significance of ravens.

In the old stories special folk were attributed with 'Raven Knowledge.' This meant that they could mediate healing, make prophesies and protect. The raven was a messenger between the two worlds—the world we lived in, and the next, the After Life. Which was why ravens were often found at the bottom of burial pits. These so-called 'shafts' were the connection between the world of the living and that of the dead. Today the association of the raven with prophecy and protection was still fostered in the heart of London.

"In the legend of Bran the Blessed, the prophetic god-king (whose name, Bran, means Raven), asks that upon his death, his head be cut off and buried on the White Cliffs facing the channel to France," the Ravenmaster said. "The magic and protective power of the head is symbolized by the presence of the birds, which have been kept at the Tower to this day to ensure the safety of the realm." He sighed. "But sadly, yesterday morning, all six disappeared from the grounds." He paused for emphasis as Drey and Angeline's interest wakened further.

"Do the authorities believe someone stole them?" Angeline asked.

"Or maybe it was Animal Rights activists. Maybe they just set them free," Drey suggested.

Surely no Animal rights group could be so naïve as to release a half dozen helpless birds into the busy streets of London where they could get run over by cars or if they took refuge in the treed areas, they might be fodder for badgers and foxes.

"They cannot survive in the wild with clipped wings," the Ravenmaster said. But there is hope for their safe recovery. Each individual is easily identifiable by different colored bands around their ankles." He removed a smartphone from the heavy tartan folds of his robe, and scrolled through some photos until he came to those of the ravens. "This one with the turquoise blue band around his right leg is George, and this here is Grog. He wears yellow."

One of the guards in red and black stared meaningfully across the green at the Ravenmaster and he quickly withdrew his phone and tucked it away. "I probably shouldn't be showing these. The police will release official photographs and hopefully members of the public will sight them."

"Don't worry," Drey said. "The city is in good hands. It's not going to collapse just because of a few missing mascots."

Angeline thanked the kind man for his time and she and Drey went into the Wakefield Tower.

The archaeologist and the Interpol agent were nowhere to be found, and by the time they returned outside, the light was fading.

***

The shuttle bus dropped them off in front of the hotel. Angeline was surprised to sight the fugitives walking out the front doors of the Savoy Hotel. Whatever their business at the famous tourist site it had not kept them long, and they had returned before their pursuers.

From his casual attitude, Jake seemed unaware that he was on Scotland Yard's wanted list, and Angeline sincerely wondered why Chancellor hadn't told him.

The men cut through a courtyard towards a traditional English pub. It had a colorful coat of arms above the doorway and was called the *Dog and Saddle*. Drey was all for accosting them immediately and demanding they explain themselves, but Angeline felt something—an unsettling feeling that caused her to hold back. This unsettling feeling—more like a strong desire—insisted she corner Jake alone.

Would either of them recognize her when they finally caught up? She grabbed Drey by the arm and lunged toward the pub door. Why did she want to confront Jake by herself? She had no explanation, except for a queer feeling. And that queerness was inexplicable even to her. She only knew that if she could get him alone, a lot of nagging questions would be answered.

The fugitives were not inside the pub. Angeline and Drey stood on the threshold scanning the room. The two men had walked with heads close, increasing Angeline's suspicions.

"I didn't think they even knew each other until the night of Diana Lune's talk," she said in a low voice. "Don't you find it strange that they're acting like best friends?"

She waved away the waiter who wanted to seat them. "Sorry, wrong place. We were supposed to meet some friends at a different pub. Can we leave through that back door?"

The waiter scowled. "No. That's a service entrance. Employees only."

The fellow was obviously having a bad day. Angeline gave him a tip of two pounds. "Thanks," she said, and he stepped out of the way as she exited by the front door.

She gestured to Drey to hurry. They made a sharp left and saw that they were on an office-lined street and were now headed onto Cromwell Road. The men were about a block ahead of them. Angeline and Drey stopped to wait for the streetlight to change, giving their quarry an even bigger head start. Thirty minutes later the men disappeared.

There were few places of interest here and the only one where they might have gone to was the Natural History Museum. The afternoon was waning. Why were they visiting the museum so late?

Inside, after paying the admission, Angeline observed the bustling lobby. What exhibits did Jake and Chancellor intend to visit, and why? A prominent sign promoting a special exhibition of Native North American shamanic cedar carvings caught Angeline's eye. This might be something that would draw an archaeologist's attention. She knew that mythical animals were subjects of Haida art. There was a special collection of shamanic bird masks. Was this what he had come to see?

She was just about to follow Drey to the exhibit when she was struck by a strange sensation. She popped into one of the annexing galleries and was greeted with eerie lighting and giant creatures in shadowy corners. Apparently this was some sort of interactive prehistoric display.

"Go to the Haida art exhibit," Angeline urged. "See if you can't locate Chancellor and keep him occupied. I'll catch up with you in a minute." She tapped her purse where her phone was lodged. "Stay in touch."

As Drey left, Angeline squinted into the shadows, hoping to catch a glimpse of the mysterious figure that had fired her imagination. She didn't know why, but it had brought the archaeologist to mind. Why had she taken to thinking of him by his first name?

It felt comfortable and right somehow, and yet she knew if she ever came face to face with him again, she would address him as Dr. Lalonde.

Some robotic dinosaurs roared and growled in the center of the massive space. It really made no sense but she thought he might be here. A glass wall lined the side where she stood. As she wove her way between the excited visitors she noticed that the outside wall was composed of glass, and reflected the moving dinosaurs, exaggerating the prehistoric effect.

The room danced with crazy lights mimicking a lightning storm, and fake thunder boomed. A holographic volcano spewed lava in the background. Most of the visitors in here were children with their parents or young adults. Amidst all of the activity her eye landed on a prehistoric bird display. The sight of it at first sent shivers over her skin, but then it dawned on her that she had experienced something similar before.

She dodged some people, wove through the crowd, desperate to find Drey. She glanced back once and a large robotic bird caught her eye. It was the thing that had drawn her into this gallery in the first place.

CHAPTER THIRTEEN

Angeline searched for an exit. There were a number of exits in this gallery. She was about to step through a door when a powerful figure blocked her path.

She gasped before recognition turned fear into annoyance. It was the Interpol agent, and he frowned at her. He stepped into a dimly lit passageway with her elbow reluctantly in tow. Not ready with a trumped up story to explain her presence here, all she could think of was that she had just as much right to be at the Natural History Museum as he. It was London after all.

Where was Drey? She was supposed to be keeping him occupied or at least within view. It was only when Angeline and her captor were out of sight of any potential eavesdroppers did he allow her to disengage herself from his grip. For a second, as they stood face to face, there was something ethereal about his expression.

"Come with me," he instructed.

He looked around before he shuffled her forward. A resurgence of fright threatened to make her bolt, and she resisted. What did she know about this man? Next to nothing. But how else was she to get any answers unless she cooperated?

Chancellor led her down the escalator to a cafeteria. It was late and the cafeteria was half empty. He ushered her in the direction of a quiet table along the wall, and indicated that she be seated, before he sat opposite her.

He studied her face in the bright light. She could see the thoughts churning around in his mind but he wasn't quite ready to divulge them.

She self-consciously dipped her head, allowed her hair to fall slightly forward to hide a faint scar on her right temple, near the hairline.

Just exactly what was he looking for?

"How did you get that?" he asked, lightly moving her hair to reveal the scar.

"How did I get what?" She slid a hand up to pull her hair forward, but he was insistent.

He reached out and gingerly lifted the long black forelock. "How did you get that scar?"

She hesitated, then said, "I don't know. I think I fell when I was a kid. What of it?" She frowned. It was hard enough for a woman to be evaluated so thoroughly on looks, but pointing out flaws was simply rude.

He observed her thoughtfully.

Had he known where Jake was all the time, even this morning during the superintendent's queries? She weighed his expression, then said, "You *know* that Scotland Yard is searching for Jake Lalonde. Why are you protecting him? You should be taking him to Superintendent Pettigrew for questioning, instead of hiding out at a museum like a couple of nerds."

He ignored her reference to him as a 'nerd.' After all, wasn't she one herself since she spent most of her time inside museums? He answered dispassionately. "I am not officially on the case."

"And exactly what *is* the case? Because I suspect it has to do with a little more than just my boss's disappearance."

Angeline did not respond to the obvious lift of his eyebrows. She felt a strange affinity with Jake. Why? She had only met him yesterday. And she had to admit that she felt something eerily similar with Chancellor too.

"You seem to have an unusual interest in Dr. Lalonde's activities," he remarked.

How was she to answer this loaded question? Should she disclose her fears, her suspicions? Should she indulge her curiosity? He seemed to think she was showing more than a natural interest in a crime that had been perpetrated in her presence. Was her concern so odd? This was a missing persons case and she was obligated to reveal any information she uncovered to the authorities.

"Why this sudden interest in a stranger, Ms. Lisbon?"

"I might ask you the same question. I thought you met Jake for the first time yesterday. Since when did you and he become so chummy?"

"Since when did you start calling him *Jake*?"

Now, Angeline was even more perturbed. It seemed to her that he knew more about why she felt this connection with Jake—correction Dr. Lalonde—than she did herself.

"Do you believe in ghosts, Ms. Lisbon?" he asked.

Her mouth dropped open.

"Look, Ms. Lisbon, I don't know what's going on with these standing stones. Why they have faces of ravens in them when previously they didn't. And why Maia Pickerton's face has appeared in the Barber Stone now that she is missing. That is the big mystery, and I'd like to help solve it. My issue with Lalonde, on the other hand, is—well, it's personal."

Chancellor got to his feet. He clearly meant to cut short the interrogation. "Meet me tomorrow—at Stonehenge. You can get a lift with the Ghost Hunter University group expedition. He glanced at his watch. Register at the front desk. They have tourist tickets there. I'll explain more to you then." He gave her a time, and then turned to leave. He threw over his shoulder: "I'm staying at the Savoy Hotel. Room 2114. But I guess you already know that."

***

There was no way to contact Drey. Angeline's phone was dead. Why hadn't she remembered to charge it? This museum was enormous; they would never find each other by physically searching. They would have to make their way back to the hotel separately.

Drey was no longer in the Native North American art exhibit. She must have followed some other clue to Jake's whereabouts.

When they failed to reconnect after a half hour of searching, Angeline returned to the Savoy Hotel alone to retrieve her luggage from the broom closet. She flagged a cab and proceeded on to the cheaper accommodations that Drey had booked on the east side. Once there, she unpacked her things, reclaimed her computer tablet and collapsed onto one of the twin beds in the room.

Ghosts. What was that Interpol agent talking about? Was he suggesting: that those faces were ghosts frozen in stone? She knew he studied the paranormal, but did he really believe this stuff? And seriously, was he attending the Ghost Hunter University's hokey field trips?

Angeline splayed herself over the bedcovers and placed a hand onto her cellphone that was on the nightstand being recharged. She should call Drey now that her phone was working again, and let her know she had spoken to Chancellor.

No answer.

Maybe *her* battery had died too. Angeline gave up, dropped her cellphone onto the pillow, and examined her surroundings. Despite the expense she should move to the Savoy—for the convenience, if nothing else. She checked out the time on her phone. It was almost eight o'clock.

She got up and grabbed her jacket, went to the window and dragged wide the drapes.

Where are you?

Her answer was silence.

CHAPTER FOURTEEN

The registration desk for the Ghost Hunter University's excursion to Stonehenge was open late. Angeline walked down the brightly lit corridor towards the elevator. Out of her peripheral vision she caught movement.

Was someone following her? Or was she just spooked by the whole idea of ghosts. She thought she had heard footsteps but when she turned to look, she was alone. She listened a few seconds more, squinted down a side passage. No hotel staff or visitors, no one at all. This ghost-hunting thing must be getting to her.

She hurried, the sensation of being followed growing with every step. Gooseflesh crept up her arms and she felt a sudden urge to run. The elevator was so far away.

Was that the click of heels? She darted a look and saw that she was still alone. Those footsteps must be coming from the intersecting corridor. She shrugged but could not shake off the feeling. Why was she afraid? Many women in this hotel wore dress shoes, and it was probably just some party girl. She looked behind her and saw nothing. Now a soft padding of footsteps, more like someone in running shoes. So what?

She sprinted down the corridor like an Olympic runner. She had practically leaped the last three paces and now she jammed her finger onto the Down button, pressing and pressing and pressing—as though that would make the elevator arrive sooner. The clicking of the heels had ceased, and again she heard the sound of soft footfalls continuing down the corridor.

The elevator ground open. Why did everything function so slowly when you were in a hurry? The doors closed at a snail's pace before the lift responded to her command. At the main floor, the elevator door slid open and several people entered as she departed. She was met by warm air from the lobby, and the chatter and noise of hotel business. She glanced at the front entrance, walked up to the reception desk and asked them to call her a cab. It took five minutes to get the taxi and another half hour to arrive at the Savoy.

Angeline entered the swanky hotel and sought out the Ghost Hunter University registration desk. She tossed a cursory look behind; she was alone. She was unsteady, still unnerved by whoever had chased her into the elevator back at her own hotel. First thing tomorrow, she decided, they were checking into the Savoy.

She listened to the concierge's directions and went down the corridor to a room bustling with people chatting about ghosts, hauntings, unusual sightings and other paranormal events. She found the desk and signed up for the trip to Stonehenge. The group leader of the Ghost Hunter University was a man named Gill Ames. He was pleased she would be joining his students and their three-day seminar.

Three-day seminar? She had not signed on for *this!*

There were refreshments of beer and some awful white wine. Angeline declined the hospitality and begged off with the excuse of needing a good night's sleep for the exciting adventure the next day. She dodged some drunk, ghost-hunting enthusiasts waving unrecognizable gadgets in her face and returned to her hotel room two and a half hours later, to see that Drey was there and already asleep.

***

She awoke with a start. She hadn't slept well. Her conversation with Chancellor had sent ghosts flooding her dreams and was probably what had caused that paranoid race down the hallway last night.

After a quick shower, she gave Drey a brief rundown on her encounter with the Interpol agent at the museum, and the cryptozoologist related her uneventful evening tailing the archaeologist. He had disappeared she said.

Drey had not yet showered so she insisted Angeline grab a quick breakfast, and join the seminar of the Ghost Hunter University without her; she'd catch up later.

The talk scheduled first was called *Time Travelling ghosts: the Other Side of the Truth*. "Are ghosts spirits of deceased people who remain in touch with our plane of existence?" Gill Ames asked. "Perhaps. But then again. Perhaps not. Could it be that what we see or experience as a ghost represents a break in the continuum of time? In other words," he suggested, "if we view time as nonlinear, but rather as a wave or a loop, could we be looking backwards or even forwards in time when we observe a ghost?"

This was an astounding theory. Why were Chancellor and Jake interested in time travel or ghosts? Because if she wasn't mistaken—there they were again.

Now Angeline understood her own hesitation to draw attention to herself last night. She had sensed something peculiar about the fact that Chancellor and Jake were at this convention for paranormal phenomena. Jake Lalonde was a world-renowned archaeologist. What was he doing studying the supernatural?

She sat back in the upholstered folding chair as Gill Ames made his concluding remarks. "The person—assuming they are from the past—is seen through a portal. In effect, what we perceive as a ghost is a live human being—existing in their own time."

Angeline rose, and shot a quick glance at the two men before she exited the seminar to visit the Ladies Room. She met Drey just joining the talk as she returned.

The next presenter had already been introduced. The eloquent speaker was a woman sporting a broad-brimmed hat, her hair tucked in beneath it. She wore enormous tinted glasses and virtually no makeup. Angeline was seated too far away to make out her features, and she was dressed very conservatively in wide slacks and boxy jacket, which did absolutely nothing for her figure. People obsessed with ghosts and the supernatural tended to disdain vanity. They also leaned towards exceptional flakiness, which explained the hat. Her voice was deep and modulated as though she was deliberately controlling the intonation. Angeline searched both of her pockets for the speaker abstracts to learn the presenter's name. Drat. She must have lost the booklet, or left it in the room. She nudged Drey who was seated beside her. She too was empty-handed.

Angeline returned her attention to the speaker. She was investigating time travel, and claimed to have been part of a government study in teleportation, where a hundred people in the early millennium were recruited to participate in a time-space experiment called *Project Pegasus*. The researchers succeeded in harnessing 'radiant energy', a universal force, which bent space and time, and allowed for 'real time' teleportation as well as time travel, using advanced holographic technology in the form of tunnels.

***

Like most of these seminars the discussion afterwards was mainly anecdotal experiences from the participants and the speakers. Gill Ames was the moderator and he stood at the podium as one after the other ghostly time-travelling stories were recounted. Finally the woman in the large hat shared a chilling experience. She was now seated among the audience in the front row but when she was called to comment, she rose to face the audience. She was still too far away so Angeline could not make out her face. Again both she and Drey missed her name when the scrape of a chair being adjusted drowned it out.

She was found trespassing at the Stonehenge circle, she declared. That is, she had slipped under the rope barriers to experience the energy of the ancient temple, and was taken to a mental health hospital where she abruptly teleported from her locked room.

Angeline and Drey exchanged shrewd glances. Drey was a cryptozoologist and had seen unexplained creatures, but unexplained phenomena based on anecdotal evidence had her just as unnerved as Angeline. No one else seemed shocked or disturbed by the confession. Everyone here was a believer.

It occurred to Angeline that the woman's voice was vaguely familiar.

"Do you recognize her?" she whispered.

Drey shook her head. "I don't think so, but I can't see her face with that giant hat slipping over her face."

When the discussion was over Angeline left the auditorium to meet up with the others for the field trip. Chancellor had told her to meet him at Stonehenge. Where was he? She had seen both him and Jake Lalonde at the seminar earlier. But it seemed they had both left before the discussions even began. If there was something the Interpol agent had wanted her to see at Stonehenge, couldn't he have waited around and offered her a lift? No, of course not. That was not his way. His way was to be cryptic, annoying and a bully. So, she would have to hitch a ride with the Ghost Hunter group, but first she had to ditch Drey. Chancellor had warned her to arrive alone, so she gave some excuse about a hair appointment, and then doubled back to the meeting place of the Ghost Hunter University.

The trip would take a little longer than she would have liked, approximately one and a half hours in a crowded, smelly bus filled with loud, manic, believers of the paranormal.

***

One thing that always put people off was to start playing with your smartphone. That was what Angeline would have to do to avoid conversation with the chatting bus riders seated around her. She proceeded to do just that, first pretending to be receiving multiple texts. The result was effective, and the chatterers gave up on her and chatted to each other.

To while the time away, Angeline conducted some research on her phone. She was curious about the woman at the seminar who had claimed to be a time-traveller. She vaguely remembered the news item in the papers. A linked story said that a woman had been arrested years earlier at a military facility, somewhere near Casterley Camp high atop Salisbury Plain along the Great Stones Way. It was rumored that the firing range meant for military training was a front for some Top Secret project, similar to the Hadron Collider. The fugitive claimed to have travelled from the future in order to prevent the scientists from Casterley Camp from destroying the world. She insisted that countries did not exist where she came from. Like the first woman, she later disappeared from a mental health ward in London and had not been heard of since.

Not until now, Angeline thought. Clearly she wasn't considered dangerous, and wasn't on anyone's 'most wanted' list. Otherwise she wouldn't be free to attend conventions. Angeline tapped her phone screen to read further.

It was just as she suspected. Speculation suggested that these two events involved the same individual. Yes, it was very peculiar indeed.

The bus drove through Salisbury and eventually arrived at the site. After debarking, the group assembled noisily outside the visitor center to await instructions. Here was the car park, the displays, a cafeteria, gift shop and washrooms. The ghost hunters were eager to roam the ancient landscape where legends of ghosts and hauntings abounded.

Angeline searched high and low between the crowds for a glimpse of a tall, conservatively dressed man in a navy blue suit and yellow tie, and beige trench coat. He was nowhere in sight. While group leader Gill Ames was busy explaining how to use some of the ghost-detection gadgets, Angeline slipped away and headed east on the path—away from the

Stonehenge visitor center.

The stone circle sat on the open plain, far away from the main car park on the A303. It was located one mile apart from the visitor center, and from where the tourists stood waiting for the shuttle to take them to the famous sight. Stonehenge itself was not visible. It was out of view beyond the skyline.

All around her were casually dressed tourists in khaki's, denim, summer cottons, sneakers and sunhats. Her own group didn't seem to notice that she was missing, so engrossed were they in the idea of detecting paranormal activity.

A man suddenly approached her. He was one of the site guides. He told her in a cockney accent that a bloke in a yellow tie and trench coat had asked him to give her a message. It was written on a scrap of yellow paper, and read:

Meet me at the Long Barrow.
T.C.

She hadn't a clue where that was, and she was beginning to regret blowing off Drey. She could have used her company. There was safety in numbers. After all, what did she really know about Thomas Chancellor? Just because he was an Interpol agent didn't mean he wasn't crazy.

Overhead the skylarks and curlews wheeled. Exmoor ponies grazed among yellow wildflowers that grew in the distance. Low scrubby plants spread roots under most of the track breaking up the chalk grass. She had a clear view of the plain. Bridleways and footpaths crisscrossed the area. In the distance she could make out what looked to be an elongated hill or mound—a barrow. Was that the one he meant?

The track crossed a meadow of sparse vegetation, mostly knapweed that gradually eroded to chalk. She meandered over birdsfoot trefoil, cowslip and yellow rattle and other plants that sprang from the cracks in the thin soil. Her pathway zigged and zagged around chalk outcrops and took a sharp jog left and then right. Grass flourished here, enjoying the late afternoon sun, and she noted that she had stopped on the edge of an earthwork.

Her pamphlet identified it as the Stonehenge cursus, a ditch and bank, whose purpose remained unknown, and which took an east-west course. On the top of the barrow she thought she detected movement.

Was that Chancellor? She hoped this tête-à-tête would be quick. They mustn't linger on the open plain at night. The Ghost Hunter group had warned her that the weather could be rough at night. Not to mention the fact that Drey would be wondering what had become of her. It was important not to miss the bus. She wondered if the ghost hunters would notice her absence and wait for her.

In the several hours that she had been hiking she hadn't seen a soul except for the tourists at the visitor center. She headed in the direction of the barrow, and climbed up over the ridge. As she reached the curved plateau, a figure moved forward to greet her.

"So you came," Chancellor said.

"You sound like you didn't think I would."

Over his shoulder she saw the magnificent stone circle of Stonehenge. The fading light gleamed pink on the stone and the shadows formed long, blue oblongs that seemed to have a life of their own. From this height, the plain sloped and she could follow the trails that crossed the landscape leading to and from the famous monument. Hours had passed since she left the Ghost Hunter group and the tourists were mostly gone.

She returned her attention to him. His heavy shoulders lifted in a shrug. "You have good reason to believe that I am some kind of delusional person. But believe me, Angeline, we are no strangers."

"So you say. I feel like I should know you, but for the life of me, I know I don't."

"It's obvious that we need to talk," he agreed.

"What is going on?" she demanded. "Why am I here?"

"Angeline—"

"Stop calling me 'Angeline' as though we're good friends. I hardly know you."

"All right. Ms. Lisbon if you prefer."

In the distance the shadows of the megaliths changed with the movement of the fading light. The classic circle looked exactly as it did in photographs except that there was a rope barrier preventing visitors from exploring inside and between the standing stones. And yet, wasn't there something inside the circle? It was late and by now the site was surely closed. But something moved.

"Where is Jake?" she asked.

"So, you don't want me to call you by your first name, and yet that is how you address Dr. Lalonde?"

Why was he being so evasive? All she wanted to know was the archaeologist's whereabouts. Was that so strange? The police were searching for him and Chancellor was in collusion with him. No matter if he denied it, she had seen them together.

Something was going on in the center of the stone circle. She could see clear movement now. She had uncanny long-sightedness, and that was definitely a person in the middle of the stones.

No one was allowed inside the stone circle. Not without written permission. And no ritual acts were *ever* permitted.

She squinted, stared—took in a sharp intake of air. "That's him!"

She didn't know how she knew it was him, but she did. She started to head down from the barrow, when Chancellor stopped her. He held her by one arm, and when she tried to push past, he said, "You mustn't interrupt him…. I'll explain later, I promise."

Chancellor's eyes were dark, imploring, and his mouth was drawn in a grim line, his face like concrete. His grip tightened on her as she tried to shrug him off. Her pulse raced.

"I'm sorry. I didn't mean to hurt you. But you have to

trust me," he said.

"Then you had better start explaining."

Chancellor released his grip on her. Angeline rubbed her bruised wrists. The wind blew his normally tidy hair across his forehead and her own whipped about any which way. She tucked her unruly hair behind her ears and waited, but when the Interpol agent remained silent she started to leave. His voice stopped her.

"I knew I was going to have to tell you sooner or later. I was hoping after I convinced Lalonde of the situation, the two of us could deal with it without having to involve you."

Her gaze was fixed on the shadowy figure among the ancient pillars: he appeared to be dancing. "Why is he doing that?"

His answer was stifled, as though he was still deciding what to tell her. Finally he muttered, "He...he is trying to locate *her*."

Angeline narrowed her eyes and managed to control her expression. Her voice however was another matter; she could not keep the fear out of her tone. "Locate who?"

"Do you understand anything about timelines?"

What kind of question was that? Certainly there were inexplicable things in the world. Hence groups like the Ghost Hunter University and ICOPS. Ancient druid astronomy, ley lines, and Wiccan magic fell into her academic pursuits. But good old physics? No.

"I saw you two at the seminar this morning," Angeline accused. "I saw you at the ICOPS symposia on time-travelling ghosts and holographic teleportation. Either you two are seriously unbalanced, or there is something you're hiding."

Working with druids and Wicca had shown her very odd things. But nothing even remotely resembling what was occurring inside the stone circle. Jake Lalonde was dressed like a Haida shaman and he was dancing in a ritualistic fashion. His face was covered.

Was that a mask? The Natural History Museum's special

exhibit of Haida shamanic bird masks flashed into her memory.

She managed to control her voice and said, "He knows better. He's an archaeologist. He shouldn't be breaking the law." But it was clear he had already broken it, if that was indeed a mask.

When Chancellor refused to elaborate she said, "I'm going to stop this."

She ran down the hill. Stonehenge couldn't be more than a quarter of a mile away. As she approached the now abandoned tourist site, a half-naked man rhythmically circled some kind of picture scratched into the earth. She stood at too oblique an angle to identify the symbol. She ceased trying to decipher it and fastened her focus on the dancer.

His face was indeed hidden beneath a painted mask. She recognized that mask. He mumbled some incoherent words as he dipped and bobbed in a crude circular fashion. Even from where she was—about thirty paces from the first stone—she could see that the mask was carved and painted in detail.

She drew closer, her breathing shallow as she hurried to reach the famous landmark. The dancer in the mask was naked from the waist up. Red paint was smeared on his chest. Beneath his pounding feet the scent of crushed aromatic herbs rose into the air. She came to a halt ten paces away from the rope barrier.

"Dr. Lalonde!" she called. "Please, you shouldn't be inside the circle. You could damage the site."

The masked, painted dancer went still—quiet—and paused—listening.

He was watching something over her shoulder.

She jerked her eyes to see what it was.

Chancellor caught up with her, and she tore away from his threatening hands as a black mass appeared over their heads.

She ducked.

The archaeologist stood immobile as the flock descended

into the circle. Before she could see what was happening, the ravens rose into the sky. Angeline watched in awe as they evaporated into the distance. When she turned back, Jake Lalonde no longer stood among the megaliths.

CHAPTER FIFTEEN

Had the eye slits in the mask gleamed red at the moment the birds descended? She could swear they had.

She yanked apart from Chancellor who tried to stop her from entering the circle and scrambled across the sparse grass into the dust. Half sliding, half falling she reached the rope barrier and ducked beneath it. She scrambled to her feet, and brushed herself off. Shot a long look into the fading sky. What had happened to him? There was no sign of him anywhere.

Something had fallen between two of the stones. Angeline ploughed her hands through some weeds, dragging what looked to be the mask toward her. Specks of dirt and dried stuff soiled the yellow beak and when she shook it they fell off like rain. She looked from the mask to Chancellor, and back to the ground inside the ancient temple. There were long deep grooves in the dust where the dancer had danced.

"Why is that there?" she asked, pointing to the pagan symbol.

As she stepped back to get a broader perspective on the lines, she recognized the pattern. The symbol etched in the dust was familiar: a circle with two crescents facing outward from either side.

She quickly turned to Chancellor, and he answered her before she could even ask. "I don't know what happened."

"You're lying. You know that symbol." She pointed to the marks. "You've seen it before. I can see it on your face. Where is he?"

"I am not lying, Angeline. I honestly don't know.

Her head throbbed. Her several-mile-long trek over the plain had weakened her. She sat down on the grass, and lifted the mask, cradled it in both hands. "We had better call the police. Superintendent Pettigrew will want to know about this."

"And tell him what?" he mocked. "That Jake Lalonde disappeared inside Stonehenge?"

"He must be around here somewhere. This is his mask."

Hundreds, no—thousands of black ravens had dropped from the sky, birds identical to the ravens flocking at Avebury. They had landed on Jake, buried him in their mass of feathered wings and bodies, and then flown away. Had they taken him with them? Was that even possible?

When she sent a querying gaze toward Chancellor, she saw that he had followed her line of reasoning and had come to the same conclusion. "Well?" she asked him. "Is it possible? And if they took him, where did they take him?"

His eyes lifted in surrender. The last light of day was almost gone. The skyline was a deep pink and the grey of dusk was descending even as they wasted time arguing. No matter if they started hiking back right this second, they would have to make the majority of the journey after dark.

Dark, Angeline reminded herself. Did she really want to be out here at night? There was nothing they could do by remaining here.

She held up the mask, trying to recall every detail of the peculiar event. No amount of mulling it over was helping. The longer they stayed the weaker the light.

Ahead of her, silent now, Chancellor led the way. She felt bruised and battered from her tumble under the rope barrier. She was filthy from landing in the dust and her breathing was rapid. Furthermore her legs refused to cooperate. She had been hiking all day, and her thighs were weak, shaking with every step. She could barely feel the bird mask in her numb arms. Suddenly she stopped walking.

"We *have* to report this. People don't just disappear into thin air."

He whirled to face her. "Sometimes they do."

He was referring to Maia Pickerton.

"All the more reason we need to inform Superintendent Pettigrew right away. If the birds took him, hopefully they didn't drop him and he's still alive." Even as she said this she knew how absurd it would sound to the police. But she was determined. She was an eyewitness to the event. It had happened. And Chancellor would have to corroborate her story.

"He's alive," Chancellor said. "And unhurt."

Angeline looked up at his blank expression.

She strode past him, dug out her cellphone. As she started to report the incident to the emergency 999 operator something hit her from behind.

***

If there was one thing Superintendent Simon Pettigrew knew for certain it was that Dr. Jake Lalonde was no ghost. He had been seen in many places in and about London. However the superintendent's search was now postponed. What had brought him back to the village was an official call from the office of Military Defense, after reports of the mysteriously vanishing woman had reached government ears. Maia Pickerton had simply disappeared.

Pettigrew stood amongst the standing stones in the quiet village of Avebury. His search for Jake Lalonde had yielded no leads. He had traced the renowned archaeologist to London, in fact to the Savoy Hotel. But all attempts to locate him had been fruitless.

Pettigrew studied the notorious stone. He stood a foot away from it and noted that the smooth pale surface appeared exactly as a rock should. When he stepped back the pocks and ridges, crevices and shadows aligned themselves into what appeared to be a face. "Interesting," he murmured.

The sharp smell of guano was fading. Although many of the stones were still covered in the white excrement, the ravens it seemed had vanished.

The early spring grass grew lush and wet, and cattle roamed, grazing oblivious to his scrutiny. The scene reminded him of a watercolor painting with the barns and the thatched roof cottages in the distance, so different from London where concrete and glass and massive, old stone edifices blocked out the sun, casting everything on the ground into shade.

He turned from the arch of stones and stared out across the meadowlands to the bramble and brush on the other side. He was alone wandering among the megaliths begging the stones to send him a clue. His men had been caught up in the mysteriousness of the place and had learned nothing new. It was indeed a place of mystery. He understood how the locals could get swept up in the strangeness. But to them it wasn't all that strange. They lived here among the stones. Most of them had lived here all of their lives.

The local druids were preparing for some kind of spring festival. Kindling and firewood had been collected and strategically placed throughout the site to form individual bonfires. On the doorsteps of many of the homes were baskets of flowers threaded together to form garlands. It was not his place to put a halt to the festivities. This was not your average crime scene. In fact, he wasn't sure he could even label it a crime scene. A woman was missing and the last place she had been seen was at the Alexander Keiller Museum, just off the lane. Everyone he had spoken to had claimed that she had gone home. So if she had made it home—and it seems she had, as the bus driver who had taken her there could swear to it and a neighbor had seen her enter her house—then officially the stone circle was no crime scene at all. And yet he found himself drawn to this place.

His steps faltered as he turned to take in the Great Circle. He found himself gazing up once again at the massive face of the Barber Stone.

Oddly no one was outside. The moment he entered the village the people had returned to their homes and shut their doors. What was going on in this place?

He studied the rows of thatched cottages as though they represented a wall protecting a secret. What was this secret? The late afternoon sun beat down steadily; the rolling downs seemed to wait. The megaliths stood silent, unable to divulge what they knew, their long shadows stretching across the fields. A little shiver shook him, and he scowled. He was letting his imagination get in the way of logic.

There was nothing alive about these stones.

As the light faded, one by one lamps came on inside the houses.

He shot a look at someone peering out at him from behind lace curtains.

What did these people know?

What were they refusing to tell him?

But more importantly, why was the Ministry of Defense concerned?

CHAPTER SIXTEEN

Her body was rhythmically shaking and Angeline realized that the vibrations affecting her entire self were due to the movement of the train in which she was currently seated. Her head pounded. She touched the sore spot and found she wasn't bleeding. Why couldn't she remember getting here? She looked down through heavy lids and saw on her left hip that her jeans were grass-stained, and her sneakers covered in chalk dust. As the gentle vibrations of the car over the tracks continued their monotonous song, memory gradually returned to her.

Chancellor was sitting beside her. She glared at him. "You knocked me out."

"Sorry," he said. "But you were about to inform the police. I couldn't let you do that."

"You could have knocked the phone out of my hand."

"You might have screamed. They could have traced the call."

"You are beginning to scare me."

"I'm sorry, I didn't mean to harm you. You're not hurt badly are you?"

She fished in her backpack for her cellphone.

"It's not there," he said. "I'll give it back to you when you're reasonable enough to listen."

"You're crazy," she said. "And violent. Stay away from me. I am not listening to another word you say."

"Suit yourself. But then you will never learn what all of this is about. And you do want to know, don't you?"

She got up and moved to the other side of the train and

found a seat well behind Chancellor's. She glanced outside the foggy windows. It was dark, but by the filmy light of the moon she saw they were travelling eastbound back towards London.

Ravens had kidnapped Jake Lalonde. *Birds!* At the very least he had disappeared. Why didn't Chancellor care? What was his role in all this mystery? Wasn't he supposed to be some kind of a policeman?

Trees whizzed by. She turned her attention back to the interior of the train. The lights inside were too bright and hurt her eyes. No one had ever struck her before. What kind of a maniac was he? Maybe she should get up and move to another car. But if she did that then she wouldn't be able to keep an eye on him. She studied the back of his head. *Who are you, mister? What do you want from me?* And why wasn't she more afraid of him than she was. That was the part that didn't make sense to her. He should terrify her, and although she possessed a healthy wariness about him, she was not really afraid of him.

Her legs were stiff, but she managed to stretch them and get some feeling back into her toes. As she was turning her attention back to the train car she glanced at the back of the empty passenger seat beside Chancellor. Where was the mask? Where was the black Raven mask she had found by the standing stones? Had he stolen that too? He didn't have it on his person. It wasn't on any of the seats that she could see. He had shrugged when she'd asked him, as though the mask had never existed.

For the remainder of the trip Angeline ignored him. In fact, she rose and moved to the very farthest end of the car where there was a free seat, as though to make a statement. As if he'd notice. He did not. The back of his head never moved. She scowled and glanced out of the window a second time, caught her own reflection, and the dirty stain on her face.

On leaving the station at Waterloo, she flagged a cab to the Savoy Hotel. She avoided the curious glance the cab driver gave her. She had done her best to brush off the dust and clean up her face, but without soap and water it was pretty useless.

Chancellor had acquired his own cab ahead of her and slipped into the traffic.

Thank heavens she had checked into the Savoy this morning before the seminar. She had decided to max out her credit card. She would worry about paying for it later. Her taxi wheeled in behind Chancellor's and a porter came to open the door. The porter gave her a look of offended surprise. She paid the fare, ignored the porter who looked like he was going to block her from entering the hotel, until she told him she had taken a tumble at one of their historic sites. He apologized, in the name of all England, and asked if she was all right. She nodded, smiled prettily—if that was possible with dirt on one's face—and hurried into the lobby.

The sounds of partying blared from an opened door, and Angeline popped her head in to observe the festivities. It was the welcome reception her eyes informed her as they fell to the sandwich board set kitty-corner to the doorway with the ICOPS convention signage. Inside, she saw Drey McFee hobnobbing with the conventioneers.

Angeline felt herself shrink beneath her soiled clothes. Never in her life had anyone ever seen her in such a state. She worked in museums, not in the field. Her primary function was public relations. Her pleasing FOA (front office appearance) was why people hired her. Mortified, she waved a hand at Drey hoping to catch her attention. No luck. She left for her room to shower and change.

At the gleaming marble bathroom sink of her hotel room she studied her glowing face. Her complexion, after a good scrub, was spotless. People had always told her that her porcelain-like skin was her best feature. She applied enough makeup to enhance her natural beauty. After drying her hair to a smooth black sheen, she returned to the bedroom to dress.

When she stepped out into the lift, she was clad in grey

silk. She had deliberately worn something that was less attention grabbing. She had no nametag, and had to get inside that reception hall to find Drey. She wasn't registered for the convention and waited for a likely moment to slip inside unseen.

"What happened to you?" Drey demanded as Angeline joined her. "I've been searching all over for you. Why didn't you answer your phone or return my texts?"

"I didn't hear them," Angeline said. "I was at Stonehenge."

"What were you doing there? I thought you went to the 'beauty parlour'." She made air quotes with her fingers.

"Chancellor asked me to meet him there."

Her brows rose. "Where is he then? I have a few questions I'd like to ask him myself."

"Don't bother. He'll only give you the runaround." She proceeded to relate the events of that afternoon—to Drey's total astonishment.

"He hit you?" she said.

"He must have. I don't remember how I got into that train. And I've got a bump on the back of my head to prove it. My only question is: how did he carry me so far? It had to be miles across the fields and back to the train station."

CHAPTER SEVENTEEN

"Go back to the room," Drey said. "You look beat. Get some sleep. I'll try to find out what happened."

"Not until I've had something to eat."

Angeline glanced at a lusciously laden tray that a hotel server swept in front of her. She indulged in a miniature quiche and a cube of smoked cheese, and then speared a bacon-wrapped shrimp with a toothpick.

She had no recourse but to go to Pettigrew and report exactly what had happened. But would he believe her? She wasn't even certain of what she would be implying. That the Interpol agent was an accessory to Jake's disappearance? But how? What kind of magician had control over thousands of birds that way?

The idea sent shivers over her spine. The more she thought about it, the more her skin crawled. Her head boomed from the knock she had taken at the hands of Chancellor that afternoon. She needed some Tylenol and some rest. She decided to take Drey's advice and return to the room.

She kicked off the pumps and peeled out of the grey silk, and hung the dress by its straps inside the large closet. Then she slipped on her nightgown and bathrobe.

All things considered, it was too early to go to sleep. Her mind was churning. Nevertheless, she went to climb into the luxurious bed when something occurred to her. Jake Lalonde had vanished into thin air beneath a cloud of ravens. That woman at the seminar this morning had also done a disappearing act.

Angeline went to the desk where her computer tablet sat. She started her search by collecting all the information she could find on Diana Lune. Diana seemed to come out of nowhere. Her first appearance was three years ago on a TV interview. Next she Googled Chancellor and every Interpol connection to him she could find. He was not even listed as an agent—former *or* current. However, he did come up on several links to paranormal investigations concerning ghosts, missing persons and time travel.

What was the link between him and Diana, and Jake?

She glanced at the clock on the nightstand. Half past nine. If she returned to the scene of Jake's disappearance would she find anything? She must see that Triple Moon symbol again, the one etched into the dust, before the wind swept it away. Something about it would surely tell her why Jake had been dancing around it. The moon shone in at the window. It would be dark, she thought, but not completely dark.

She dressed quickly, left the room and hurried out of the bustling hotel lobby and made her way to the Underground. There was only one train headed to Salisbury. The trip was fast; there were virtually no passengers. She patted the pockets of her jacket where she had tucked a flashlight, and hitched a ride with a kindly looking English tourist couple that were headed her way. "I don't feel right about leaving you in the dark here," the husband said as he pulled over to let her out. "How are you going to get home?"

"It's all right. I work for the English Heritage Board, (which she did on weekends). I have a key to the visitor center (which she did not). And look, the custodians' cars are still here. They work past midnight. I'll catch a ride with one of them."

She fully intended to do that. She didn't know what sort of tale she'd spin them, but she had to admit it hadn't been very wise of her to set out on this excursion without a plan for returning to her hotel.

The English tourists smiled anxiously, wished her luck

with her mission (whatever it was) and drove away.

***

The interior of the visitor center was dark, except for the southern end where she could detect lights through a window. Out in the car park it was well lit. She left the near empty parking lot and headed along the main path until she came over the rise to greet the eerie shapes of Stonehenge. The stones stood tall, and reflected the light of the moon. They were still quite a ways into the distance, and resembled the ogres and trolls, and other fairytale creatures of her childhood. She reminded herself vehemently that she was not afraid of the night.

If not for the moon it would have been impossibly dark. Shivers coursed up her spine to her neck and down her arms. The plain at night was unspeakably lonely and fear traversed her entire being. Just walk, she told herself. The only way to overcome her fear was to face it. Blue shadows closed in around her. This was not what she feared. The voice of her group therapy leader resounded in her brain:

Walk into the fear
Face the fear
Survive

She used to think that she was afraid of the dark. But since her therapy she realized now that it wasn't the dark that she was afraid of. It was getting lost.

It should not be a problem here, for she knew exactly where she was.

And with that fact firmly in mind she ordered the fear within her to vanish. She could not possibly get lost.

Abandoning the track, she took a short cut over the downs. Now that she was out in the open, moonlight illuminated the path. She crossed a vast expanse of black where patches of silver disturbed the grassy surface. She looked to her left and saw nothing except the long barrow, the grass on its open plateau swept by the wind.

On the track where she now walked were rubble and chunks of chalk. The wind was sharp but moderated by the relatively mild temperature. She buttoned her jacket, switched off the flashlight and tucked it into one of her pockets. No point in drawing too much attention to herself. She didn't want the custodians rushing out to explore the grounds because of a suspicious light bobbing across the plain. The place had enough of a reputation for being haunted.

Her only company was the whipping of the wind. Her footsteps crunched where sparse grass gave out to gravelly soil.

Her breath shortened; her legs slowed as though she slogged through mud. She had reached the great henge and now nothing stood between her and the megaliths—not even the flimsy rope barrier, which was stored away at night. The circle loomed large and ominous. It was nowhere near as grand as the stone circle of Avebury, but it was so much more intimidating. She fetched out her flashlight and aimed it at the ground. From behind her a shadow crossed her path, sending her heart to her throat.

CHAPTER EIGHTEEN

"I've been waiting for you."

She slowly raised her eyes to seek the face of the speaker. The woman did not smile. Angeline glanced at the gleaming stones of the circle, white now from the light of the moon—a perfect hiding place—before refastening her gaze on the intruder. Diana Lune had stepped out from behind one of the sarsens.

"You were waiting for me?"

She nodded.

Angeline tried to show no fear or surprise when she had recognized whom it was. After all, she had had her suspicions.

A curious mist had arisen from somewhere in the distance. She knew there was a river nearby and this was probably the fog's source. It was apt that it should be misty. The whole scene was heavy with intrigue and her curiosity had overcome her fear. She was not lost. And Diana Lune was only a woman after all.

By now her hair and skin felt damp and dreary. The sooner she got this interview over and done with the sooner she could go back to the hotel to a hot bath and a warm bed. With the adrenalin under control she felt a calmness envelop her. She wasted no time with niceties. This woman had a lot of explaining to do, and she had better start talking fast.

"I saw you at the talk today. It *was* you, wasn't it, in that big hat? I don't understand. How are you mixed up in this?" The celebrated author and the visiting archaeologist had not seemed to know each other at the lecture the other night, and yet Angeline knew Diana was involved. Was she acquainted with Chancellor, too, before the talk at the Alexander Keiller Museum? Were both men former acquaintances of hers?

When she did not respond immediately, Angeline frowned. "I believe you did know him, and Jake too, but for some reason they both think they only just met you for the first time... *You* were the one who was put in that mental institution. You have a new identity." When she remained silent, Angeline said, "When did you change your name?"

Diana shrugged. "What does it matter?"

Angeline didn't know why it mattered, but something told her it did. "What is your *real* name?" she demanded.

The woman's mouth curled into a smile. "I've had many names. How do you think I managed to stay off the radar?"

"Tell me what they are."

"Does the Black Goddess ring any bells? How about Asherah, Branwen?"

What did she take her for? A fool?

"You've been having strange dreams, haven't you? Hearing voices?"

Angeline's head jerked up. Her hands were cold. Her heartbeats quickened. How did she know? How *could* she know? She was the crazy woman who thought she could travel through time. She had been avoiding the authorities by changing her identity every time they came close. Both times when they caught her, they had put her in a mental institution.

"Don't you get it? You are a pivotal part of this whole thing. At first I thought I merely had to get rid of you. Now I think in order to make Jake embrace his destiny, I need you. You must come back to Avebury with me," Diana urged.

"You're going to turn *yourself* into the police?"

"Why would I do that? No, I am going to help you find Jake."

Angeline frowned. "Why? So that you can turn *him* into the police?"

"The police have nothing to do with my agenda," Diana

said.

"I am not going anywhere with you until you tell me the truth. Did you have anything to do with Maia's disappearance?"

"Why would I want her to disappear?"

I don't know, Angeline thought.

"How much has Chancellor told you?" Diana asked her.

Her eyes narrowed. There was some logic to this illogic. She only had to think hard about it. She glanced down at the diamond ring on her hand. Diana noticed it too. She smiled. "Who gave that to you?"

Angeline squeezed her eyes closed. Tears of frustration threatened. She had thought it was an heirloom belonging to her grandmother. But now she knew it wasn't. She frowned, concentrated.

Where are you my love?
I need you to give me some answers.

The voice did not reply.

The delusional woman nodded, looked into the darkness beyond the cluster of stones inward of the large circle. Angeline could see a long shadow stretch out across the chalky soil into the moonlight. She gasped when she recognized the shape. It looked to be a huge elongated bird.

She covered her lips with her hand. Her tongue felt glued to the roof of her mouth. She did not trust herself to speak. The shadow faded. Her eyes rolled up to take in the entire shadowy circle of stones to the exact spot where she had seen the archaeologist disappear earlier that evening.

Diana spoke. "Don't believe a word Tom Chancellor tells you."

"Why not?"

"Because he's dangerous. He says he's an Interpol cop, but is he? He doesn't seem to be investigating anything, except the supernatural."

Isn't that what you do?

Angeline suspected the self-professed antiquarian did not believe that any of her own theories were based on the paranormal. Right now that really wasn't important. The real question was: What was she doing out here in the middle of the night?

No logical explanations came to her mind and Diana's answers to her questions were elusive. Was the woman mentally unbalanced? She did not seem unstable. She seemed more rational than Chancellor. Did she truly believe that she could teleport?

When Diana resumed talking it wasn't to answer any obvious questions. Jake Lalonde, she informed her, was the Haida descendent of a 10,000-year-old shaman. This shaman was the originator of the Raven myths and Jake had inherited his memories.

There were no such things as inherited memories, Angeline mused. A random thought occurred to her. She chuckled at the idea, even though inside she was shaking. But now that her reasoning was on this path, she pursued it although she felt ever more confused. Something in their conversation had triggered a further memory.

"He told me he can feel the shaman inside him," Diana said. "His thoughts, his vision, his sense of smell—everything changes."

He had even sought therapy from a psychiatrist, she explained. The shrink concluded that he carried deep-seeded emotional baggage. The burden was causing him to hallucinate, and it was all because he was an orphaned infant raised by the foster system. The psychiatrist interpreted his visions as some sort of defense mechanism, that his desire to escape his reality had caused him to create a substitute reality. As for her, Diana did not think Jake insane. He may have emotional baggage from being passed from home to home, but that was in the past. Whatever was happening to him now were not delusions.

"I think that Interpol cop is using him for some vile purpose. He created an elaborate hoax to get us off his trail.

Jake is in danger, and we have to get him away from Chancellor," Diana warned.

Angeline could not deny that she felt a strange affinity to both men. She felt as though she knew Chancellor well, even though logic told her otherwise. And there was no doubt that Jake Lalonde had an unprecedented and frightening attraction for her, but she was aware of what they said about the fine line between genius and insanity. If he was still alive, was he hanging by a thread? Were they both?

Diana sighed. "On top of all of that he has the ability to dream his ancestors dreams."

No wonder both he and Diana Lune had ended up in psychiatric care.

"He told you all of this last night?"

"We spent the night together," she said. "A man will tell you a lot of things after a night of love."

There were a million things spinning in Angeline's head, jealousy least of all. She could see Diana choosing her words carefully. "Here's what I believe happened. Clearly the raven phenomenon is not limited to Avebury. They are also attracted to the standing stones at Stonehenge. When that flock of ravens landed in the circle, Lalonde took advantage of it for cover and made his escape. He was trying to ditch Chancellor."

How did she know about the flock of ravens? Angeline had not mentioned anything about that incident. Was there more to Diana Lune than the Internet had revealed?

"How long were you in that mental health ward?" she asked.

"Long enough to meet Chancellor."

Angeline widened her eyes in disbelief. *He* was in a psychiatric hospital too?

"That's why you can't trust him. He thinks he's a ghost."

Angeline was speechless. But eventually she managed to say: "I looked up your story on the Internet. They say you disappeared and never returned."

"I never returned to the hospital. Why would I? I am *not*

crazy."

"You told the doctors you could time travel."

"I also told a group of scholars that Native North Americans crossed the Atlantic and built the stone circle of Avebury."

"You don't believe the theories you're espousing?"

"Do you? I tell the people what they want to hear. It sells books and it gets me gigs."

"And those simulacra? Those faces of ravens in the standing stones, that image of Maia…how do you explain that?"

"I don't. I don't know what's going on there, but I use it to my advantage. It brings in the crowds."

"But you're telling people *lies*," Angeline insisted.

"My postulations are not lies. They are simply inconclusive *theories*. I have enough evidence to keep them viable. You were there at my lecture. Why didn't you challenge me then?" When Angeline failed to answer, she added, "Why do you think Maia Pickerton invited me to give that talk at the museum?"

She knew very well why Maia Pickerton had invited Diana Lune to give a talk at the museum.

That phenomenon with the flocks of ravens had seriously disturbed her. They were scaring visitors away. When she discovered the 'faces in stone' she went to the experts. Diana Lune and Thomas Chancellor could put Avebury back on the map. The only question remaining was: who would want Maia out of the way? Who wanted to scare off the tourists?

Diana shrugged. "Just face it, honey. There is no place for the truth in tourism. People want to be excited about something. They want to believe in greater powers."

Angeline looked around at the dark. The stone circle before them loomed over the black plain like an ancient temple. Everything that Diana was saying was beginning to make sense. They had to find Jake.

***

Through the fog, memory lurked on the edges of his mind. His head felt heavy. His heart thudded and he gasped for breath while flashes of heat consumed his body. Sweat broke out on his face, although the palms of his hands were icy. The sensations lasted a minute and were replaced by calm. He breathed easier, widening his eyes against the blackness.

He moved blindly, feeling his way. His surroundings felt rough and cold like stone on his groping fingers. A sense of foreboding afflicted him. He struggled to stay glued to his senses as his heart pulsed and his mouth went dry. He could not trust his senses any more than he could trust his thoughts. But now something seemed to speak into his ear.

Are you there? Can you hear me? I need you!

He trembled with memory, tried to answer with his mind but found his thoughts blocked. He gave up trying to think, trying to speak, and moved towards the shimmering. Was he dead? Was this the passage to the After World? He felt a scream well inside him. Before him a pattern materialized on what appeared to be a wall. It was decorated with symbols. He recognized them—the simulacra of the Ravens.

The shimmering he had been following now surrounded him. On the Barber Stone in the circle of Avebury, Jake Lalonde's face appeared carved into the rock.

CHAPTER NINETEEN

Everything Diana had told her rang true. Angeline knew she should not trust Diana, but she was compelled to stay close. She accepted a lift back to the city in her rental.

"Stay away from Chancellor," Diana warned as they parted ways inside the Savoy Hotel.

"Don't worry, I will." But that was a lie. No one was going to tell her what to do. Her own thoughts and memories seemed to be bits and pieces of lies. Chancellor knew much more than he was telling and no matter what he had done to her, she had to speak to him. There was something the crazy woman had said that needed clarification. And only Chancellor could do that.

She racked her brain to recall the number of his room. What had he told her at that museum cafeteria? Room 2114. She took the lift to the twenty-first floor and banged on his door. It was 2:00am. She waited a moment then heard footfalls and the door clicked open. Obviously she had awakened him from sleep. He wore sweatpants and a t-shirt.

"Angeline," he said. "What are you doing here? What's happened?" He had dropped all formalities, no longer referring to her as Ms. Lisbon.

She pushed her way into the room. A lamp was on by the nightstand. She went over to stand by the sofa in his suite. "Diana Lune is that whack job who escaped the mental hospital—twice. I saw her at the conference this morning. You know her, don't you?" She did not let on that she had just come from an encounter with her.

"Of course, I know her. I met her at her lecture in

Avebury."

"Don't mess with me," Angeline said. "I know you knew her before that. She admitted as much."

"So, why ask me?"

"Because I don't trust her. She was committed to psychiatric care. *Twice.*"

"I see… you still haven't answered my question. Why are you here? It's the middle of the night." He massaged his stubbly chin, yawned. "As you can see I was asleep."

"I … oh damn it. There's something about you. I—" She bit her words off before saying anything she couldn't retract. Then she realized that she had to tell him the truth. "Just tell me this. Diana said something really peculiar tonight. She said: 'Don't you get it? You are a pivotal part of this whole thing.' You made a similar claim. Something like: 'I knew I was going to have to tell you sooner or later. I was hoping after I convinced Lalonde, we could deal with the situation alone, and not have to involve you.'" She scowled. "What is it that I don't know? What is it that I'm supposed to be a pivotal part of?"

"Jake is missing," Chancellor said.

"I know that!" She was getting thoroughly frustrated. You said he was all right. You said you knew where he was!"

"I didn't exactly say that. I said he probably wasn't hurt and I'm pretty certain he isn't. I'm just not sure where he ended up."

She was silent for a few moments. Chancellor smoothed his tousled hair back from his head. He said, "Angeline, sit down. I'm going to tell you everything I know. But before I do that, I want you to promise not to interrupt me or ask any questions until I'm finished—because some of this you are not going to believe."

At the moment she thought she could believe anything. She nodded, sat down on the sofa. He went to the sidebar to make himself a cup of coffee. There was a Tassimo coffee maker there.

"No. No thanks," she said when he indicated the

porcelain teacups. "Now tell me who is Jake Lalonde." She paused while he pressed the button to the machine.

She was half afraid of the answer. What she had learned from speaking to Diana Lune made her wonder if she too hadn't been, at some point, committed to a mental institution. The thought had occurred to her during their encounter.

Was that how she knew him? Were they patients in the same facility? Were Diana Lune, Tom Chancellor, Jake Lalonde and herself once inmates together? That was the only thing that made sense. There were gaps in her memory. Not to mention the fact that she heard voices in her head. In fact, she talked to the voice inside her head. Up until now she had not thought that was strange. It seemed to her she had always felt his presence. But now, for the first time in her life, she was questioning her own sanity. Maybe what she had thought was a telepathic ability was nothing more than mental illness. Had she been incarcerated in a mental hospital with those three, and had her memory been erased? Had she been involved in some sort of clinical experiment? The idea terrified her. The only way to find out was to ask the man in front of her what he knew.

"Who do you really work for?" she demanded. "Do you work for the government? That Project Pegasus that was revived at the turn of the millennium—was that it? Were the four of us used in some experiment and then had our memories erased?"

Chancellor's brows rose, then he smiled. "Is that what you think?"

"Isn't that what you and Jake were trying to find out? Why we all have gaps in our memories? Because apparently we all know each other."

"What makes you think that?"

She glanced down at the diamond on her finger, raised her hand. "Where did this come from?"

"You don't know?"

"No," she said despairingly. She scowled, lifted her eyes to Chancellor. "But it seems to me that you do."

"Oh, no. No, it wasn't me." Amusement transformed his normally stiff-jawed expression. "We never knew each other that well."

"But we knew each other."

"Yes."

"Why are you the only one that remembers?"

"It's not just me. Diana Lune remembers too."

"So, I'm right. The four of us were involved in something together, something that I have no memory of and I'm pretty certain Jake has no memory of either."

Chancellor shrugged. "He may have no memory of it, but he believes me."

Angeline closed her eyes. What was he implying? That somehow the life she had now wasn't the way it was supposed to be?

Something was stirring in her mind. The vision she had experienced in the empty theatre after Diana Lune's talk in Avebury. Angeline had assumed it was a hallucination triggered by exhaustion and too much wine. Now she was beginning to think it was a... premonition? No—not a premonition—the opposite of that. What was the opposite of a premonition? What was the word for something that had happened already? A flashback.

Chancellor rose from the armchair where he had been seated opposite her. He went to a wardrobe and removed a briefcase. Inside that briefcase he retrieved a black object. She saw as soon as he brought it into the light that it was the Raven mask.

"You stole it from me," she accused him.

"You already knew that."

"Why did you take it?"

"Because it belongs to Jake."

He passed it to her and she held it at arm's length. The yellow beak curved sharply downward and the eyes were slits with white ovoids painted around them. The cheekbones were high and angular. And then the scene, the scene she had thought she had imagined in the theater at the Alexander

Keiller Museum flashed across her memory. Only this time it came in much greater detail.

She saw a shrine and an eerie, mystical stone figure. The statue swirled before her eyes in preternatural, nebulous transfigurations. She felt in that instant the same feelings she had felt before—feelings she had experienced in another life. She stared at Chancellor with full knowledge dawning. She finally recognized the man in the dark muddle of her dreams. It was Jake.

"Tell me what you're recalling, Angeline." His face was serious, his eyes reaching out as though they could see what she was seeing in the deepest recesses of her mind.

***

The man was in trouble. He stood in shadow, and was dressed in some sort of outrageous priest's costume. The dark-haired woman and Jake were trying to stop the priest from hurting himself. It had something to do with…the statue. Angeline clasped her hands to her mouth and slowly breathed as the scene revealed itself to her. The dark-haired woman was speaking to Jake and her voice echoed clearly in Angeline's thoughts. *"We are going to have a hell of a time explaining what just happened here. The authorities are going to come after you. They'll think you killed him."*

Angeline's eyes locked onto Chancellor's as the significance of that vision crashed down on her. It wasn't exactly a memory; it was more like a vision. Jake Lalonde, and another man and two women were inside a subterranean shrine. Chancellor encouraged her to continue. "Tell me what happened next."

Jake had taken the woman by both hands and lifted her from where she knelt on the ground until she stood with him, face to face. He had said something unexpected, something startling. *"I love you. Don't ever forget that."*

Somewhere in her heart she had already known it. The look that had been on his face was indescribable. It was the kind of look you saw on the face of someone who was terminally ill. Chancellor's voice broke into the silence. "What's the matter?"

"Nothing…" She paused. "He…. he wanted—"

He had been desperate. He had wanted to escape the shrine. That much was clear. But there had still been the matter of the dead body. Yes, someone had died there that night—the man in the outrageous priest's costume. All the time she watched the scene, one question looped in her mind. What to do with the body? What to tell the police? Yes, something terrible had happened, something that required the attention of the police. Then she felt someone pinch her arm. She felt the pinch as though it were happening to her—and that it was happening right now. It was the journalist. Angeline couldn't drum up a name for her, but for some reason she knew the other woman was a journalist.

And then, everyone in the temple had turned to look at where the dead man was lying, except that he had vanished. Only a puddle of folded clothing remained where his body had lain.

All she remembered now was feeling fear. The vision terrified her. It was at this moment that the outlandish thought sank in. What had happened to the body?

But that wasn't the end of it. As her eyes raked in the walls of the temple in her mind, finally landing on the floor at the foot of one of the benches, something shiny gleamed there. She recognized it, and saw herself go over, lift it from the ground, and switch it on. An ISD meter. How she could possibly identify the gadget, stymied her. But she recognized it nonetheless. The man, a paranormal investigator had brought the ghost-hunting device and dropped it to the ground when the statue had spellbound him.

Even now, as she recalled the scene, she saw herself raise the infrasound device to chest-level and wave it in the air. It began to beep out a high-pitched shrill.

A voice oscillated to a squeak—the journalist's. Her head now flashed from side to side as she tried to see what the device had detected. *"Oh my god, that's a ghost-tracking gadget, isn't it? He's here. Oh shit. He's here!"* She ran to the exit of the temple.

Angeline snapped her eyes shut. The clarity of the images, the dream or memory or whatever it was frightened her. Chancellor did not speak, but encouraged her to continue her story. "What happened next?" he demanded. "This is important."

The journalist had disappeared. Jake was still there. He nodded and rose, and she could see that something weighed heavily on his mind. The voices came to her as though they were speaking right now. The dark-haired woman, whom she realized was herself, seized his wrist and clasped both of her hands around his. He spoke and the words came out hoarse and desperate:

"Promise me you won't forget me. Promise me!"

She was mesmerized by the images that followed. Jake let out a pained laugh. *None of this would have happened if I had stayed put. And now...now I have to think of a way to keep us connected. So we don't forget each other."*

Sadness, longing, regret, all reflected in a look of—of farewell? Angeline stiffened. His face had suddenly changed. This was the part of the dream that rendered her the most confused. She looked up at Chancellor and he encouraged her with a nod.

She squeezed her eyes shut to bring back the images.

There she was, suddenly excited. Her hand reached out and grabbed his, and then they ran towards the exit, but an invisible electrified barrier appeared and as she struck it, the impact twisted her body, snapped her onto her side, causing her head to hit the ground, hard.

CHAPTER TWENTY

Angeline slapped a hand to the scar on her temple. "I'm engaged to Jake!" she whispered.

Chancellor smiled. "Not now. But yes, in that life, you were."

"Does he know?" She answered her own question before Chancellor could. Of course, he didn't know. If he knew, he would have recognized her.

"He had been experiencing strange feelings just like you, Angeline. Ever since he got to England. He told me it was as though some greater force were drawing us together. He doesn't know how right he was. Some greater force *is* drawing us together."

"It's Diana."

Her eyes lowered before she returned his gaze. She saw again in her memory the man in the priest's robe, his prostrate body. Her jaw dropped before she spoke. "You were there. You were there in my flashback."

Chancellor nodded but did not elaborate.

"What was our relationship? Why were we all in that underground shrine? And what was that statue all about? And…. You were dressed in some strange religious outfit. You were performing some kind of ritual… Oh my gosh—" She bit off her words as he continued to nod his head in silence. "You died!" Her last statement came out in hushed excitement.

When still he said nothing, she added, although this time her voice was hushed: "It was *your* body that disappeared. But…If we return to that timeline…won't you be dead again?"

"I don't know."

She sighed. "But you're willing to take the risk."

"I have to take it. There are greater stakes here. What happened in your flashback was real. She is manipulating our every action. She has taken Jake and we must get him back."

"You think Diana is *her*?" Angeline stared at him. Of course she was. She had practically confessed to it. "I think I'll have that coffee after all."

Chancellor brewed her coffee after she made a choice from the diverse selection. When they were both seated opposite each other sipping at the hot beverages, she resumed, "How is it that I can remember all of this, and why now?"

"Do you know anything about Chaos magic?" Chancellor asked.

She shook her head.

"Its main purpose is to bring the practitioner to an altered state of consciousness—in order to manipulate reality.

Manipulate reality? That was the only phrase that registered.

"To eradicate all doubt by bypassing the 'Psychic Censor'—the faculties of the mind adverse to the magical control of reality."

She halted him with a raised hand before he could elaborate. What did any of this have to do with the dream? He requested that she keep her promise and refrain from asking questions until he had finished. She frowned, nodded reluctantly, and became attentive. He continued to talk and she stifled her frustration. Eventually he must come to the point.

"Ever since I began to suspect that there was something wrong with me, and the world I was living in I started to research traditional shamanism. I recognized that modern practices had adopted the methods of the aboriginal. Ritual involving the use of meditation, dance, music, costumes and psychoactive drugs all contribute to the altered state of consciousness. The point of all the ritual is to believe in a different reality."

It was impossible to digest what he was saying. Was he suggesting that Diana Lune was some kind of a witch? That she could manipulate minds to make innocent people live alternate lives?

Angeline's head pounded. He was getting too far ahead of her now with his explanations, which didn't really explain anything at all. As his voice broke through her thoughts, her mind latched onto his next point: that those who practiced Chaos magic could also change past events.

This time she had to object. "How can anyone change past events? It just isn't possible."

"This power is what Lalonde was striving for in his experiments with Haida shamanism."

"Are you saying that this person—who might now be going by the name of Diana Lune—somehow convinced us to live in an altered reality?"

"Not only convinced us. She made it happen. She made it so that you and Jake never met."

Angeline frowned. "But we *did* meet."

"Yes, and the reason for that meeting was something *she* with all her power of changing identities and realities could not change. She didn't reckon on the power of love. You somehow maintained a connection with Jake, didn't you?"

Suddenly the identity of her telepathic companion was obvious. But why couldn't she reach him now? She put all her thought and will into seeking him.

Where are you? Why don't you answer me?

The truth was he had not answered her since his disappearance. Did he know it was she with whom he had been communicating? For the first time, she used his name.

Jake!

"Let me finish," Chancellor said. "Then maybe you will understand better."

She could scarcely breathe. What he was telling her was absurd. And yet it could be nothing short of the truth. She was certain now that Diana Lune was not normal. She shut her eyes. Her mind screamed: *You can't have him!*

"I know it's a lot to take in," he said. "But if we're to save him, then we have to form a plan."

"What is she?" Angeline asked. "Is she really a goddess? Or a witch? Are there actually such things? Or is she just some charismatic mental patient who has somehow hypnotized us all into believing what she wants us to believe?" She got up and went to him. He set his coffee cup down on the glass top of the marble coffee table. She touched him gingerly like he might break. "She said you think you're a *ghost*."

The Interpol agent did not answer her. "Do you want to save him or not?"

CHAPTER TWENTY-ONE

By the time she had finished relating her dream or memory or flashback—whatever it was, and Chancellor had espoused his theories of altered realities—a red sky was peeking through the crack in the curtains of the hotel room. Angeline called Drey on her cellphone, and told her to meet them for breakfast at a restaurant around the corner from the Savoy.

She was not in the least bit surprised or incredulous of the story that Angeline and Chancellor had to tell. She was, after all, a cryptozoologist, and she dealt with the incredible every day. Diana Lune they informed her was the culprit. She was the quack biblical archaeologist (albeit in a different guise) who had enchanted Chancellor during his sojourn in Italy, drugged him into believing that he could cross the two planes—co-exist between the living and the dead. But it was always Jake that she had wanted, and it was Jake she intended to keep. The question (or *questions*) was how had she kidnapped him, and where had she stashed him, and what did she intend to do with him?

There were two artefacts, Chancellor had decided, that they needed in order to release him from her power once they located him: one was the Raven mask that they already had in their possession. The other was a physical representation of her symbol—the Triple Moon. They had to get that necklace that she had worn on the night of her lecture in Avebury. Their next move was obvious. But who among them would make the best thief?

Before anyone could answer the question, the ringtone of

a cellphone chimed. All three of them reached into their respective bags and pockets to fetch out their devices. It turned out that none of their devices was the source of the ringtone. Then Chancellor grinned sheepishly. "It's Lalonde's. He gave me his phone for safekeeping."

He glanced at the caller ID. Jake had removed his password protect from the older device so that Chancellor could answer it if his fiancée called. She was calling now. Drey had no idea why Angeline and Chancellor were so nervous. She said, "Just tell her he's not available right now."

"She'll wonder why I have his phone."

"Here, *I'll* tell her."

"He has a fiancée?" Angeline asked, disturbed.

Chancellor shook off Drey's attempts to interfere and answered the call, and told the fiancée that Jake was currently lecturing at the conference. Then his eyebrows rose and both women noted the quiver in his voice. "You've just arrived at the Savoy? You're in his room?"

It was clear that the fiancée whose name they all learned was Serena Dunnel was not fooled for even a second. She was well aware that Jake was not giving a talk; she had checked the program. "All right. I'm a friend of Lalonde's. Come down to the coffee shop—I'm having breakfast—and I'll explain."

He ended the call and brought their heads together over the table. "Before Serena Dunnel gets here, we have to split up. Drey, I want you to be our thief. Find that necklace. Angeline—" Before he could complete his sentence his eyes rose and she knew that the fiancée had already arrived. She was standing at the door scanning the restaurant for them. Chancellor instructed in a low voice: "Drey. Leave the premises so that I don't have to introduce you. As far as Ms. Dunnel will be concerned, two other women in Jake Lalonde's life is two women too many."

Drey slid out of the booth and left in the opposite direction, just as the fiancée approached. Fortunately, her back had been to the door, so as she slipped by, the tall, thirtyish woman paid her no mind.

Serena Dunnel was strikingly good-looking. Her clothes were stylish in a sloppy California kind of way. Her hair was brown with sunny highlights, cut in fashionable layers, and hung past her deeply suntanned shoulders in heavy waves. She exuded confidence and self-esteem in a double tank top, and a sweater tied around her narrow waist. Chancellor knew he wasn't going to escape with a lame story. She strode up to the table and introduced herself, and he did likewise before he introduced his breakfast companion. He explained that he and Jake were old friends, which Angeline supposed was true. He revealed also that Angeline was a colleague, and *that* she supposed was also true.

"He told me that you were on an expedition to prove an archaeological theory concerning the earliest human migrations to the New World?"

"I was," Serena answered. "But it got delayed because of a fire aboard the boat. It looks like I won't be going until next month. After our wedding."

"Oh," Chancellor said.

"What's going on, Mr. Chancellor? Where's Jake?"

Angeline wondered if he was going to expose the whole sordid story about Diana Lune. If he did, just exactly how well would that go over? She barely believed it herself and she had excellent reasons for believing it.

But Serena would think they were all quacks. And Angeline wasn't sure if her first surmise wasn't the correct one. It would make a lot more sense if she, Chancellor, Jake and Diana Lune had all somehow been experimented on and ended up in the same mental institution.

But there was something familiar about Serena as well. Although she was certain that she had never met the woman in her life. The marine archaeologist had her hands on the table, and Angeline could see the large diamond on her third left-hand finger. If Jake had chosen this bling then the man had superb taste, but it seemed more likely that the woman had selected this ring. As she let her eyes linger on her own delicate little diamond she could see a clear difference in the buyers' tastes. Jake had purchased *her* ring himself.

When she looked up, she was aware of a pair of clear eyes watching her. Serena Dunnel was Jake's current fiancée. And there was only room for *one* fiancée.

***

"So what's going on?" she repeated.

Chancellor was silent for a moment. Angeline refused to answer either.

"It has something to do with these stone circles, doesn't it?"

"How much did Jake tell you?" he asked cautiously.

"Well…" Serena heaved a sigh of total exasperation. "He was supposed to be here studying the Raven images in the megaliths, but when I last spoke to him, he said he was intent on attending some conference on the paranormal. Now, I'm not stupid and neither is Jake. So my question is: what does he have to do with paranormal phenomena and stone circles?" She lowered her head and removed a computer tablet from her handbag. She buzzed it on and displayed a webpage. "This was in his hotel room. It's *his* tablet. Why was he researching this?"

The three of them hovered over the tablet that now sat in the center of the table. The website was called **Crypt of Chronos, Stone Circles of Teleportation**.

"What the hell is this all about?" Serena demanded.

Angeline read the first paragraph over Chancellor's shoulder.

> *A stone circle of teleportation is designed to allow safe travel between two locations. For two stone circles to function as intended they must be constructed so that, when activated, they operate simultaneously.*

"Are you kidding me," Serena said, her voice filled with incriminating scorn. "Stone circles of teleportation? Since when did he start believing that Stargate was real?"

Angeline doubted that Jake had ever heard of the popular television series where a military government team, known as Stargate One, visited other planets and universes via a portal, a circular Stargate, that was somehow (she had forgotten how) transported to Earth, and with sister gates established on other planets.

If she could be so presumptuous as to interpret what she had just read in the same manner as Serena, then prehistoric stone circles like Stonehenge and Avebury, and numerous others all across Europe were connected to one another.

From the look in Chancellor's eyes Angeline knew exactly why Jake was researching stone circles. He was trying to find a way back to their original timeline. But was this even the same thing?

Chancellor's slight shake of the head warned her not to speak her mind in the presence of Serena. Why not? Serena Dunnel was Jake's fiancée. She had a right to know. But he continued to be elusive. "The police are out looking for him," he said. This much was true. Superintendent Simon Pettigrew was actively hunting for Jake. "Don't worry, he'll be found. In fact, why don't you contact the police yourself? I'm sure they'd be interested in interviewing you, since you're the closest thing he has to a family."

The look on the cocksure face made it obvious that she was none too pleased with the idea of contacting the police. But if she were really concerned with his whereabouts, wouldn't she do that on her own? Clearly, Chancellor wasn't handing out any invitations for her to join them in their search. Angeline was glad. There was something about Serena.... Was the woman just jealous? Jealous of *her* for some imagined connection with Jake? Or did she have information that she wasn't sharing?

Finally Serena rose, after barely touching her latte, and

made to leave. "Here's my number," she said, handing over a business card. "Call me if you hear anything."

Chancellor's phone rang before Angeline could comment on Serena's abrupt departure. He waited for three rings before he answered it. "Hey Drey," he said. He watched the restaurant door close behind the irate fiancée before he set the device to speakerphone, and placed it onto the well-scrubbed tabletop between their plates of half-eaten oatmeal and eggs. "Find anything?"

When Drey left them earlier her intent was to check out Diana Lune's accommodations. She had managed to disguise herself as a maid and wander through the unlocked door when the real chambermaid left to fetch some coffee for the unit.

"I couldn't find anything in the room; the maid came back and I had to leave before she started asking questions, but I'm pretty sure I didn't miss anything. That chick is unusually neat and tidy. You won't believe this but she hardly brought any luggage with her: one small suitcase with two outfits in it. I couldn't find any jewellery so she must be wearing it... Since I was here I decided to check out Lalonde's room, and you'll never guess what I found..." Drey spent the next ten minutes describing her adventures snooping about.

"Be careful McFee," Chancellor warned. "Lalonde's fiancée is on her way back. She just left us—"

"Oh-oh."

"What? What's happening?"

"Gotta go, Chancellor. I think she just came in the door."

The phone went dead and Chancellor switched it off. He looked up and Angeline said, "I wonder what she found?"

"Well, hopefully Serena will fall for the guise and not detain her. And she can make her way back to us. Meanwhile..." He pulled out his computer tablet and started searching Google Maps.

"What exactly are you looking for?"

"Some pattern to these stone circles."

"Why? What will that do?"

He looked up. "There was a time when I would have thought that all of this talk about stone circles was bunk, but experience has changed that. I don't know if any of what we heard in that lecture last night is true, but I am going to go on the assumption that it is. That means these stone circles, according to *her* theory…." He proceeded to explain the theory and why he had finally decided to adopt it as his own—while Angeline grew more and more incredulous. "Jake was inside the stone circle when he disappeared. And so, my next point is: the only person who has an explanation for where he disappeared to is Diana Lune."

"So shouldn't we be confronting *her*?"

"How? If she doesn't want to be found, we won't be able to find her. And even if we did locate her, we wouldn't be able to make her return him to us or convince her to return the timeline to the way it is supposed to be—if she is actually responsible for all of this. Besides, I'm sure as far as she is concerned who's to say the way things are now isn't the way things are supposed to be. Everything happens by chance, and if there is a grand design, who's designing it? God? Not if you live in a world where Diana Lune exists."

Angeline fell silent for a moment. "Was that why you stayed quiet on the subject while Serena Dunnel was here?"

"Bad enough that the police will think we're loony as a bat house, but no point in dragging the fiancée into it."

"What are we going to do, then?"

"I'm hoping Drey found the Triple Moon symbol. I think that is the device we need if we are to succeed in this venture."

"But Jake didn't have that symbol."

"But he did have the Raven mask. I think it needs both. The symbol of the goddess and the Raven."

Angeline clasped her hands together as the truth descended. Why hadn't she thought of this earlier? "The symbol was scratched into the earth. She was there before *he* was."

"But that symbol wasn't permanent. It was placed there as bait."

"So what are you saying? That the.... Oh, I see..." The local Wicca and druids had adopted Branwen as their goddess. June was a sacred month because it was the time of year when the goddess chose her mate. The event was honoured by the festooning of the village and her followers with her chosen symbol—the three moons. "Oh my gosh. You are talking about the Handfast!"

"You're catching on."

CHAPTER TWENTY-TWO

The Handfast was the union of the Goddess with her mate. From what Chancellor recounted of the events in the previous timeline, her dream or flashback—whatever it was—was a memory of the first attempt to bind the Raven. Together they would have ultimate power. And Angeline? Well, she will have lost him forever. "We must stop her!"

"That's the plan. We just have to figure out how she was able to abduct him from Stonehenge without leaving behind any visible evidence. Even those ravens are all gone. They're not like the ones haunting Avebury..." Or were they? Chancellor paused, a puzzled look distorting his handsome features. He shook off the troubling thoughts and added, "And then we must find out where she's hidden him. Best guess is that she uses the stone circles. I think I have an idea as to how they work."

He proceeded to describe the symbol he saw engraved on one of Avebury's megaliths—the night Maia Pickerton went missing. There was also a similar symbol scratched onto one of the Stonehenge sarsens. That was why he had chosen the site of Stonehenge for Jake's attempt at reversing the timeline through a Haida Spirit dance. What he hadn't anticipated was that she would have predicted their move, and arrived first.

"So, 'she'"—Angeline felt a compulsion to emulate quotes with her fingers when she spoke the word—"could pass through with her own symbol, the three moons?"

"Yes, and Jake could pass through with *his* symbol."

Something suddenly struck Angeline with crushing

clarity. "Jake *is* the Raven."

"Exactly."

Somehow, all of this was beginning to make sense. The idea that he was the Raven did not seem outlandish to her. "How does Maia fit into this?"

"All I can think of is that she somehow interfered in Diana's plans."

"Then you really do believe that *she* is the person we're looking for?"

"I do."

The problem was: who was she really? Supernatural entity or mental patient? Angeline shook her head helplessly. "She just doesn't give up, does she?"

"Why do you say that?"

"I don't know. But for some peculiar reason, I have a feeling I've done something like this before."

"You have."

Before he could elaborate, Drey came waltzing through the door. She looked furtively behind her before she joined them at their table.

"What did you find?" Angeline demanded.

Drey stole one last look around her, then dipped her hand into her pocket and pulled out a chunky piece of costume jewellery. But it wasn't just any piece of costume jewellery; it was a fake gold replica of Diana Lune's necklace. Or else it was the original, and at some point in their acquaintance, she had left that necklace in Jake's possession.

The first thing that entered Angeline's mind was that Diana had been speaking the truth when she said that she and Jake had spent a night together. While Angeline had no reason to object or to feel as rotten as she did (since in this timeline she and Jake were new acquaintances with no relationship whatsoever), Serena would certainly have every right to be distressed. "Where was it in his room?"

"Well, that's the odd thing," Drey said. "It was right on the dresser top, right in the open. Anyone walking in there would see it."

"That *is* strange," Chancellor mumbled. "But it doesn't change anything. We need that necklace. Angeline, go and fetch the Raven mask from my room. Here's my key. Drey, you accompany her. It's inside my briefcase. It will be locked. Meet me outside the hotel. I'm on my way to the lobby to rent us a vehicle. We are going for a drive."

"Our destination?" Angeline asked.

"The starting point of the Great Stone's Way."

"And where would that be?"

"Depends which direction we take. North-south or south-north. Myself, I would choose north-south, Barbury Castle to Old Sarum."

The rental was a Ford Fusion, roomy enough for three and any supplies they wished to bring with them. Chancellor pulled up in front of the hotel and the two women entered the car with the briefcase containing the Raven mask. "Put the necklace into the briefcase for safekeeping," he instructed.

Drey followed his directions for releasing the lock, and then laid the piece of jewellery alongside it before closing the lid and relocking it. By the time they reached Barbury Castle, Chancellor had once again altered his plan. Mostly because Barbury Castle (which was actually a hill fort, and not a castle at all) was in fact not readily accessible by car, and although they had plans to walk the famous trail, he was not keen on leaving his vehicle in such an isolated area of farmland. So he decided they would start at a more natural starting point, and that was a return to Avebury. It made more sense, on reflection, to follow the trail between the two most famous historic monuments (Avebury and Stonehenge); and hopefully somewhere along the way they would become enlightened.

They abandoned their vehicle at the car park in the village, and absorbed the scene of megaliths surrounded by massive, dark green earthworks, crawling with pale yellow cowslips. A river of grey mist steamed from the ground and quickly dissipated as they strolled through it. Oddly there

were no ravens visible today, only their guano, thickly
layered on the peaks of most of the sarsens.

Chancellor made directly for the Barber Stone. He
inspected it up close, and then stepped back. Unexpectedly,
he choked on a breath and Angeline ran up to him. "What is
it? What's the matter?"

He made no sound, merely pointed. He, like Angeline,
was expecting to see the simulacrum of Maia Pickerton.
Instead, they saw Jake Lalonde's sculptured features.

"I don't understand." She gulped. "Why is Jake's face
represented in this rock?" Drey came up to study the standing
stone as well.

"I'm not sure." Chancellor moved away and began to
study the ground and the other stones. Angeline mimicked
him, but then turned back when she heard a sharp intake of
breath from beside her. "Come look at it now."

At first glance, the megalith before her was the same
enormous rock, tipped upright to stand on its narrow base. It
was not artificially crafted in any manner. What was
occurring was a trick of perception. Their brains were
playing tricks with their eyes, combining the bumps and
grooves and cracks and pocks in the surface texture, and
encouraging their imaginations to shape images into the
rocky surface. And all of that would have been acceptable if
it wasn't for the fact that it was the archaeologist's face they
were imagining.

Perhaps it was wishful thinking that was making her see
his face, but whether or not that was true was irrelevant.
Because now, on the surface of the very same rock was
something else. The image had changed. It was no longer a
resemblance of the missing archaeologist. What they were
seeing—at least what Angeline was seeing—was the image
of a large, hooked-beaked bird.

Their imaginations were doing double time. In reality no
bird was carved into the rock face, and yet whatever angle
she observed it, she continued to perceive the head and
shoulders of a raven. And it wasn't only her. From the

expressions on her companions' faces, she knew they saw the identical image.

Drey was first to break the silence. "Chancellor. Wasn't it here, near this stone, that we caught that sighting of 'Big Bird'?"

Angeline looked from the one to the other. What were they talking about? Then she recalled the evening of the infamous lecture. According to the cryptozoologist she and the Interpol agent had glimpsed a human-sized bird in the dark.

Chancellor fetched out his iPad; Drey withdrew her smartphone. They both began flipping through their stored images. Each had photographed the sighting. And then Angeline realized that she too had had a similar sighting. Only hers was inside the museum, after everyone had left— and she had gone back into the theater to find Diana's PowerPoint still running.

*   *   *

"What *is* that hideous thing?" Angeline asked, touching the photograph on his tablet.

Chancellor did not wish to elaborate for fear that the answer would frighten her. He had his own theories about the 'Big Bird' sighting, and was pretty certain it would not jive with the cryptozoologist's concept. Drey was not privy to his personal knowledge of the archaeologist. And Angeline clearly did not recall, although in her subconscious he suspected she knew. The only thing he was clear on was that the creature was a representation of the Raven. And to find Jake, and possibly Maia, they would have to follow any sighting of it.

Drey, for some miraculous reason, seemed to read his mind. "Last sighting of 'Big Bird' was near the Nine Ladies circle," she said. She was a member of Cryptid Chasers International who kept track of recent sightings.

The Nine Ladies is a Bronze Age stone circle, an ancient

megalithic structure consisting of nine stones, each of which stands approximately one meter high. Legend alleged that nine women transformed into stone when they danced in the woods on the Sabbath. A tenth stone rested slightly apart from the others. This stone was supposedly the fiddler who strummed the music for their dance, and is known as the King Stone. It was held that this stone circle formed a link between earth and sky—and hence a connection between living and dead. *We shall see,* Chancellor thought.

If this was the locale of the bird creature sighting, then that must be their next destination. More and more it seemed the stone circles were the secret to locating the missing archaeologist and curator. The Nine Ladies were dwarfs in comparison to Stonehenge or Avebury, but there must be a reason they had been brought to his attention. The only connection that came to mind was that the henges were all erected within a certain time frame. And that was about 4,000 years in the past.

He herded the women to the car without explanation, and once they were settled and belted in, he backtracked onto the motorway.

"Where are we going?" Angeline demanded.

"To Stanton Moor in northwest Derbyshire."

"But that's got to be a three or four hour drive," Drey protested.

"Doesn't matter. If that's the location of the last sighting, then that's where we have to go. You said the last report of 'Big Bird' was near the Nine Ladies. It's a stone circle. Something tells me that all of these stone circles are linked somehow."

The first couple of hours of the drive were uneventful. Drey slept in the backseat while Angeline kept peering nervously out her side passenger window. The scenery skated by, towns and small villages, and as they drew farther north, the landscape gave way to open farmland. Cattle and sheep grazed on lush green fields and manmade canals cut through the meadows. Eventually it seemed as if the traffic was lighter, and then remarkably the road became quite empty.

He steered off the A6 between Bakewell and Rowsley onto the B5056 Ashbourne road, and then made a left where the road to Youlgrave forked off to the right. To the west were the shining waters of the river Derwent.

A railroad track ran parallel to the road and he continued driving, the sun beating relentlessly into his vision. He glanced at the GPS. It instructed him to drive 500 meters further, and then to veer left to Stanton in Peak. They were almost there. He was supposed to pass through a village before taking a left onto the moor. The vales now transforming the landscape were the Derwent and Wye valleys. "Keep an eye out for the turnoff to the Stanton Moor Peak District National Park."

Angeline moved her head in soundless agreement, and then turned back to the side window. Woodland had replaced the farmland, and stands of birches, beeches and ash trees dotted the landscape. "The GPS insists we're here," she said, tapping the console.

"I don't see any signage."

"There's a side road, maybe that's it."

"I don't think so. I'm going to keep following the train tracks."

She shrugged. She seemed to have something on her mind, but he refrained from meddling.

In the distant horizon, the road and the train tracks seemed interminable, but there was no sign of civilization anywhere. Could he have taken a wrong turn? There was a station platform up ahead. It had a sign above it that read: Stanton Moor. Okay, so they were in the correct place. He had not expected it to be quite so isolated. He parked the car and exited. Angeline followed and Drey who had just woken up, climbed out of the backseat yawning, and asked, "So where is it? I don't see any stone circle."

A large transformer stood in the field beside the train platform enclosed by a chain link fence. A red and white sign hung from it:

No Trespassing. Danger of Death.

All around was nothing but open fields. Not even any livestock. It was unnervingly quiet. Only the wind blew through a few straggling trees, and beat at the long grasses at the edge of the tracks. The sky had shifted to a leaden grey.

"Hmm," Chancellor said. "Maybe you were right, Angeline. Maybe that turnoff we passed is the road to the stone circle."

He reversed the car and drove the three kilometers back to the side road. There was no sign, but the road appeared well used. It was paved, although in sore need of repairs. Several varieties of weeds pushed up between the cracks and potholes. They came to a dead end where the road crumbled to gravel. There was a semicircular space where drivers could reverse their cars, or park. Chancellor parked.

They hiked through the birch and beech trees until they arrived at a diverging path. They chose the left fork and emerged from out of the ash trees to the moor. The nine stones stood in a circle, and to the south was a small boulder—the King Stone.

Chancellor approached the largest of the stones and pushed at the purple heather that had partially hidden its surface. There was nothing of significance here, zero markings or symbols—only a smattering of modern graffiti. If these stone circles operated according to his suspicions, there must be some sort of sigil to activate them.

"What *are* you looking for?" Angeline asked.

"A symbol scratched onto the stones."

"I don't see anything except some modern vandalism. And this—" It was the name 'Bill Stumps', notoriously mentioned by Charles Dickens in the *Pickwick Papers*, and carved onto the surface of the King Stone. Well, that couldn't have anything to do with Diana Lune.

He continued to inspect the stones while his companions wandered off in different directions. Suddenly Angeline called out, "I found something."

In her hand was a curious round lens, about two inches in diameter, like the lens had fallen out of someone's eyeglasses. The find wouldn't have been so unusual, and she might have ignored it if it weren't for the object that was clearly visible in the glass. Embedded in the thick lens was a tiny gold emblem—a circle with two crescents, one on either side, outward-facing.

He took it from her and held it up to the light. It was transparent as though it were made of amber.

"Why is this here?" she asked. "That tiny emblem is the same design as Diana Lune's necklace.

"So, she's been here." He gave the lens to Angeline for safekeeping and traveled deeper into the site, searching the ground for further signs of an unearthly visit.

CHAPTER TWENTY-THREE

The landscape had a fairylike quality about it, especially with the dappled sunlight filtering through the foliage. Chancellor stood dead center of the sacred site. There were no signs on the ground. Other than the modern graffiti the stones were also unmarked. Was this circle a nexus to the others? If so there should be a symbol scored onto one of the stones or in the earth as there had been at both Stonehenge and Avebury.

He turned to Angeline. "Let me see that lens again."

She handed the object to him. He concentrated on the design before restoring it to her and requesting that she keep the lens safe in her handbag. She peered at it one last time and then fumbled with the zipper of her bag to do so. "What have you got there?" Drey asked, returning from her exploration of the shallow woods. She too squinted at the lens, but instead of exclaiming as her friend had done, she raised her shoulders. "It looks like the lens from somebody's eyeglasses. Big deal."

The inflection in the cryptozoologist's tone of voice induced a rather unexpected suspicion in Chancellor. He retrieved the item from her, and indeed it did resemble a lens from a pair of eyeglasses, only now the golden emblem that had been center-stage of the lens had vanished. The incredulous look on Angeline's face told him that he wasn't imagining things. He had been observing the interaction between the two women, and neither had tampered with the lens. The tiny symbol previously embedded in that piece of glass was gone.

"I think we've been had." He pierced the vast empty landscape with a hard stare and sighed. It would take a half a day to get back to the Great Stone's Way. They were running out of time. If the event that he suspected were to occur, then it would happen tonight on the night of the summer solstice, which was June 20th. "What's the nearest big city from here?"

"Manchester, why?" It was Angeline who replied.

"Because we need to hire a helicopter to return us to Avebury ASAP."

She frowned. "The drive will still take about an hour."

"That's better than four. Let's go."

***

The name of the village had its origins in prehistory and the words 'ave' and 'bury' meant 'female serpent of the sun'. If one followed this line of thinking, the pathway of Avebury passed through a large circular Temple of the Sun, emerging, winding and ending in an oblong head, directly in line with Hackpen, a conservation area in Oxfordshire, affectionately labeled Snakes Head Hill by the locals. The central circle symbolized the sun and was the male principle in the creative process. Once the serpent had passed through the sun circle it was recharged with new life. Prehistoric folk used to walk outside the pathway of the serpent, leaving the inner pathway for the priests. According to Diana Lune's bestseller, this was the means by which the living could achieve new life. The dead had their own means via the tombs of nearby West Kennet.

Chancellor removed his mini iPad and matched the view below with the sketch he had made a few nights previous. From this vantage point in the helicopter he could identify linear indentations in the ground, filled in with grass. He had to squint to clear his vision as the light was painfully glaring and the scene below was bathed in shades of green and yellow, and deep shadowy blue. Throughout the Great Circle he detected a familiar pattern. On the other hand, with the late afternoon sun as steep as it was, what he thought he was seeing could merely be a trick of light and shadow.

He focused on the center of the North Circle at the locale of the remaining stones of the Cove. There seemed to be a gentle depression where the stones used to be. To either side of it more curving linear impressions flowed in an easterly and westerly course, identical in each direction.

He shuddered, his suspicions escalating. The Great Circle was more than what it appeared when seen from the ground. It seemed strangely elongated from the angle in which they were flying now, in preparation to descend. Diana's words from her lecture returned to haunt him.

The avenues were the serpent's tail and the Great Circle its head. The inner circles formed the figure of a raven with the obelisk representing the beak and the stones of the cove, an eye. Like Native Haida art, the two figures intertwined. And then he recalled how she had ended her talk. She had recited a Celtic folktale passed down for generations about the Snake and the Raven.

What exactly was she planning? Was it really as simple as a Handfast? She had tried that once before—and had failed. The creepy sensation he was experiencing told him that it was something more.

The wind from the rotors cruelly slapped their clothes and their hair with raw force as they debarked from the helicopter in the newly mown field. Chancellor gave the pilot a thumbs-up and waved him away.

"Now what?" Angeline asked.

"Yeah, now what?" Drey echoed.

"I'm not certain. I only know that we need to be *here*."

Drey wandered away and began to explore the various megaliths. Angeline stared at him then turned away to see the familiar megalith that was causing them so much anguish. The accursed stone showed no face on its pocked surface.

She said, "I don't know about you, but I could use a drink and a bite to eat. Where's Drey? I'll go fetch her."

Chancellor suddenly yanked her by the wrist, dragged her back. "Look at it now. What do you see?"

She shrugged his hand off and studied the megalith. She stepped back in horror. "Oh no. Chancellor, it's the spitting image of Drey...Drey!" she shouted. "Where are you?"

She ran off toward the South Circle, he following, his worst fears materializing. Suddenly she disappeared. He ran towards a massive stone, the one they called the Devil's Chair—to where he last saw her—and was startled to see a single black raven with a yellow band around its ankle perched on its summit.

**

Angeline glanced to either side of her, terror rising. Where was she? And where was Chancellor? He *was* right behind her and now everything was dark. She rapidly blinked. Now, as she studied the walls around her she realized it wasn't as dark as it had originally seemed. She was inside a sewer-like tunnel, and at the junction of the tunnel where a single light bulb burned she caught a glimpse of someone familiar.

"Drey?" she called, but dared not raise her voice too loudly. She still wasn't certain where she was. At first she thought somehow she'd had a blackout and then ended up inside the subbasement of the Alexander Keiller Museum, but now as she glanced around she saw that she wasn't there at all. An arm slunk out of the shadows and touched her elbow.

"Oh my God, Drey. You scared me!"

"I'm sorry," she said. "But I didn't know how else to get your attention. You looked so desperate, and I have a creepy feeling that that's the worst thing we can do right now."

"Where are we? Where's Chancellor? He was right behind me."

"I'm not sure, but I don't think we're in Avebury anymore. As for Chancellor, I haven't seen him. Just you."

"How can we not be in Avebury anymore?"

"I don't know, but follow me. Do as I do and don't draw attention to yourself."

"How can I draw attention to myself? There's nobody else here."

"I wouldn't be too sure of that."

There were faint voices coming from somewhere. It sounded like the mindless jabber of tourists.

"I swear I saw you go in the opposite direction," Angeline whispered. "You were acting like you were stalking someone. How did you end up behind me so fast, when I just saw you go down that tunnel a split second ago?"

Drey frowned. Something was troubling her. She told Angeline that she had been among the tourists, and had picked up something off the floor from the litter around their feet. There was a single light bulb hanging from one section of the ceiling, and she nudged Angeline under it. Angeline looked at the pamphlet and saw that it was indeed a tourist guide, but before she got a chance to ascertain exactly what kind of tourist site this was, Drey pointed to the date of the copyright. "Oh my God," Angeline said.

Drey nodded, "The only thing I don't understand is how we got to Seattle."

"But the date says it's—. Oh my. We are in the future!"

"The future, yes, but in *Seattle*." She tapped the address on the pamphlet. "To be exact."

"Isn't that Jake Lalonde's hometown?

Drey nodded again.

A man's figure crossed the tunnel and it was unmistakable who it was. The ubiquitous navy blue suit, yellow tie and beige trench coat looked incongruous in this setting. It was going to be plenty hard for him to blend in with the tourists when they caught up. Angeline cupped her hands to shout, when Drey dragged her arm down, and placed a finger to her lips. She indicated with her thumb the direction they should go—the same direction the man had disappeared. Angeline gave her a puzzled look.

"That's not who you think it is," Drey said.

"What do you mean? Of course it is. That was Thomas Chancellor. I recognized his clothes."

"No, it's not."

Angeline didn't waste anymore time arguing. They had approached the place where the voices originated and stopped at the rear of a fifteen-person group.

Just in front of them was a young woman. Her hair was covered with a brown hoodie, but trails of red hair escaped the sides. She wore nondescript khaki jeans, with a mustard T-shirt, loose over the low-rise waistband. Angeline turned to Drey after glimpsing the other woman's face in full profile. Her eyes widened in astonishment, and she almost spoke, when Drey once more shook her head, and motioned her back out of sight.

But that woman looks identical to you!

She shook her head again, and pointed at the date on the pamphlet. Now Angeline understood. That *was* Drey. But it was a Drey McFee from one year into the future. She was dressed differently from when Angeline lost sight of her in the South Circle.

The lighting was dim, shadowy. It seemed Drey McFee's doppelganger was searching for someone. Drey indicated with hand gestures that they both move deeper out of sight. "We can't let her see us."

"You really believe that stuff about paradoxes?"

"Yes. And just imagine how disturbing it would be to meet someone you know from the past. Especially your own self?"

By now, it was clear that they were underground somewhere. The smell was dank, like damp, unwashed laundry. The air was cool, and the walls breathed moisture. The floor was uneven and in some parts unpaved, and what they stood on now was raw trampled earth. A set of rickety steps appeared and Angeline and Drey followed the dark figures of the tourists down the wooden stairs. At least there were handrails to prevent anyone from falling. A woman in front of her wore high-heels. Her husband (or was it boyfriend?) kept clutching at her arm when she stumbled. The dead voice of the tour operator rumbled through the funnel they were descending.

"Where are we going?" Angeline whispered.

"Same place she is." By 'she' Drey meant her double.

They reached level ground and Angeline could see the brick arches of the ceiling over the underground corridors, which looked to be street sidewalks. The tour guide pointed out the former meat market of Seattle's old Pioneer Square, and a bank. Most of these structures were red brick. They were in ruins with standing columns and walls. Much had been cleaned up since the great disaster, but it was far from being restored to its former glory.

In the late 1800s a massive fire had burned down thirty-one blocks of mostly wooden buildings, and instead of rebuilding in the same manner, city officials had decided to elevate the city two stories higher than the original plan. This left the original shops and businesses below ground, to be eventually abandoned. One day a local businessman realized the profit potential as a tourist draw, and restored the underground city just enough to make it safe for tourists to prowl through.

"Please stay on the path," the tour operator, said. The tour group moved on. Angeline looked down to see a boardwalk of planks covering the ground. A shadow fell across the floor and she frowned, although when she glanced up nobody was there. On the wall however was a man-sized shadow that reminded her of something she had seen before. A creeping sense of unease began to prickle along her spine. She twisted to locate the source of the shadow and saw no one. The tunnel where she and Drey had stopped was dead silent. No voices could be heard, not even the voices of the tour operator and his group. When she looked back, the shadow had vanished.

She exchanged glances with Drey who had seen it too. What's more, she had observed the doppelganger's behaviour, and it seemed she was following the mysterious shadow.

They hurried through the tunnel down another flight of stairs until they reached the bottom and caught up with the group at a subterranean gift shop. They waited in the shadow of the doorway and watched someone push a souvenir-type book on Drey's future self. A display caught the doppelganger's eye. These were posters crowding the walls, reproductions of the soldiers who had been summoned to help douse out the great fire of Seattle. They stood in a single line on the grass at the city's perimeter with a forested area in the background, while the foreground showed a dead creature with enormous wings. Its wingspan stretched the entire length of the row of soldiers, and one of them had his foot on the creature's belly; the others stood with arms crossed and feet spread, in triumph. Again, Angeline felt that shiver of déjà vu.

The woman in the high-heels said to her husband, "That's what people have been seeing near the cliffs."

The husband shook his head. "That looks like a pterodactyl. Pterodactyls are extinct. What people saw at the cliffs looked more like a giant bird."

Drey's double cocked an ear to listen. The couple moved out of hearing range. She glanced around, annoyed. While she was distracted, the person she had been tracking gave her the slip.

CHAPTER TWENTY-FOUR

They followed the doppelganger to her hotel, a small inexpensive place near Pioneer Square. When they had determined where she was staying they decided to book rooms at the Edgewater Hotel on the waterfront. They didn't dare stay at the same hotel as Drey's future self, for fear of running into her.

"From what we witnessed of your future self this afternoon," Angeline said, "it was Chancellor that your double was tailing. The question is: why?"

"I'm more concerned about getting out of this time warp or whatever it is. What's our plan? Any ideas?"

"I think we'll find our way out of this time if we follow your double and Chancellor. There is a reason why we are here. Once we find it, I think we'll be able to leave."

"You think they have something to do with how we got here?"

"I think they have something to do with *why* we are here. But first I want to go to the library and do some research."

Drey couldn't think of a better plan so they agreed to go to the University of Washington's library.

At the imposing building, they followed the stairs to a room filled with ceiling to floor shelves. The library was not crowded and most of the people were studiously attached to computers. Not many rummaged among the stacks.

They went to a terminal, and with their heads lowered, did a search. Angeline typed while Drey speculated over the events that had brought them to this impasse in muted whispers. Angeline mumbled her agreement but really heard little of what was said. It wasn't everyday a person found herself in the situation of witnessing the future, and although she was apprehensive of learning her own prospects she was keen to cobble together information on her friend's… and to know what she was doing in this time period. Aha. So that was what became of Drey McFee. It was only a year into the future, but Holy Crow! She never expected this—

"You and Thomas Chancellor are partners in a cryptozoology outfit based in Vancouver," Angeline announced in an excited whisper.

"What?" Drey could barely keep from rolling her eyes at this incredible turn of events. "Chancellor and I are what?"

"Shush, keep your voice down. Partners. You two run a cryptid hunter business. You investigate strange sightings."

"With that amateur?"

"He's not an amateur. He's got loads of experience with the supernatural."

Drey shook her head. "I don't believe it."

Angeline twisted the computer screen toward her. "See for yourself."

This was the future, and things were what they were. Drey was stymied by what she read on the Internet, but in the end she had to accept it. "Okay, now you. Let's find out what you do after grad school. A link led to some professional websites. But that wasn't the one that caught their eye. Drey clicked onto a wedding announcement—and they both stifled a gasp. Angeline Lisbon of the future was married to the archaeologist Jake Lalonde.

All of a sudden Angeline caught a flash of a tall man in a trench coat. She looked up and saw him at a far terminal searching online. No time to ponder her future husband. For some strange reason she was not surprised. She was filled with a kind of elation and maybe embarrassment as Drey turned to her, eyes wide, but rather than respond to the unspoken query, she jerked her own toward the trench-coated man.

When he was done on the computer, she nudged Drey

and they waited until he had left for the stacks before they tiptoed to his vacated keyboard and searched his history.

Myths and Monsters was the first thing that came up. They shared puzzled glances.

"That *was* Chanellor, wasn't it?" Angeline asked. "How do we know that that's not the real Chancellor? I mean *our* Chancellor?"

"We don't. But I'm pretty sure he's not from our time, so if he comes back don't let him see you."

They both wore disguises. Angeline had rolled her hair up into a tight bun on the top of her head, and wore much more makeup than usual, while Drey had tucked her red hair under a small-brimmed floppy hat. Their clothes were as drab as they could make them: khaki's and T-shirts bought from a local thrift shop.

Angeline clicked onto the link. The first article explored creatures of myth, ancient fantastic beings that stalked the globe, and which included huge panthers with bird's claws for feet, horned serpents with wings, and humans that could transform into great birds.

None of it was making any sense. Why was Chancellor researching mythical creatures?

When they had finished reading that article, Angeline clicked onto the next link. This essay concerned the discovery of megalithic fauna—mammoth bones and the like—and how they may have led to aboriginal beliefs in strange creatures like giant cannibal birds. For some reason a dark haired, casually dressed man in blue jeans flashed into her memory. She glanced at the author name. That explained it. Their missing archaeologist (and her future husband?) had written the essay. Drey sent her a questioning face. She shrugged. So far this search explained nothing.

"Chancellor seemed unusually nervous," Drey whispered from beneath her hat, "What do you suppose was making him so nervous?"

The lights were dim in the library and long shadows leaped across the floor in the open space beyond the book stacks. Angeline saw a man standing between the shelving. His eyes flickered in their direction and her heart raced as she urged Drey to look down. But when she got up the nerve to cast a quick glance in the direction his eyes were fixed, she saw it wasn't she he was staring at, but Drey. Not *her* Drey, but Drey McFee of the future.

Future Drey stood in the doorway, half hidden by the doorjamb. She was acting strange too, for her eyes also seemed to dart toward the shadows, especially the shadow cast by something behind Chancellor. As Angeline's gaze lingered on the shadow, she blinked, thinking she saw something that couldn't possibly be there. She looked away, but when she heard the click of the keyboard she returned her gaze to the next series of links on Chancellor's search history.

She felt a nudge on her upper arm, saw Drey remove her hand from the keyboard and motion to follow the double. Why didn't she confront him? Angeline wondered. If the two of them were partners in the future, why was she hiding from him?

The double left the campus in a Mini Cooper. After a few seconds Angeline breathed a sigh of relief. Lame though their disguises were they had not been sighted. She urged Drey to hurry. She suggested that they follow her until in her side vision she caught sight of two men. She slowly raised a warning hand to Drey. Thomas Chancellor and Jake Lalonde had met up, and were walking towards the parking lot, their heads locked deep in conversation.

It was dusk by now and the streetlamps were lit. She removed her sunglasses, and watched the two men cross the campus and enter a dark Bronco. In this light it was hard to tell the exact shade.

She ran to the road frantically flagging a taxi. Who should they chase? Future Drey or these two? One glance at Drey told her they were in agreement. They finally succeeded in acquiring a cab, and chased the Bronco onto Vine Street. It turned onto Elliot Avenue. They drove a few more miles then asked the driver to let them out at the next intersection. They had lost them. Drey had just paid the fare with the little cash they had left between them, when Angeline saw a man across the street entering a Target store. It was Chancellor. But where was Jake?

They pursued the trench-coated figure into the building behind a pair of skinny-jeaned, high-booted girls, reeking of smoke. Department store music came from somewhere above and people dressed in street clothes, some consuming drinks and food on the fly, pushed grocery carts across the floor. Narrow full-length mirrors lined the side of one wall where clothing racks offered bargain deals. Angeline squinted into the bright lighting hoping to catch a glimpse of the Interpol agent. As she wove her way between the shoppers she noticed that the place was huge. How was she going to find him again, or Drey for that matter? She seemed to have lost her friend as well.

The vastness of the store and the odd lighting, bright in some spots, dim in others, was giving her a feeling of agoraphobia. Angeline's eye landed on her own reflection in one of the mirrors, hanging over a family of shoppers.

Then she saw Drey.

Next, they both glimpsed their quarry.

Unafraid, the cryptozoologist steadied her eyes in the mirror. For Angeline it was a different story. The tremors creeping up her arms were real.

Drey rotated to come face-to-face with Thomas Chancellor, while Angeline ducked out of sight.

CHAPTER TWENTY-FIVE

This Chancellor was oblivious of her presence, and unaware that the person he had waylaid was an imposter. Angeline tucked herself further beside a shelf of folded clothing and realized, as a skeleton hung down between her and her vision that she was in the costume department. On a shelf just at waist level sat trays of theatrical makeup. She craned ever so slightly forward to eavesdrop on their meeting.

"What are you doing here, McFee."

"I might ask you the same question." She answered, calm returning when she realized he had no suspicions of her identity. Angeline on the other hand was trembling.

"I'm on a case. And it's got nothing to do with you. This one's personal, so go home. I'll see you in a few days. I'll explain then."

Drey resisted by bracing her feet on the tiled floor and crossing her arms. She planned to take advantage of the situation and rout out as much information as she could. "No. I want an explanation now. We're partners, Chancellor. If I can't trust you, then what kind of a business relationship do we have?"

They were next to the exit to the corridor that led to the employee lounge, and he shoved the swinging door open and nudged her through. Angeline tucked her head down before venturing a peek through the small square window. Blocked from view by shelves of dense goods, it was quiet here. At the end of the aisle two women in Target uniforms swept by. She stepped back, lowering her head as though examining a piece of merchandise until they had passed. Then she returned to the swinging door and nudged it ajar.

"It obviously has something to do with Jake Lalonde," Drey was saying.

Chancellor's face was in three-quarter profile away from her view. He froze at the suggestion. So did Angeline. Drey was taking a big chance talking to him. "What makes you say that?"

"I saw you leaving campus with him. So where is he?" She paused, before deciding to continue. "I want to know what's going on. As you well know, his significant other is a good friend of mine."

Angeline perked up at this comment. Chancellor frowned, pulled at his chin. She was beginning to notice that this particular Chancellor perpetrated the mannerism when uneasy. "So now, you're playing detective? If you tell me she hired you I will just laugh in your face."

"Of course she didn't hire me." Drey glared. "Is he involved with that giant bird shadow I've been seeing?"

"You saw it? Where did you see it? Do you think anyone else saw it?"

Clearly he was on edge. His voice was pitched at least an octave higher.

"I doubt it. No one reacted. You would have to be looking for it to see it."

"And you were looking for it?"

"Well, not specifically. I was looking for anything unusual, and that's what I saw. It was in the underground city, and so were you. And yes, I was following you. Now, obviously you've seen it too. So tell me what it is. What are we dealing with here?"

"*We*—are not dealing with anything. This is just a leisure trip. I'm here visiting a friend."

Drey took another risk, and disagreed. "Since when did Jake Lalonde and you become cryptid hunters?"

Chancellor shrugged. It looked like he was about to explain, but before he did a scowl passed across his features;

he had changed his mind. He raised his hands briefly. "Okay, we've had our differences."

Drey grinned. "I'll say. And her name is Angeline Lisbon."

Angeline's eyes shot up as she heard her name. Her heart had jerked and a breath had escaped, but she reigned in her reactions. Did she have some kind of relationship with Chancellor in the near future? And if she did, how would Drey know?

"*She* has nothing to do with this… Look, Lalonde asked me down here. He's worried about something that has absolutely nothing to do with you. Like I said. It's personal. So, I am not talking about this anymore."

"Then answer me this. What are you doing here at the Target store? Shopping for bargains?" Drey laughed. She was really sticking her neck out now, and Angeline wanted to stop her. However, if she did she would expose herself, and possibly blow both their covers.

"I'm warning you, McFee. Go home. This is not one of your close encounters—or anything to do with cryptozoology—or any sort of mysterious sighting. Go home."

"What were you doing in the underground city this morning?"

Chancellor laughed, and went silent. His smile changed into a grim line and he started toward the swinging door. Angeline ducked behind a rack of hanging sweaters, and Drey exited a second later. They both watched as Chancellor went to the checkout and paid for a tray of costume makeup.

***

The book was like a bible, a dictionary… an encyclopedia to all of the unexplained cryptid sightings on the west coast. The cover fascinated her with its colorful drawing of a giant raven-like bird. Drey flipped the pages, consumed with excitement. This book was delicious; she could gobble it up.

"Keep an eye on the hallway," she called to Angeline who was acting as lookout. They had pilfered the big *Book of Monsters* from out of the double's luggage and now Drey was flopped on the bed skimming through it.

Big birds that fell into this category were transformational. What exactly did that mean? Her eyes widened as she read the explanation. What had Future Chancellor gotten himself involved in? A cloak of invisibility? Sheesh. This was getting wilder and wilder. She read the description of Big Birds' personality. It was restless, curious and, to an intense degree, quickly bored. It was always looking for stimulation, which was why campers, hikers, mountain climbers and dirt bikers were its usual witnesses. It was seen in the thick of things. But a supermarket? Well, supermarkets could be considered stimulating if you liked shopping.

So why was he interested in this particular sighting? And what was he doing with costume makeup? And why did he insist that these Big Bird sightings were personal? If it should be personal to anyone, it should be to *her* (and to her future self). Although no one believed her, she *had* seen her mother turn into a monstrous bird and fly away when she was a girl.

"Okay, Angeline, I'm done. Did you want to have a look at it?"

Her accomplice turned her head. "No time. I think we'd better get out of here before your double returns."

Drey was about to stuff the big book back into the suitcase where she had found it, when a thought occurred to her. She didn't pause to consider the consequences of her rash decision but it was made. They were going to get to the bottom of this mystery if it was the last thing they ever did. And it well might be.

She went to the window and opened the curtains. The lights of the city glittered across the street. No sign of the double or her Mini Cooper.

"Let's go before we get caught."

She snatched her oversized handbag, now bulging with its stolen property, from the foot of the bed, and joined her accomplice at the door. A smell, salty like the sea flooded the passageway.

Angeline closed the door behind them, and jiggled the lever to ensure that it was locked. It had been easy to get another key from the front desk. All Drey had had to do was claim she had misplaced hers. She frowned. "What a weird smell." Not only that but she had the feeling they weren't alone. She turned to Angeline, had she felt it too? Apparently she had, because now she was motioning for Drey to follow her.

The elevator was at the end of the hall but Angeline gestured for her to head for the stairwell. Someone had been eavesdropping on them. Whoever it was fled through the emergency exit and the glimpse they had snatched was too vague to identify.

Drey ran after Angeline who had swung open the door to the exit. She hastened down the dimly lit steps, as she sighted a descending form. Angeline was ahead of her and had practically leaped down three flights of stairs and now had to stop to catch her breath. The padding of her sneakers stopped, but the footsteps did not. The sound of soft footfalls continued down the stairs as it spiraled toward ground level. The two women hurried, practically sliding down the handrails. Every hair on Drey's body stood on end.

They heard the sound of the door on the main floor open. As they reached ground level, the door hinged closed, ending with a *snick*. A rush of cool air washed over them, bringing with it the smell of the street. Ahead of her, Angeline rammed her elbow against the bar and shoved the door wide to catch the flight of a winged shadow. A light rain had fallen and the sidewalks were wet. They splashed through the puddles running hard. They turned the corner and stopped at the intersection. Whatever or whoever it was had vanished.

CHAPTER TWENTY-SIX

This time, Drey manned the keyboard. The article she clicked onto was called *Birth of the Dragon Myth.* The author proposed the theory that, on occasion, primitive people the world over encountered dinosaur bones, the magnitude of which made them believe in giant man-eating birds and carnivorous flying reptiles the size of elephants. Over the millennia these sightings were repeatedly told in story form until they became dragons rather than pterodactyls. *And some of them still exist,* Drey thought.

Why was Chancellor's future self interested in the origins of the dragon myth? She sat slumped in the smooth upholstered seat as she read the conclusions, before clicking onto the next link. The article was written by a woman scholar. She had conducted research in the Seattle area and had discovered the bones of a huge, unidentified ancient bird displayed in the city's aboriginal cultural center. Strange stories surrounded the discovery. "His shadow," Drey read aloud to Angeline, "is sometimes seen by the local people."

It was day two of their bizarre adventure and they had returned to the university library and appropriated the computer that Chancellor had used. His sessions were still logged. Drey absorbed every word intently. She had the sense that this was something important, something they needed to know. Since the discovery of the bones, the scholar went on to describe several sightings to the local press, the university's zoology department and even the police. "These are big birds," she read aloud, although in a very quiet voice. "Giant winged creatures like something out of Jurassic Park."

Furthermore, a pilot reported spotting the creature while flying passengers from Seattle to Vancouver. He estimated its wingspan to be around twenty feet.

A federal government researcher (a raptor specialist) reported that he was unaware of anything with a twenty-foot wingspan that had been alive for the last hundred thousand years. Those sightings may have been an Asian Steller's sea eagle, one of the world's largest birds. "It can be nearly twice the size of a bald eagle," Drey whispered. However, that hardly matched the description.

They finished reading the essay and looked at each other. They decided to exit the library and search for the double. Did she know about these bird bones? Drey was pretty certain that she must. Aboriginal people believed that the bones were the remains of a great shaman. The paper had said that the bones were housed in a cultural center on Marginal Way. Drey and Angeline rented a car, a Honda Civic, and drove there.

A Mini Cooper was parked in the visitor's lot in front of a two-story glass and wood building. No one was around, and they located the exhibit but it was now empty. There were no bones behind the glass display but the signage remained. At the base of the display was a card that read:

Pegasus

Apparently 'Pegasus' was a nickname for the skeleton. Scientists were notorious for nicknaming their discoveries. The bones were described as very large—man-sized in fact—with a yellowish color due to age. Fossilized remains were sometimes found amongst stratified rock, and these were the biggest bird bones ever unearthed in the cliffs of Discovery Park. A small earthquake at the turn of the millennium had broken them loose.

Drey saw someone who might be a curator and stopped him as he passed by. "Oh, that display was requisitioned by the government," he explained. "It's already on its way home."

"And where is home?"

"DARPA. The Defense Advanced Research Projects Agency."

"What?" Angeline cut in, her voice sounding totally incredulous.

"Is there any chance they would let us see the bones?" Drey asked. "My colleague here is an archaeologist, and I'm a cryptozoologist."

"Hey, weren't you just in here?" the curator inquired of Drey. "I swear I just spoke to someone who looked very similar to you. She was also a cryptozoologist."

"Oh, well, you know what they say, there's a doppelganger of every one of us somewhere in the world." She proffered a smile.

The curator returned her smile, but skeptically, and replied, "You will have to call or write to the department if you want any more information. Government scientists were the ones who made the original discovery. It was like pulling teeth to even get them to give the specimen to us on temporary loan. I can't imagine what they want a bundle of bones for. One thing I do know however is that they have it stored at a military base somewhere around here. Its location however has not been disclosed. The department picked up the specimen themselves." He shrugged. "Sorry, I can't help you any further."

"That's okay, thanks," Drey said.

They left the cultural center and made their way to the parking lot. The Mini Cooper was gone. "We have to go to the military base to see those bones," Drey decided.

"Why? It was just a big bird."

She wasn't sure why, but her instinct was telling her that this big bird had something do with their missing archaeologist.

When the GPS took them through a route currently under construction they stopped at a gas station to ask directions to the nearest military base. Neither she nor

Angeline knew the city, and the detour signs were confusing.

"Sorry ladies," the gas station attendant inside the store said. "There are Coast Guard stations and an Air Force base nearby, but no other functioning military institutions. What ya lookin' for exactly?" He paused for a second. "Well, there *is* Fort Lawton but it hasn't been used as a base for decades and was officially closed in 2011 and the land handed over to the city as part of Discovery Park."

Why did that name ring a bell? Wasn't it from the cliffs of Discovery Park that the giant bird bones were extricated?

"Thanks," Drey said, and nudged Angeline back to their rented Honda Civic.

"Discovery Park?" Angeline intoned.

"I was thinking the same thing."

"I don't know why, but I think we should go there."

"Does it have anything to do with the bird's nickname, *Pegasus*?"

Angeline's head reared upright. "Yeah, you're right. That's what struck a chord in my memory. *Pegasus.* Where did I hear that name just recently?" She frowned and when she glanced over at Drey she nodded. They both recalled the Ghost Hunter University's seminar moderated by its leader Gill Ames. One of the speakers, the woman in the giant hat, had claimed to have participated in a time-space program called Project Pegasus.

"What do you think, Angeline? Could this be our ride home?"

"If it really exists? Maybe. But what I want to know is why are we here, and how did we get here? There was no secret government project in the middle of Avebury's stone circle. I just ran to look for you near the Devil's Chair and *bam*, I was in the underground city of Seattle."

"That's the way I remember it too."

"So shouldn't our portal home be back in the underground city?"

"How should I know? I think this government facility is a better bet. And I really don't feel like hanging around here much longer. Let's go."

***

They couldn't exactly drive up to the compound in full view, blatantly announcing their arrival, so Drey parked the car on the beach lot at sea level, and they headed onto the trails. It would be a roundabout route of getting there, but safer until they knew the lay of the land. They were in possession of a pamphlet that they had acquired from the gas station attendant showing a map of the park grounds.

Rolling hills with steep cliffs that sloped down to the sea formed most of the landscape. It was to those cliffs that they needed to go. Vegetation was low and spare with broad expanses of grass and clover and other weeds. These stretched across intermittent rocky terrain, which grew steeper as the ground rose up from the sea. The cliffs were well ahead and they started for the rocks just below the creeping vegetation. Apparently the military facility originally covered five hundred and thirty-four acres and had buildings scattered throughout. Most of these had been turned into park buildings, but a few were unused, or so they said.

The trail meandered steadily upward over rocky outcrops crusted with lichens and moss. Other vegetation surfaced in the fissures of the rocks. The path they followed was indirect, and at times twisted and turned, forcing them to climb uphill before descending and emerging on a flat rocky ledge. Grasses and dandelions grew out of the crevices, and they paused for breath just under the bluff. A wedge of sea showed between the folding rock, and far out ahead more cliffs continued along the shoreline composed of sedimentary layers. Alternating levels of dark and light rippled parallel to the plane of the sea, and the base of the cliffs ended where the water began. On the sandy bank driftwood and dried logs, bleached pale by the sun, bathed in the cold Pacific spray. Seagulls screamed amidst the surf; and a single solitary raven flew towards the clouds. Was that a yellow band on its leg? Drey watched it a few moments before turning to Angeline.

"Yes, I saw it too," she said.

Drey clamored down into a gully before ascending once more. The going was tough and there were shrubs and small trees, which she used for handholds to get across the rocky terrain. "Almost there," she said encouragingly.

When finally they reached their destination, the plateau was flat and several buildings stood out in the near distance.

"Now what?" Angeline asked.

"Now we go into the compound without being seen."

Fortunately there were few people around. Not many even among the cliffs or below, on the beach.

From the map Drey noted they were in the range of the former Post Exchange and Gymnasium and, in the near distance, was the locale of the Guard House and Quartermaster Stables. Beyond that she could see the dome of the radar tower. The administrative building was further away. There was one more building, a modern structure made of solid concrete. It was sinister in appearance because it had no windows, was the most distant, and half hidden by trees.

"That's probably where we should go," Drey suggested, pointing it out.

They walked at least half a mile before they met a sign that read:

Government Property
NO TRESPASSING
D.A.R.P.A.

"What does DARPA stand for again?" Angeline asked.

"Defense Advanced Research Projects Agency."

They crept up to the building, still no sign of any people. There was a large army truck parked outside with several crates on the ground waiting to be loaded or unloaded. Angeline peeked at the lettering on one of the boxes. It stated clearly: *Pegasus*.

"This is the place," she said.

Every door they tried was locked. The locks were digital, which meant they would need a special keycard. "How are we supposed to get inside?" Angeline whispered. "And now that I come to think of it, maybe we're just letting our imaginations run away with us. We should get out of here before we get caught. Or shot."

"No one's going to shoot us."

They hid behind a bush as a metal door opened. A man in a lab coat exited and climbed onto the truck to remove another crate. It was too bulky, however, for him to shift alone. He pulled out a cellphone and made a call, then went over to unlock the door by tapping the keycard. Then he propped the door open with a wedge of wood. He tried dragging the boxes toward the door, gave up and went around to the hood of the truck to have a smoke.

Now was their chance. Drey and her accomplice ducked through the open door and found themselves inside a long corridor. All of the doors were locked along the way using the same kind of digital technology. Finally they found a door that gave, and they entered. It led them up a short set of stairs to a platform with a domed window. It looked like some kind of observation room, and when Drey looked down through the glass she saw that she was right. A small console with a computer and controls was built into the lower ledge of the clear pane.

"Drey," Angeline said. "Isn't that Chancellor?"

She looked down. The yellow tie and navy suit beneath a beige trench coat were unmistakable.

"Doesn't he own any other clothes, even in the future?"

Drey touched a button on the console with a speaker icon and voices filled the dome. Chancellor's voice came first:

"If this doesn't work, Lalonde, then we'll have to try it your way. But I'd rather experiment with science first."

"All right. Anything... I have to know. I have to know

if—"

"We'll find out. Keep your voice down."

Drey stared in fascination. She had always deemed this material conspiracy theory. In her courses at the Institute of Metaphysical and Humanistic Sciences there was an elective that dealt with teleportation. She remembered reading about 'The Philadelphia Experiment' and 'Project Pegasus'.

Pegasus was a classified, defense-related research and development program under DARPA where apparently the U.S. and U.K. had joined their technical teams to experiment with time travel. The mission statement of Project Pegasus was to study the effects of time travel and teleportation on the human body and to relay important data concerning past and future events. She had honestly never considered it to be real.

She looked down as a sound caught her ear and Angeline gasped. There was some sort of machine down there and a shimmering curtain glowed between two elliptical booms. "When you pass through this curtain of energy," Chancellor was saying, "you will enter a vortal tunnel that will send you to your destination."

Angeline was frantically pointing to the computer screen in front of them. Neon blue lines indicating structural features inside the lower lab, and glowing red dots, possibly a heat signature, indicating human movement had appeared. It was a digital floor plan labeled with "Plasma Confinement Chamber" and "Jump Room."

"This holographic technology," Chancellor continued explaining to Lalonde will allow you to travel both physically and virtually."

"My God, Drey. Do you hear what he's saying? They are planning to time travel."

"Calm down," Drey said. "Don't forget. Somehow, *we* have already done that."

Angeline sat down on one of the five chairs that were in the observation deck. "Oh, you are so right. But why? Why does Jake want to teleport?" She paused. "Wait a minute.

Maybe that's *our* Jake? And he's trying to return home!"

Drey grabbed Angeline by the wrist as she rose to race out of the observation deck.

"No. I'm pretty sure it's not."

"How can you be sure?"

"Let's wait."

While they were talking, Jake had disappeared behind the shimmering. While it seemed he was only gone for about five minutes, to Angeline it seemed an eternity. When he returned, the shimmering dissipated and he stepped out of the Confinement Chamber toward Chancellor. "Well?" Chancellor said, his voice echoing eerily out of the speaker.

"It's worse than we thought. I have to do something. I have to do something before Angeline finds out."

"Before I find out what?" Angeline demanded turning to Drey. "What on earth is he talking about?"

"Can't imagine," she said. "But if that thing down there really works, then it's our ticket home."

By the time the two of them returned their attention to the Jump Room Chancellor and Jake were gone.

***

The rhythmic pounding of drums came dully out of the distance. In the half-hour or so that they had been trying to find Chancellor so that they could ask him to help send them home, not a soul had crossed their path, except for a rare hiker. Now Angeline realized that the sounds she was hearing were not the sounds drums make. It was the thrum of someone chanting. Well, that was even stranger.

They climbed up over the next ridge to where the scent of burning pine resin was strong. A man dressed in a black hooded cape danced around another man who stood near the edge of the cliff. The first man had a rattle and he chanted as he shook it. The rattle was carved in the shape of a flying raven. A few feet away from them a small fire burned within a ring of cobbles. Angeline suddenly had a bad feeling about this and dragged Drey down behind some bushes. She had recognized the man who was the focus of the dance. It was Jake, of course, and he was naked from the waist up and wore what looked to be a string of bird beaks around his throat. Some kind of pigment or costume makeup was painted on his chest and face in sharp red slashes. The scene triggered a strong image in her memory.

The chanting suddenly ceased. Pebbles clattered down the gully and now someone stepped on a twig.

Angeline remained hidden in the bushes, but Drey was already rising from her crouched position, and spun to see that it was Chancellor. This Chancellor looked exactly like the Chancellor of their time. He was wearing the same clothes that Angeline had seen him in last. His eyes narrowed and his mouth was grim, and he grabbed Drey's arm when she tried to bully past him.

He stifled a sardonic smile before he spoke. "If you absolutely must know," he said. "It's an exorcism."

Drey managed to control her expression, did not utter a word. He clearly had no suspicions that the Drey McFee he was talking to was not the Drey McFee he was acquainted with. Because he spoke as though he knew why she was there.

"Not an exorcism of the devil," he said. "It's an exorcism of something more insidious. That man in black with the rattle is a shaman."

Drey stood dead still, while Angeline shivered, hunched down as small as possible in the bushes, hoping to remain concealed. "He doesn't *seem* possessed," Drey said, warily.

Chancellor was serious. "It's not possession in the way you think of it. This is something he has inherited. An ability that could change his entire existence." He paused at her stark silence before he added, "You mustn't tell Angeline. Lalonde doesn't want her to know. Now get out of here before he sees you."

He marched toward the shaman and the dancer. Drey retreated to the bushes and to Angeline.

"He's right," Angeline said, shaking with fear. "We *have* to get out of here."

CHAPTER TWENTY-SEVEN

They took the beach route, which was below the cliffs and where they were the least likely to be seen. It was faster going downhill than it had been going up. The sea was curiously calm along the rocky shoreline. The sun was still warm but rapidly sloping with the dying afternoon, sending a bright glare into their eyes. It was hard to see, but Drey had noticed something and was now rolling up her pant legs to her knees. She kicked off her shoes, and waded into the shallows and looked up.

"What is it?" Angeline asked, anxiously. She wanted to get as far away from this place as she could. She didn't know why she felt so apprehensive. But something bad was about to happen.

"A very weird thing is going on up there. I'm not sure we should have left."

"I disagree. It didn't feel right, Drey. I can't explain it, but it just didn't feel right. I want to get out of here."

Drey ploughed her way deeper into the water, disregarding her soon-to-be soaked jeans. She was trying to get something into her field of vision. She squinted, moved a few paces to the side and looked up again.

Angeline followed her gaze. Was the sun playing tricks on her? The brilliance was irritating and distorted her vision. She moved a few steps sideways, avoiding taking the plunge into the water. When the glare was under control she looked upward again.

Her eyes landed on some long deep scars, oblique on the cliff face. She sent Drey a look of query but the cryptozoologist was fully engaged, attention fixed on the bluff, working out her own theories. The angle at which she was standing gave her a poorer view than Drey's who was knee-deep in the sea. She had a good hunch, however. If Drey was that fascinated, it didn't take much guessing to arrive at an explanation.

Drey finally glanced her way. Angeline was no expert, but the scars, in her opinion, were talon and beak marks. This would have been a reasonable account except for their size. They were enormous. In her cryptozoological studies, Drey explained, such marks were credible, made by large birds, most of which turned out to be natural marks made by eagles or condors.

Angeline watched Drey drag herself out of the water, the edges of her wet pants, clamping onto her legs. Her shoes refused to go on at first but after a minor struggle she managed to lace them up.

Angeline returned her attention to the mysterious scars on the cliff. If the scratch marks belonged to a birdlike individual, then—

"What do *you* think?" Drey asked, staring hard once again at the marks on the cliff face.

Then it would be the largest bird she had ever seen.

***

They hiked for another hour before they reached the car. They were wet through and chilled by the sea mist, and wind. Both breathing fast, worst of all daylight was fading swiftly, although the parking lot was lit.

Drey crawled into the driver's seat and collapsed her head for a brief moment onto the steering wheel. Angeline got into the passenger side, while Drey raised her weary head, and switched on the ignition. The lights blinked on. All around the trees dipped and swayed, heavy with moisture. With the heat turned on and the engine warming up, she was beginning to feel better. They were both stiff with cold, but she managed to place her foot on the gas and pull out of the parking lot. As she was turning onto the road she glanced at Angeline who sat next to her, rubbing the blood back into her fingers.

Angeline sent a brief backward nod over her shoulder. "What do you *really* think made those marks back there?"

No other traffic appeared on the road and Drey braked to squint between the headrests and past the backseats through the rear window. Those marks were huge, and Drey was pretty damned sure they weren't made by any avian species recorded in Audubon, or any other wildlife encyclopedia.

It was approaching dark. She drove to the Edgewater Hotel and parked. They entered the lobby where they caught the attention of several guests who turned to stare at them. Sure they looked a bedraggled mess. They were still paying customers... Drey sloughed it off. What people thought of her appearance had never bothered her. Clearly, it was not the same for Angeline. That one looked desperate for hot water and soap. So they agreed that Angeline should avoid Jake; she was too emotionally involved. And heaven knew what would happen if she should speak to her future husband. But they also agreed that Chancellor was their best bet for help.

Angeline went upstairs to shower and change while Drey rolled down her stiff pants and strolled up to ask the man at the reception desk for Chancellor's room number. He said it was against hotel policy to provide room numbers to unannounced visitors, but if she would wait while he called the room? She shook her head, and hooked a left for the elevators. It was better if she spoke to him in person. As she looked ahead she swore she saw Chancellor and the shaman waiting, but no Lalonde. She hurried to enter the elevator simultaneously but the door closed in her face.

She watched until the elevator stopped at the eighth floor. She ran to the stairwell and raced up the steps. By the time she reached the eighth floor she was thoroughly winded. She opened the door and saw two men outside the elevator talking, then the shaman went to the left corridor and

Chancellor turned to the right.

Was it really such a terribly good idea to enlist his help? Would he even believe her? Of course he would. Hadn't he just helped Lalonde peek into the future? Clearly, Lalonde was frightened by what he had seen. She chased down Chancellor and just as he was unlocking the door to his room, she tapped his shoulder. He swung around, saw who it was.

"I need your help," she demanded.

When Chancellor was silent she said without hesitation, "Project *Pegasus*."

He stared at her, his face turning several shades darker.

"I thought I told you to go home."

"I can't—until you tell me how Project Pegasus works."

His silence was excruciating. His eyes bore into hers like he wished to see inside her brain. "What do you know about Project Pegasus?"

"I was on the observation deck today, when I saw you and Jake Lalonde in the 'Jump Room'… I know you sent him into the future and back again."

Chancellor fell silent. Was he angry or relieved? From the expression on his face it could have been either. The only thing she was certain of was that he still hadn't caught on that she wasn't *his* McFee. She would soon change that.

"What do you want in exchange for your silence?" he finally said.

She told him in as few words as she could. Her story took less time than she had anticipated, and the shattering silence that followed was exactly what she expected. She could elaborate further if necessary, but it wasn't. Just as she had surmised—and hoped—he listened, although with skepticism.

"You expect me to believe that fancy yarn?"

"Yes. I need you to help me—to help *us*—get home."

"Us?"

"Angeline is with me. Did I forget to mention that?"

She had deliberately left out any mention of Angeline but now she realized her involvement might give Chancellor just the nudge he needed. He looked her up and down, and then nodded. "You have her face and her build, and you dress like her. But you *aren't* her, are you?"

"I just told you I wasn't."

His lips pressed together in a thin line. He was wasting time, and she had no more time to waste.

"Why do I believe you?"

"Because it's the truth. So…do we have a deal?"

"On one condition," he said. "You help me first.

CHAPTER TWENTY-EIGHT

When Drey returned to the room, Angeline was gone. Something caught her eye as she gazed across the room over the beds.

Her mouth dropped open. She ran to the balcony door. Behind the open curtains, the sliding glass door was ajar. She ducked outside and stared across the street and toward the sky. Her vision slipped down to the floor where some faint scratch marks marred the concrete. Large bird prints.

She rushed indoors and grabbed her hotel key, then flew out the door to the elevator. When she reached the lobby she went directly to the reception desk. "Did someone come into my room while I was out?" she demanded.

The girl on night duty behind the desk looked surprised. "Just your roommate… what's wrong? Did someone break into your room?" She picked up the phone. "I'll send Security up straight away."

Drey shook her head. No. *No*, this wouldn't do. She didn't want Security snooping around. They might damage any other evidence that had been left. "It's okay," she said.

"Perhaps it was just the maid. They service the rooms every day. Did she disturb something? Remove something she wasn't supposed to?"

"No. It's okay. If my roommate returns will you ask her to wait upstairs for me? Thanks."

Drey returned to the room, studied the claw marks again. They were for sure the real thing. But who had left them? *Did Angeline find these and then go to look for me?*

She glanced at the clock on the nightstand. She had

made a promise to Chancellor and now it was time to keep it.

She opened the Book of Monsters that she had stolen from her double. She flipped to the chapter on Big Birds. By the time she had finished reading it her heart was racing. Now she knew who had left the claw marks. And now she understood why Chancellor wanted the book. But she still needed proof before she surrendered it to him.

She left the room and hurried out of the hotel lobby to the car where it was parked in the guest lot. She started the engine, listening to it purr as she pondered all that had happened in the last little while. This was their best chance.

She drove to Discovery Park, left the car, and crossed her loaded carryall over her shoulder, and started to walk. Out in the open she could see her way by moonlight.

The sea beyond was a vast expanse of black, and patches of silver mirrored the surface. She left the main trail, and kept to the beach. Behind her were sand dunes swept high by the winds. On the shore it was a veritable maze as she meandered between and over dried logs, the odd low-lying boulder and driftwood. It was breezy but not uncomfortably cold. The slap of the waves against the sand and the rushing of the wind were her only companions. Her footsteps crunched on the odd pebble, shell and dead crab. The smells of the intertidal zone reached her nostrils in a stinging piquancy. The wind burned on her face. Was the tide going in or out? She had to make sure she stayed high above the shoreline so as not to get trapped if the tide were returning.

The beach seemed to be getting wider, and that meant the tide was ebbing. From the trees and shrubbery beyond the dunes came the song of cicadas, night insects.

In the beam of her flashlight huge four-clawed prints disturbed the sand. She raised her eyes, searched the sky, and saw that she was nearing the cliff where she and Angeline had seen Lalonde with the shaman. Her flashlight danced over the sand and across the rock wall. She recognized the way the bluff jutted out into the sea and the pink and grey striations in the stone. The tide was far out now and left the cliff appearing higher and the beach broader than they had seemed before. Tidal pools appeared, exposing previously submerged blocks crusted with mussels, barnacles and starfish. Rubbery kelp bulbs with their long fronds and stipes lay beached high and dry, their smooth bodies gleaming in the pale light like abandoned wine bottles.

Over her shoulder was her carryall with the book. The book—the great Book of Monsters. She removed it and cradled it in her arms.

"I see you've come to keep your end of the bargain," a voice said. "Rest assured, I intend to keep mine."

She slowly turned to face Chancellor. He looked into the darkness beyond the cluster of trees inward of the beach to where a long shadow stretched out across the sand into the moonlight. She recognized the shape. It was tall and massive, wings folded, with a sharp downward pointing beak.

But the thing that was making the shadow was not a bird. It was a man. He stood with the moon's silver light, casting his shadow sharply ahead of him. It was then that Drey gasped. She had been expecting something, but not this. Behind him was a second shadow. The first was shaped like a raven; the one behind was the outline of a man.

"Do you have something in that book that will help me out of this fix?" Lalonde asked. She tried not to flinch as the shadow spoke.

"Ye…yes." She stuttered. She did have something—something that would help them *all* out of their current predicaments. But it wasn't in this book. She had to go back to the hotel room and hope that Angeline had returned. The thing that ailed Jake Lalonde was a problem that only her future self could solve. She and Angeline no longer needed to be here.

She passed Jake Lalonde the book.

She had kept her end of the bargain, now it was up to Chancellor to keep his.

CHAPTER TWENTY-NINE

"Where are you?"

Chancellor was frantic. She was just there in the South Circle a moment ago. He followed the circumference of the ring of stones, and then his head shot up when he heard a sound. Across the field, two figures, female figures were waving at him from the vicinity of the Devil's Chair. They approached at a run, and he hurried to meet them.

"Drey? Angeline? Where the hell have you been?"

"How long have we been gone?" Drey asked him.

"Only a few minutes, why?"

The two women traded taut glances. "Because for us, it's been a few days."

Chancellor was silent. Suddenly he asked, "Where did you go?"

"No time for that now," Angeline said. "She's playing with us—that bloody goddess of yours. She isn't just planning to bind Jake to her through the Handfast. She is planning to transform him, body and soul into a physical incarnation of the Raven."

"And what we've seen of his image, it isn't pretty," Drey said. "It's downright evil-looking."

It all made sense now. *She* wanted Maia Pickerton out of the way to clear the path for her use of the greatest, and most ancient outdoor temple in Europe. The curator had wanted to bring back the tourists, entice the millions of visitors that were drawn to Stonehenge over to Avebury, but that would defeat *her* purpose. She could not perform her evil deed with millions of spectators watching.

Chancellor let his eyes roam over the enormous site. Where in this vast circle of standing stones was the event to take place?

"Chancellor," Angeline said.

His head jerked up.

"Do you remember what Diana said at the end of her lecture at the Alexander Keiller Museum?"

Indeed he did. "The Serpent and the Raven. The Celtic tale. The Raven is poisoned by the serpent's bite. What she failed to tell us was that invariably the Raven is reborn."

"Just like in the Haida myths."

"Yes. She was hinting at her plan all along. Only we failed to see it."

Avebury was to be the site of the Raven's rebirth.

***

The head of the Ghost Hunter University had reported that one of his students was missing. A Ms. Angeline Lisbon. She had gone on the Stonehenge expedition, but when the participants had regrouped to board the return bus she was not among them. He had done a head count. He assumed she had found some other means by which to return, except that when they reassembled the next morning she had failed to appear for the seminar. She was registered and had neglected to inform anyone that she wished to withdraw, nor had she requested a refund.

Students sometimes behaved in an irregular fashion, and had it not been for Pettigrew tracking both Lalonde and Lisbon to this convention, the leader of the Ghost Hunters, a Mr. Gill Ames, would have thought nothing of it. But now on reflection he informed the police; he believed that she was still missing. The windswept plains of Salisbury were cruel even in summertime at night. The plains spread out for kilometers on either side of the towering sarsens and if she had lost her way in the dark she might still be wandering the downs. He had sent a search team to scour the area, and had come up empty.

Superintendent Pettigrew glared at the report on his desk. The graduate student's disappearance coincided with the archaeologist's and the curator's. He had just learned that Drey McFee, the cryptozoologist who roomed with Ms. Lisbon was also missing. Or, if not missing, then absent. Neither of the women had been seen for twenty-four hours.

Their presence at the convention and subsequent absence would have seemed normal were it not for the fact that the Interpol agent Thomas Chancellor was also registered at the convention. What, he wondered, was the connection between these four individuals? And how were they connected to the vanished curator?

He had gained access to Chancellor's room after having searched the archaeologist's, and the accommodation of the two missing women. He had become suspicious when he learned from Interpol that Mr. Chancellor was no longer in their employ.

In the ex agent's suitcase in lieu of clothes, he'd had stacks of printed articles on Chaos magic. Because of the dubious circumstances, Pettigrew had obtained a warrant and removed the evidence. He now selected one of the articles that had been atop the stack, and flipped through the pages, eyes enlarging as he read.

The main purpose of Chaos magic, a modern practice that borrowed from ancient cultures, was to bring the practitioner to an altered state of consciousness—what practitioners called gnosis—in order to manipulate reality.

Was that genuinely possible?

The purpose was to force out negative thoughts and, through a single idea experienced during the altered state, to instantly forget. In other words, to eradicate all doubt by bypassing the faculties of the mind (what Pettigrew preferred to think of as reason) that would inform any rational person that the magical manipulation of reality was impossible.

Changing belief systems at will was the goal, and the whole purpose of the user was to accept a new reality.

Well, well, well, he thought. *Now, we are getting somewhere.* His mind harkened back to a previous case, a very old one when he was but a rookie assigned to simple cases of public nuisance and parking tickets. This one had long gone cold, and concerned a lunatic who believed she could time travel. Was there a link between the two cases?

The lunatic, a woman, was in the habit of performing public rituals; they had suspected her of engaging in psychoactive drugs, which might have contributed to what the article termed the 'gnostic state.' The point of all the ritual was to have the practitioner believe in a different reality. Well, that woman had certainly lived in some sort of fantasy. She was most certainly experiencing an invented reality according to the psychiatrists that had examined her.

The name 'Black Goddess' and some curious notations were scribbled in the margins beside the paragraph he had just read. She was some kind of witch that could manipulate innocent people's minds? Pettigrew scratched his brow. Curious indeed.

Now here was something that was underlined in red ink. Retrochronal magic—the changing of past events.

> *This is a skill requiring a deep understanding of the nature of memory and belief, and is the proposed mechanism through which all forms of magic works. It requires the practitioner* (the Black Goddess?) *to replace his/her subjects' memory of how things used to be with a belief that things are in constant flux, that change will occur and that the resulting change is real.*

Pettigrew was stunned, but not surprised. Changing past events. How did one do that, even hypothetically? The key, here, he mused was that all four of these people, and perhaps Maia Pickerton, as well, believed that they were living in an altered reality. The question that nagged at him was: what exactly *was* this altered reality?

Success depends upon using belief as a tool to create an alternate reality, one that benefits the practitioner; and then to convince those around them that the invented reality is the true one. Different forms of Chaos magic adopt different sigils like the triple moon or idols like the Venus figurine.

He stopped reading and put the article down. It was obvious to him that he must expose the identity of this 'practitioner'.

So, what or who was he looking for? A witch or a goddess? Outwardly, he laughed, but inside his stomach went cold. The person he was searching for most certainly must be some mental patient who had hypnotized a group of formerly sane people into believing what she wanted them to believe.

A knock came at his door. A blue uniformed police officer informed him that his guest had arrived. He closed the article and replaced it on the neatly arranged stack, before he nodded for the informant to enter.

"Ms. Dunnel," he said, as an attractive young woman materialised in his doorway. She had sunny brown hair and looked to be in her thirties, with the build and attitude and style of a fashion model. "So glad that you could spare the time to meet with me. "I understand that you are Dr. Jake Lalonde's fiancée, and that you have something you wanted to show me?"

"I do," she said. She was carrying a black briefcase with her as she swung her hips in a runway walk to his desk. This she now set down in front of him. She unlatched it before seating herself across from him. "I followed Thomas Chancellor and his 'girls' to Bakewell, to the park where the Nine Ladies stone circle is located. After their visit there, they abandoned their car in Manchester. It was a rental. Luckily I was able to search the interior before it was reclaimed by the rental agent. The fugitives hired a helicopter. The company refused to tell me where they went. Company policy they said. I suppose that makes sense. But I found this inside the rental car. In their hurry they must have forgotten it."

Lodged in the briefcase was a black Raven mask, with white painted ovoids around the eye slits and a yellow beak. Pettigrew frowned. It reminded him of the Haida art that he had seen inside the Natural History Museum's Native North American special exhibit.

The helicopter company may have a privacy policy for customers, but it would not apply to a police investigation. He rang up the front desk and requested the information ASAP.

PART 2: THE GREAT STONE'S WAY

CHAPTER THIRTY

The darkness was clearing, along with the hallucinations, the visions of interminable tunnels. Was he losing his mind? Or had the dizzying ritual disoriented his senses, and caused some catastrophic imbalance in his middle ear? In that case it had also affected his vision. Because at first he was totally blind.

Now, what he was seeing seemed to be a perfect scene of the English countryside. But if that were the case what was he doing here in the middle of the road, miles away from any town or sign of civilization? He forced himself to recall what had happened during his frantic dance inside the circle of Stonehenge. He blamed the man in the yellow tie and beige trench coat for this entire debacle… because if it weren't for him he'd be warm and lazy in some London pub, not lost and disoriented. And he wouldn't have Diana Lune's name running over and over in his head.

Admittedly if he hadn't been doing that, repeating her name as though his life depended on it, his mind might have stayed fuzzy. It was as though her name was the one thing that kept him grounded. And he was stuck in the middle of nowhere, totally useless and uncertain of exactly who she was or what she meant to him. His thoughts were still muddled bits and pieces, disconnected images returning to memory—like the sections of a jigsaw puzzle.

He did remember the uncanny descent of the ravens onto his person. There were hundreds of them. Maybe thousands. He had been dancing inside the stone circle, engrossed in his chanting when a collective cry from the birds had seized his attention, and then suddenly the landscape had changed. What struck him barmy was why he was dancing inside the stone circle in the first place.

And then all had gone dark. Blackness and numbness had filled him with apprehension, a feeling he had experienced before. The most frightening part was the sensation of total abandonment. He had groped his way through the darkness, following the perceived tunnels until a shimmering had guided him out. Now he was alone on the motorway, dazed and befuddled, and with the sun shining brilliantly overhead, but as his head continued to clear all he felt was a compulsion to return to Stonehenge.

A sign ahead of him said: The **Great Stones Way**. That, he recognized as a project of the British government—a walking trail that led from Avebury to Stonehenge over a landscape covered with Neolithic monuments. His interest in the monuments reminded him of his profession—an archaeologist. Good, that much of his memory was restored. And he knew his name, Jake Lalonde. He knew that the man in the yellow tie and beige trench coat was a friend or at least had claimed to be. That much was clear. What was not clear was Diana Lune, and everything that preceded this moment of epiphany.

He must return to Stonehenge, and much as he would love to have followed the ancient people's trail, he decided to adhere to the road where it was likely he could hitch a ride. The odd thing was the seemingly total absence of highway traffic.

He stole a brief downward glance at the tourist map pinched between his trembling fingertips. His mind drew a blank as to how he had acquired it, and although the area was vaguely familiar he could not recall ever having visited. The landmarks were clearly indicated and corresponded to the signage along the road. According to the map he should be at a place called Figheldean. Marked with a starred accommodation symbol was the only B&B in the village. It was labeled the Thatched Inn and should be sitting on his right.

But it wasn't. If he had kept his cellphone with him, he would have succumbed to the convenience of technology and used the GPS. But he had only this paper map—and his memory. And that wasn't, at the moment, terribly reliable. He had the unnerving feeling that something was still wrong with him. He ruled out amnesia because he knew who he was, and he sort of understood *where* he was. The thing escaping him was how he had arrived here.

If he had reached as far as Figheldean, then he must have been wandering aimlessly down the road in a mental haze or he had sleepwalked onto a bus, and then exited without remembering. It was a little disconcerting to think that one might have had a brain seizure. And yet it was the most plausible explanation. That name kept returning to his memory. Diana Lune. Who was she? What did she have to do with him and the man in the trench coat?

He stopped at the side of the road. There was a dilapidated grey barn with an enormous hollow through its center, the wooden doors at either end long since gone. It was a wonder that the structure still held. Many of the boards had been split or torn away by wind and rain, the posts and rafters exposed, the general state of the building suffering from sheer neglect.

Yet, if there was a barn here (or the ruins of a barn here) at the side of the road, shouldn't there be a farm? There was no sign of a farmhouse, or of any livestock or crops. In fact the place was eerily unpopulated by people or animals, and the fields were untilled meadowland.

He tried to fix his thoughts on the task at hand. His mind persisted in wandering, and that was troubling. *Focus,* he chided himself. Was the village just around the corner? If it was, he could get help there. He could locate a telephone and call…call who?

What was Beige Trench Coat's name? Ah…Chancellor. His name was Chancellor. He could call and ask him to come and fetch him.

He shaded his eyes from the sun's glare and squinted. No, there was no village. All he could see were some scattered trees with chalk hills in the background, and plume-like clouds rolling in from the distant skyline. Something must be wrong with this map.

The sun was angling low and a loose cloud darkened his view of the landscape, drowning everything in shade. Something moved along the downs, a light swimming silently in the shadows. Was someone there? He hurried in the direction of the floating light but then just as quickly as it had appeared, it vanished. The sun broke through the scattered cloud and blinded him in copper brightness.

Was he seeing things? He needed rest, food and drink. Those three necessities would go a long way towards restoring his mental faculties. He rubbed a sweaty palm on the hem of his T-shirt and only now realized he was fully clothed; when inside the stone circle he had been shirtless. *That's good,* he thought. *That much I remember.* The mask was missing too (Yes, there had been a mask). Had the descent of so many ravens just freaked him out to the point that he had suffered some sort of blackout? Oh, if only he could find some kind of inn and grab a hot shower and some food, then maybe the remainder of his memory would return. He was so thirsty his tongue felt like a sponge filling his mouth, and his lips cracked. Oh, how he wished he had his cellphone.

The moving light was gone. It had reminded him of the wavering of a flashlight or a lantern. Why would anyone be using a lantern in broad daylight? Yes, it was a dark day, and yes, it was gloomy, but using a lantern was just weird. His eyes returned to the road from where they had been roving over the meadow. He had been standing here for ten minutes churning his thoughts like a muddled top to no avail. There should be coffee shops, pubs, restaurants, B&Bs and other businesses. Jake slumped against the fragile peeling boards of the hollow barn, the wind rushing in his ears. A small, clear canal flowed alongside the ancient farm structure, bubbling in spots before jutting sharply to his right cutting a path through the downs. The moving water gurgled glaringly loud in the peaceful countryside, and seemed clean enough. Was it safe to drink? He stooped, and cupped a handful and sniffed before taking a tentative sip.

His stomach rumbled. Soon he would collapse from hunger. Wind crackled through the long grasses. The silence was unnatural. Still no traffic.

Then Jake glimpsed what might be a pub ahead in the rising mist. Odd that it should be stranded here all alone, odd that the mist should only hover about the pub. He crossed the road and a few paces further he trod over the grassy spit now also swirling in mist. Even before he had reached the front door he knew something was amiss. No glass blocked the weather from entering through the windows, and the wooden shutters were askew, black with rot. There were no signs of life—anywhere.

The door handle yielded to his efforts. Whatever lock had once sealed out trespassers had long since eroded. He peered inside, disappointment temporarily appeasing his hunger. The place looked ancient, like a medieval tavern. Filmy cobwebs covered the naked struts and joists of the ceiling.

From wall to wall wooden tables stood cloaked in dust or ash, and some of them were laid with long unused oil lamps and crockery with the petrified remnants of food and drink. The smell was musty and scratched at his throat. No one had visited this establishment in decades, maybe centuries. If it wasn't for the fact that the structure was built almost exclusively from stone it would have long since crumbled away. The rotten floorboards moaned as he stepped on them. He tried calling out, but he knew from the appearance of things that shouting was useless.

Outside, he heard a familiar sound. He glanced sharply through the glassless window and saw a large black raven sway from the top of the barn in the near distance.

The rafters were precarious and jutted out from beneath

the broken roof. Jake didn't know why he did this, but he shouted, as though somehow he could communicate with the bird. Then he moved toward the door that had swung partway shut. He heard the raven *quork* as he forced open the door, and stepped outside to witness the bird take flight.

***

Jake drew in a sharp breath and ventured out into the clearing. If he wasn't totally losing his mind, it appeared almost as though the bird were encouraging him to abandon the place. His situation was truly disconcerting. Bewildering. What exactly had happened to him?

He scanned his surroundings and saw a man appear out of the growing fog. He was clad in a peculiar outfit of coarse wool tunic with leggings, and wooden clogs on his feet, carrying an even more ancient appearing satchel, an oddly shaped pair of scissors in his hands and—a lantern? This must be some sort of costume. He was dressed as a medieval barber. Admittedly Jake was still a bit foggy in the brain, but this whole area was part of the National Trust heritage lands, wasn't it?

Maybe the oddly dressed fellow worked for a nearby museum and could tell him where he was.

Jake called out. "Sir? I've been in some sort of accident and don't know where I am." The man strolled past him. Jake sprang to action and dashed towards the man but he disappeared behind the crumbling stone building. Jake followed his wet tracks, crushing the long grass, chasing the fleeing figure. He expelled the pent up air in his lungs. "Mister? Please. I need your help."

The costumed man disintegrated into wisps of pale mist. The landscape was silent. Shadows leaned into each other while the low sunlight from above filtered blindingly through gaps in the scant lime-green foliage. Now Jake understood what people meant when they said 'the silence was deafening'. It was. Not even a leaf rustled. No birdsong or insects humming, not a squirrel or snake. And certainly no traffic sounds from the road. Where *was* the road? He turned to look and saw all around him a strange landscape. But through the mist and the dying daylight he could swear there was a light. It moved as though someone holding a lantern or a flashlight were searching the fogged-in corners of the field. And then it melted, blending in with the fuzzy dampness.

The meadow onto which he had wandered was like no meadow he had seen before. For miles into the distance beyond the sparse trees lay large depressions giving the terrain the appearance of a moonscape covered in grass. Except for a few raw open pits that gleamed white through the fog because the chalky matrix was exposed, the rest of the scenery rose and fell in wide shallow depressions of pale green. Either he had been transported to an alien planet or this was one of those ancient flint quarry sites he'd read about. Had the man descended into one of those pits? And if so, why would he do that?

The fog swam and broke over the strange meadow-scape revealing different sections of the abandoned quarry. Jake peered deeper into the gaps in the mist; it seemed to him that the quarry was not entirely abandoned. He knew prehistoric peoples used to mine for flint in the chalk, but he had never heard of a flint quarry near Figheldean.

The drifting mist made it dangerous to investigate further. He was better off returning to the road—if he could find it. He rotated a full ninety degrees and started walking when he glimpsed a bobbing light in his peripheral vision. He jerked around and hurried across the dented terrain, careful to stay on the rims of the shallow grass-covered pits to avoid falling into a deeper hole and breaking a leg.

The silhouette of the same barber man drifted through the moving fog and suddenly evaporated. Jake stared at the last position in which he had seen him. The only place he could have gone was down. At his feet was a hole, pale, glowing in the vanishing daylight. The chalky ground had been removed in chunks and dumped into an adjacent hole, leaving a pit twelve meters wide and at least fourteen meters deep. A rope ladder led down into its murky depths. A light below flashed and Jake lowered himself unthinkingly into the quarry. There seemed to be levels made up of wood beams where workers apparently dug tunnels into the walls seeking flint veins. When these seams of rock were exhausted they had apparently lowered the platforms to chase new sources of the stone.

He had no light and it was dark down here. The fog was dissipating as he reached bottom, and he could see by the whiteness of the chalk walls. Down here there were more tunnels. Light glowed from one of them and Jake dropped to his knees and crawled into the crevice. At first he had thought this was an archaeological site, an ancient quarry, but it looked to be active. There had been mounds of chalk chipped out and piled high ready to be removed, and here at his knees was a piece of antler, the tool that had been used to scrape out the chalk. Someone had hit the mother lode, a clear vein of flint. Nodules of the stone lay scattered about, along with large chips of flint. How he was able to see was beyond him, all he could say was that the walls had an unearthly glow. In the distant tunnel he heard the tinkle of flint chips, the tone of which sounded like the pings of crystal glasses.

Something seemed familiar about his situation, although he knew he had never been down here before, or inside a flint quarry of any sort. It was the tunnels that fascinated him. Were these the tunnels that he was inside before he awoke on the motorway? Had he gone that badly astray?

The bobbing light in front of his eyes disappeared. He was surrounded by darkness and suddenly Jake knew he had to get out of here. Terror flooded his bloodstream and he inched his way backwards until he exited the tunnel. He sat at the bottom of the pit, knees drawn up until his breathing returned to normal and his head cleared. What did he know about Neolithic flint quarries? That they were a valuable source of stone. Flint was cherished like gold in prehistoric times. And people would go to extremes to obtain it. In fact, the more difficult it was to mine the material, the more valuable it was. Flint was made into polished axe heads and razor sharp blades, without which Stone Age life would be impossible. It was thought by these people to be a gift of their ancestors and so they tunneled underground following deep veins of rock to their endpoints.

He was getting cold. His fingers were locked by numbness and his legs felt stiff. It occurred to him, just then, how odd it was that this seemed to be an active quarry site. Why would people in the 21st century be quarrying flint with antler tools? What use did they have for flint at all? But none of that mattered. His only thought was that he had to escape this rabbit's warren of a flint mine before he froze to death, for the temperature below the surface was ten degrees colder than it was above ground.

CHAPTER THIRTY-ONE

Back on the moonlike meadow Jake surveyed his surroundings. The shallow craters of backfilled pits overgrown with new grass filled his vision. Wherever that costumed man had gone, Jake would never find him in the dark. He was on his own, and his best hope was to return to the motorway.

Where was it? He would have to trust his instincts—and his gut was telling him that left was the proper direction.

A piece of asphalt broke off under his heel. The ground was cracked and clumping in places along a gravelly shoulder. This was no doubt the road. He skirted a puddle, recognizing it as such by its dark shine, and stepped into the middle of the empty highway. Now that he had found the road, which direction should he head? Although by now the mist was thinning, he had no way of accurately orienting himself. The fading sunset was to the west. So in order to reach Stonehenge he must continue south. Truth be told, he was getting seriously worried. His faculties were still dubious, his reasoning equally so. Had he fallen and hit his head while performing that ritual dance, and was everything he had experienced since merely hallucination? He didn't think so. He had no wounds on his head that he could detect. Yet all he could remember clearly were those ravens descending on top of him.

There could only be three explanations for why he was feeling like this.

1. He had fallen, struck his head on a stone, and this

was a dream and any minute he would wake up.

2. He was having a mental fit. When he was young he had been sent to several psychiatrists to analyze the visions he had experienced and which no one would believe.

3. This was an inherited memory. But if so what was he remembering?

Or number 4. All of this was real. As he mused over these possibilities a hunched couple seated on a horse-drawn cart broke though a clot of fog to his side. The horse was stocky, heavy-footed—a Clydesdale? Jake stepped aside, raised a hand, and the horse and cart stopped. More jokers dressed in period costume. There must be some sort of festival scheduled in these parts. But none of that interested him. The only thing on his mind was a speedy return to Stonehenge. A woman muffled in a long woolen shift with a shawl about her shoulders sat beside a man, a cold pinched expression on her face.

"Can you tell me where we are? My map seems to be outdated," Jake said.

"Be quick about," the woman replied in a strange accent. "We haven't all day."

When the man climbed down to check his horse's hoof for a stone Jake realized that the couple had not heard him. The shifting fog may have hidden them from his view temporarily, but at the moment he could see them clearly so surely his presence was clear to them.

Jake turned to the man face flushed, and realized he was clenching his fist. "I'm trying to find my way to Stonehenge. Do you know how much farther it is? Could I possibly get a lift with you if you're going that way?"

The peasant stared at Jake, (yes, he looked like an old-fashioned peasant), a hanging shadow obscuring his face. It was difficult to make out his eyes although he had turned his face upward after stooping to attend the horse's hoof.

"According to this map I should be in Figheldean. But there is no sign of the village anywhere."

The grubbiness of the man's costume and his voluminous facial hair made it impossible to determine his age or the expression on his face. Had he even heard Jake's request? He did turn his eyes in the direction in which Jake had come—before climbing back onto the cart and slapping the reins.

The couple had abandoned him in the dusk.

At first Jake did not move because he was so confused. Now he darted forward but could only stare incredulous at their backs, as they vanished into the distance.

There was nothing to do but move on. Then he thought he detected something, a figure, floating in the darkness across the downs. He stiffened for a moment, and went to investigate. Maybe the man he had sighted in the flint quarry had returned, and was, at this moment, coming toward him. Jake hesitated before crossing the street to the meadow. The widely pitted field was vast, and in the fog had no endpoints. There were cracks in the ground, and chalk outcrops, where low-lying jagged peaks could trip an unwary foot.

A blustery wind followed, and the figure melded with the landscape. The grasses on the ground stirred. A door slammed in the distance and Jake jumped. The old barn? It was devoid of doors as far as he could remember. Must be the rotting door of the public house. The leaves on the nearby bushes rattled. His adrenaline was high. He was a brave man, but for the life of him, and at this moment, terror crawled up his skin.

A shudder of wings drew his attention back to the abandoned barn. The splintered shutters hung lopsided and the raven hunched outside on a short spindly tree nearby. The last of the reddish glow of sunset made a dramatic background against its black form, and the raucous cries sounded inanely human. It flew over and landed on another tree just above him. He noticed something now that he failed to notice before. The raven wore a blue band around its left ankle. Ravens in the territory had once been almost eradicated by hunters. In the last few decades they had made a comeback. Was this one part of a tracking system to measure their reproductive success or to determine their migration patterns? It didn't matter. Why waste time puzzling over how a wild raven came to have a colored tag affixed to its leg.

The motorway was deserted. He wandered an unknown distance before he heard the thunder of racing hooves, closing in fast. He stuck out his hand to flag down the rider, but the horse failed to reduce its speed. Jake dodged to the side of the road to avoid getting hit. The runaway horse kept running, the rider never even glancing down. The force of the wind as the horse pounded by almost rocked him off his feet. My God! Why was it that no one could see him? Was he in the throes of a psychotic episode?

He tried to remember what Chancellor had told him about Diana Lune. How he felt she was responsible for the strange sensations he had experienced all of his life, the feeling that something wasn't quite right. Would never be right—unless something changed.

Just exactly what did any of that mean? He still had no recollection of Diana Lune, her profession, or why her name refused to leave his thoughts.

The shadows stretched long and menacing. The air was chill and damp on his skin. No further traffic, either equine or motorized appeared ahead or behind. How long had he been wandering? The sweat on his face and the back of his shirt was cold.

A light was approaching; his eyes widened in disbelief. Was that the man he had seen earlier, the one dressed like a barber from out of the past?

He shook his head, blinked his eyes rapidly to dissipate the gloom, but the man was as real as the feet he was walking on.

Yes, a man in wooden clogs, ruddy-skinned as though he

spent most of his life outdoors, with long brown hair, and in 14th century dress no less and a pouch-like satchel, was strolling down the other side of the road in his direction, carrying a lighted lantern.

Oppressive darkness had fallen all around them, but the moon was large and shining. It cast a pearly light over the man and Jake could see him almost as clearly as though it was day.

He paused. The man was decked out like a medieval person. He must be part of the local parks program. But if so, why Medieval? Why not Neolithic, since that was the period of the famous stone circles in the vicinity? Jake knew the Stonehenge museum was about a mile west of the stones.

Jake was just about to hail him, when the man stepped over a pothole in the road, and strayed into the nearby wood. He was grubby and weathered in appearance, and by God he looked authentic. By the time Jake caught up, the man and his lantern had dissolved into shadow. Jake was certain this was the same fellow, the one he had decided was portraying a medieval barber. He chose to follow in the direction in which he had vanished, even though he was weak with hunger and thirst, and his eyes blurry.

He emerged on the other side of the thin wood at a diverging path and could see small stands of birch and beech trees reaching for the moonlight.

By now night had fully descended. He chose the left fork, and arrived from out of a clump of ash trees onto what in his dim vision looked like a moor. He did not even question why there should be a moor here. Nine stones stood in a neat ring, long grass and clover making a nest at its base, each standing stone pale as alabaster in the night. Jake approached the largest of the stones in the circle, which appeared to be partially covered with dark heather.

To the south was a small boulder. He moved over to this isolated boulder that stood well apart from the others, and bent down until his eyes were mere inches away from the surface. Moonlight turned the stone white and he could read what was carved there. How odd. The name 'Bill Stumps' was scored onto the rock. Wasn't that a character in Charles Dickens *Pickwick Papers*?

Jake continued to inspect the stones, flabbergasted. There were no other stone circles in the vicinity between Stonehenge and Avebury that he knew of. Had he just made a landmark discovery?

Something inside his pocket dug into his agitated fingers. When he withdrew his hand he was holding a curious round lens, about two inches in diameter, like the lens of someone's eyeglasses. How did that get in there? he wondered, and then shrugged and dropped it on the ground. It wasn't his.

Suddenly the lantern light appeared inside the circle. It was the man sporting the medieval barber's costume. Starting to get quite nervous now, Jake approached him. "Can you tell me where the town is?" he asked.

Pale as a soapstone figurine he walked past, between the standing stones, and continued through the ash trees. Jake stood dumbfounded, speechless. He hurried in his wake. The man looked ghostly with the white light of the moon painting his figure in quickly moving splashes of silver. Jake reacted as swiftly as he was able in the difficult light. The stranger was gaining distance quickly, so Jake picked up the pace. But the faster he walked the faster the costumed man seemed to widen the gap between them. When Jake arrived back on the motorway, the man was gone. Jake's neck twisted both ways, he exhaled in exasperation as much as fear. He turned to squint back in the direction of the small stone circle he had just left. He was damned if he could find it again. It was just too dark. At least he was back on the road. Surely a car or truck would drive by and give him a lift.

The urge to plod on was overwhelming, but he had no idea which direction he should go. He was weak now.

And then the oddest thing happened. He was in the middle of the countryside on a dark, deserted road one moment, and the next he was inundated with the sights and sounds of a bustling community.

***

Jake was relieved when he saw the rows of stone and thatch-roofed cottages on either side of the road. The last thing he sighted before he stumbled into town was a wooden arrow indicating the Great Stones Way.

Not too far in the distance were the bright lights of the Thatched Inn. Thank God. He wasn't crazy after all. This was a real place. A small sign over his head confirmed it:

WELCOME TO FIGHELDEAN

Exhaustion did funny things to the senses and he knew if he didn't get sleep soon he would collapse. He had to stop thinking about Diana Lune. Thinking about her was worsening his situation. It made him feel weak and powerless, and confused. What did she even look like? Who was she and what sort of relationship did they have with one another? All of this was a blank, and yet her name, her name was prominent in his mind. Why, oh why, couldn't he remember?

He made a B-line for the inn. Fortunately, there was a room available.

It smelled like new-washed cotton and the bathroom was recently scrubbed. Fresh rounds of soap sat in little glass holders and stiff white towels hung from wooden rails. The toilet reeked of bleach.

He gulped down several mouthfuls of tap water from the sink before he realized that that wasn't such a smart idea. He had a shower, and afterward he went to collapse on top of the colorful quilt. There was a complimentary bottle of water on the nightstand and he drank its entire contents. He wiped his lips and lay back against the dense pillow. Beside the water bottle was a package of oatmeal chocolate chip cookies. These too were complimentary and he wolfed them down. He was too spent to search for more food. Despite his frustration and confusion he was utterly exhausted.

He slept for what seemed hours before he awoke ravenously hungry. He stared up at the ceiling trying to collect his thoughts. Nothing more had come to him, nothing to tell him about Diana Lune. Furthermore, dreams had bypassed him the entire time he was asleep.

He dressed and went downstairs to see if he could get something to eat. The proprietor pointed him to a pub around the corner, and he went and sat down at the bar. He ordered bangers and mash, which the barkeep described as four highly seasoned sausages and mashed potato with beef-flavored gravy, and a side of mushy peas. In his ravenous state, this sounded delicious. While he waited for his meal to cook, he sipped on a pint of ale.

Squinting at his watch, shading it from the setting sun that filtered through the narrow windows, he noted that it was light outside. He looked up at the round, metal-framed clock with its large black numbers over the rows of spirits behind the bar. Wait a minute. It was light. Why was it *light?* It should be dark. He had arrived after sunset. His eyes jerked back to the tavern's clock. He had only slept a couple of hours before coming here to get some food. He could swear it was dark when he lay down on the bed.

The barkeep asked if he'd like another pint. "No, thanks," he answered. "Hey, can I ask you something?"

"Certainly, what about?"

"I'm a stranger here—"

"I figured you was by the way you keep looking around as though you can't believe where you are. Where do you hail from anyway?"

"America," Jake said. "Seattle."

"Ah," he said, with a slight smirk of his thin lips.

"Yeah, well. I just wanted to know the name of that small stone circle I saw south of here."

He frowned. "Not certain what you mean. Are you meaning Stonehenge? I wouldn't exactly call it small but it is a whole lot smaller than the one at Avebury."

Jake grabbed the hair on either side of his temples and snapped shut his eyes. He shook his head. He couldn't have gotten *that* disoriented that he didn't even know what he was seeing. He knew he had not imagined it.

"You okay, mate?" the barkeep asked.

Jake blinked open his eyes and nodded, even though he was far from certain that he was.

A bell jingled from the kitchen and the barkeep straightened from his slouched stance, shot a look over his shoulder. "Your supper's ready. Be right back. Want Worchestershire sauce with it?"

CHAPTER THIRTY-TWO

The plastic water bottle was on the floor alongside the cellophane cookie wrapper when Jake woke up. Nothing had changed as he opened his eyes just after dawn: same room— with two single beds, a wooden dresser—sunlight slanting through the slit in the curtains. The room had a one-cup tea maker, and He brewed himself a cup before he went to have a shower.

He checked out of the inn and asked directions to Stonehenge, just to confirm that he was on the right path. From what he was told, he should make it to the famous monument in a couple of hours. There he planned to seek out the long barrow where he had seen his trench-coated friend and a beautiful young woman on its plateau. Odd thing was, memory failed when he tried to recall the latter's identity or her purpose for being there. Something about her presence had turned everything upside down. He had to revisit the 'scene of the crime' and discover exactly what had taken place.

As he resumed his journey, he expected signs along the road somewhere to advertise the small stone circle he had discovered. There was no advertising for it, only a billboard publicizing the Stonehenge Visitor Centre. There was not a single restaurant or shop along the way. But Jake was filled with new hope. His head was clearer today and much of his academic knowledge, although rudimentary for this area, was resurfacing.

This site, the Plains of Salisbury, was 4,000 years old and once frantic with building activity, henges, burial barrows and processional avenues all crisscrossing the route he now traversed. He paused to appreciate his surroundings more thoroughly and collect his thoughts. He left the motorway, despairing of ever hitching a ride with a car, and made a conscious decision to continue along the Great Stones Way.

The trail curved to cross and then follow the Avon, a river that loomed large in the activities of Neolithic peoples. It was along this drainage that the bluestones of the Preseli hills in Wales were thought by conventional archaeologists to have been transported by boat to Stonehenge, after negotiating the Pembrokeshire and Cornish peninsulas to the river mouth at Christchurch. So much for the theory of Native Americans erecting stone circles in Britain, he thought.

He suddenly stopped. The theory. She was a colleague.

He frowned. Or was she? Something about that didn't seem right.

The valley was peaceful with splendid stretches under clouds of beech trees and cool bluebell woods. He moved on, now more confused than ever over his random thoughts. He was coming to the last leg of his journey—open plain with wide vistas of the rolling landscape, green and lush and speckled with yellow flowers. He finally reached Durrington Walls, where the trail cut through a huge enclosed area. Here at least was a sign and he didn't have to rely on his memory or on any previous knowledge. The site was where archaeologists thought the builders of Stonehenge might have lived. It faced sunset on the summer solstice. *Solstice.* Why did the idea of the solstice matter to him? Jake shook his head. That did nothing to clarify his problem. He glanced around and recognized the landforms. Here was Woodhenge, once a concentric ring of wooden poles, recently marked by concrete posts.

He passed King Barrows along the ridge, some of the few sites that remained unexcavated, and the mysterious Cursus group of Bronze Age barrows, named such because

William Stukeley (an 18th century antiquarian) deemed it to have been built for Roman chariot races. The Romans had settled much of Great Britain in the past, and their ruins were everywhere.

The sight of the ruins brought knowledge rushing back to his memory. Long barrows were tombs, originally filled with the bones of the dead. Ancestor worship for whatever reason had helped the prehistoric inhabitants of this mysterious land explain the universe. And as he thought about this it occurred to him how the descendants of these dead folk had at some point in their history gone from worshipping their forebears by interring them under stone and earth to raising their eyes to the heavens and seeking explanation of their world from sky gods—in the form of standing stones.

From where he walked amidst the sacred landscape the barrows appeared indistinguishable. Which was the one where he had spotted Chancellor and his guest? He decided to continue to the infamous tourist site.

Across the meadow, against the milk-blue horizon, Stonehenge finally appeared. He felt solidly oriented now. The tall linteled pillars appeared flat grey and majestic, and if it wasn't for the circling traffic of mostly tourist buses from the A303, he could truly have embraced the Sky God theory as the explanation for the standing stones.

Quite exhausted by the time he reached it, he spent what remained of the day exploring, before deciding to pack it in and return to London. All of the paraphernalia he had brought with him for the ritual had vanished. The mask, which he was hoping to recover, was gone. The Interpol agent had cleared the evidence or else it was the National Trust staff that had conducted the cleanup. Before he gave up entirely there was one thing he must try. He walked around to the farthest arc. There were large groups observing from every viewpoint. He began to have second thoughts. Those doubts gave way to certainty. If he went inside the rope barrier and started dancing in the center he would be arrested.

Desperation would not solve his problem. He had no reason to believe that dancing around inside that circle would magically restore sense to his life.

His best bet was to return to London and seek out Chancellor. As he strolled in the direction of the waiting shuttles that would take him back to the visitor center where he could catch a bus to London, movement beneath one of the lintels caught his eye. He did a double take, followed the movement to his right, and swore he saw someone peer around one of the sarsens from the inside. He glanced around to see if anyone else had noticed, but the place was bustling with tourists shooting photos with digital cameras and taking selfies with their smartphones. When he refocused his sight to the concentration of erect stones, anyone who had been inside the circle was gone.

Exhaustion, he reminded himself, did peculiar things to the perception.

He caught the shuttle for the short ride, and sat upright as it rolled to a stop in front of the visitor center. Most of the tourists went inside to use the restroom facilities, gift shop and restaurant. After weaving his way past the crowd, Jake located the signage directing visitors to the transport into town. He was still distracted by what he had seen or *thought* he had seen inside the stone circle. Whatever or whoever it was had disappeared, and after the bizarre experience when he had defied the authorities the first time around and slipped under the barrier, he dared not tempt fate again. Instead, he boarded a waiting vehicle and collapsed into a seat near the front, adjacent to the driver.

Nothing more could be done until he arrived in the city. He settled back to take a nap. The gentle lull of steady movement soon had him deep in slumber.

He had no idea how long he slept but he was awakened by a lurch. To his surprise the view outside was not what he had expected.

Instead of a bustling city the bus had arrived at rural Durrington to collect more passengers. Yes, that was what was printed on the sign.

Welcome to Durrington

Wasn't Durrington in the opposite direction of London? Before he could react, the scenery began to change. It seemed to him they were headed the wrong way, but he was helpless until the next scheduled stop.

The countryside blurred by as their speed increased.

"Next stop, Figheldean," the bus driver announced.

Jake now realized without a doubt that he had boarded the wrong vehicle. He was determined to stay awake for the next couple of hours. He was still perplexed as to his location at the time he saw the old grey barn with its split boards, bare rafters and hollow center, and the stone ruins of a public house abandoned in the middle of nowhere.

And what about that strange pitted landscape surfacing from the mist? He was fairly certain that he had had some kind of psychoactive reaction. What had caused it however was a mystery. Was it the ritual he had performed under Chancellor's urging? Dance and chanting could have that kind of effect on the human brain. It was not unusual for people to suffer blackouts under those conditions—even without the use of psychoactive drugs or alcohol.

He would never forget the day, when as a young teen he had been taunted into drinking excessive amounts of cheap bourbon whiskey and woken up on the train tracks.

Had he suffered a similar lapse in memory? While he was grateful that most of his memory had returned, he was still frustrated by the gaps. Much as he had mulled it over, he was stymied as to why he had been performing a Haida dance in the middle of a Neolithic stone circle. And even though he remembered the beige trench-coated Interpol agent, why had the man insisted he perform the ceremonial dance?

As they raced along the motorway, his pounding heart began to quiet. He noted some familiar landmarks, a certain bend in the road, a yellow field of rapeseed, a gap in the bluebell wood with a view of the chalk hills. A pristine canal cutting through the downs. They were coming up to the place where Jake was certain he had followed the medieval costumed man through the thin wood to a small concentration of standing stones. There was the pothole that he had stepped over. It was distinctive, shaped like Florida State. Any minute they should see the old grey barn. They slowed as they neared a red bus stop.

The barn was still there, but where was the old stone ruin? It was nowhere visible. The vehicle had come to a full halt. Everything about the scenery on either side of the road was familiar, including the tangle of bushes where the couple on the horse cart had stopped to attend to their animal. The only thing missing was the old public house—and the moonscape-like flint quarry.

Jake asked the driver how long he would be stopped here.

"Long enough to get a cup of coffee." He pointed to a Starbucks, tucked in from the road, a modern glass and stucco one-story building at the end of a manicured pink flagstone path, lined on either side with potted herbs. Starbucks. When had they built a Starbucks here? That was where the abandoned stone ruin should have been. Jake's jaw slipped, but he said nothing. Further down the road were more buildings, the Thatched Inn and the pub where he'd met the thin-lipped barkeep when he was last in Figheldean.

"What happened to the flint quarry," Jake ventured, making a wild guess, and pointing to the direction of the town. "Wasn't there some kind of quarry around these parts?"

"Quarry?" the driver said. "How did you know there was a flint quarry here?"

Jake said, "Where is it? I've been trying to locate it as we were rolling into town."

"There's not been no flint quarry here for centuries, maybe for thousands of years. The place was all backfilled before the village were developed. He paused for a second to check for his wallet in his rear pocket. You can read all about it from the tourist information booth over there." He thumbed in the direction of the Thatched Inn.

"Thanks." Jake was beginning to feel more than a little nervous.

"Twenty minutes," the driver said. "Before we leave."

Jake nodded, and then froze as the figure of a woman— whom he recognized instantly—came toward the bus.

CHAPTER THIRTY-THREE

"Ma…Maia?" he stuttered. "Maia Pickerton?"

The woman nodded. "It's Dr. Jake Lalonde, isn't it?"

At this point he did not even question how he knew instantly who she was. What are you doing in Figheldean? Everyone has been searching for you, including New Scotland Yard."

"They won't find me," she said.

He frowned. "Why not? What happened? Why are you on the run?"

"I'm not on the run. I've been trying to get back to the museum for days. Or what seems like days. Where *we* are there's no accounting for time." She pointed a finger at herself and then at him.

Jake was silent. What did she mean? He glanced down at his watch, frowned again.

"What does your watch say?" Maia asked.

"It says 5:45 pm. But it can't be 5:45. I caught the bus at 5:45."

"And I caught the bus at 7:00 pm two or was it three nights ago? I've been here ever since."

"In Figheldean?"

"Between Figheldean and Avebury."

"I don't understand," Jake said.

"Don't you? Where are you coming from?"

"Stonehenge."

"And where are you going to?"

"Well, I thought I was returning to London. But apparently I boarded the wrong bus. It seems I'm headed to

Avebury."

"Didn't you find anything strange when you were at Stonehenge?"

"Like what?" he asked suspiciously.

"You tell me."

The remark was cryptic. Come to think of it the historic site had not looked quite the same. There were a whole lot more tourists and the maze of rope barriers had expanded to accommodate them. There were also more buildings. Even something that looked like a hotel, with a full-scale upmarket restaurant, not the lone cafeteria they'd had before. Could it be that he had missed this section of the development? But honestly if there had been a hotel near Stonehenge wouldn't he have seen it the first time he was there?

He scratched his ear in confusion. Of course, only a day ago, his memory was pretty much a blank slate. But he did remember Maia. He remembered that she had gone missing. He returned his attention to her. Was it some kind of festival that had brought the crowds? None came readily to mind, and he asked Maia, who shook her head.

"There is no festival on this day, in *this* time or any other time. The festival comes near the end of the month, always on or after June 20th, summer solstice. That would be tomorrow."

Jake kept his objections to himself. What was she talking about? Nothing she was saying was making sense. Why should he be surprised? Nothing had made sense since that cloud of ravens had landed on top of him. He was just grateful that most of his recent memory, prior to the event at Stonehenge, had been restored.

"Look," he said, "just so that everyone will stop worrying about you I'll phone the police to let them know you're okay. I think Tom Chancellor mentioned that the detective in charge is named Pettigrew. Yeah, Superintendent Simon Pettigrew; I have his card."

Just then he remembered he didn't have a phone. He asked her if she had one and she did, and passed it over. The number was on a business card that Chancellor had given him, and he tapped it onto the keypad. "In fact..." He returned the cellphone to her. "You should probably tell him yourself."

"How old is your Superintendent Pettigrew?"

"Why?" He hesitated, tried to picture the man, and then realized he had never seen him. Chancellor however had described him in great detail. "I don't know how old he is. Fiftyish maybe?"

She shut off the phone, and thrust it back inside her handbag. "There's no point. Superintendent Pettigrew is retired." She smiled at his look of incredulity, and handed him a newspaper. "I picked this up at the local tavern. It's today's paper."

It was a copy of *The Guardian* and it was dated June 25th 2041.

"Did you honestly think there was a Starbuck's in 2017 Figheldean?"

Jake was speechless. It was all adding up. He had been witness to the past and the future, but was barred from his own time. But if these people and this town were the future, was that man he saw in medieval costume really the past? *That* he found impossible to accept because that man, and those other people—the people in the horse-drawn cart and the racing horseman—were oblivious to his existence. And yet *he* could see them.

Maia nodded and led him soundlessly toward the Starbucks shop. They went inside. Jake was still dumbstruck. Maia ordered coffees for both of them before sitting him down at a table. "I've been here longer than you, and I still haven't quite figured it out. How's your memory by the way? When I first got here, I hadn't a clue as to who I was or what had happened."

"It's starting to come back to me."

She nodded. "Good. There's one thing I'm glad I did keep with me when this whole thing happened." She dug out a book—an international bestseller—from her handbag. "It helped to restore my memory."

He stared at the familiar tome. The eye-catching cover showing the megaliths of Avebury with their 'faces in stone' was causing stirrings in his memory too.

"If you don't believe me. Just look around you. In our time there was no Starbucks coffee shop in tiny villages like Figheldean. The village is a village no more. It's grown up. It's a town."

"What are you saying, Maia?"

She set the paperback down on the table between them. It was the softcover version of the *Sacred Stones of Raven*, the book Diana Lune had been plugging at her lecture. Maia fastened her eyes on Jake's, and then turned a few pages before stopping and tracing a chapter heading:

THE GREAT STONES WAY

The Great Stones Way is a 36.5-mile walking route through the ancient landscape and the varied, stunning scenery of West Wiltshire, linking the World Heritage Sites of Avebury and Stonehenge. What many people don't know is that it is also a walking path of ancient magic, connecting the two most powerful stone circles in the United Kingdom. In prehistoric times, they were designed to allow safe teleportation between two locations. For two stone circles to function together they must be constructed so that they can be activated simultaneously.

To create the portals a stone circle must be configured in such a way that they will provide explicit times for activation. Each circle must be such that its counterpart will activate at exactly the same moment. When the planets and stars align in specific ways at both sites, and a special symbol is carved and placed in the center of each, the portal is opened. But for a short time only.

The complexity of its architecture dictates how often it can be used. A simple circle may open only once in a century or a millennium. The more complex the concentration of stone the more often it can be used.

If more than two portals are opened at the same moment, time travel between them can have unpredictable effects, and sometimes, disastrous consequences.

Despite himself he found that he had gone slack-jawed. Yes, everything was coming back to him. Like a dammed river suddenly released, the waters of memory flooded his brain. Sure, this—or at least a semblance of this—was what he had been searching for himself. That was the connection between him and Diana Lune. To be honest, at this very moment, he was teetering between believing and scoffing. How did the physics of such a thing work? As a scientist he was open-minded. He had to be. He was no stranger to the paranormal. A flashback sent his mind reeling to a time when he was younger and had gone on a solitary cycling trip across the Olympic Peninsula from his hometown of Seattle. He had suffered a time-lapse then, and an eerie sensation of witnessing different portals of time.

The episode was unnervingly similar to what he was currently experiencing. At the time he had chocked it up to dehydration and exhaustion, and had forgotten about it until this moment. Now, he realized that not only had he confronted things that could only be explained by the supernatural, but also he had deliberately dabbled in the paranormal through the use of psychoactive plants and mind-altering Native rituals.

But science fact was one thing, and science fiction another. In fact that was one of the things that he had been told would always hold him back—his failure to fully believe. Without fully believing in the impossible, he could not embrace his destiny. And it was Diana Lune who had offered him that bit of wisdom.

The idea of a stone circle having the power to transport a person from one place to another, from one time to another—wow—it boggled the mind. And yet wasn't that what he had been trying to do with the shamanic ritual? Hadn't he already succumbed to the possibility of unimaginable power, trapped within the circle of stones at Stonehenge?

As Maia continued to talk, breaking into his thoughts, the last vestiges of disbelief vanished. Because now... *now* it was real.

So, *she* had the answer all the time. The entire event at the Alexander Keiller Museum replayed in his mind. He should have squashed his scepticism and stayed for her entire lecture. Had she touched on this subject in her talk? All he'd had to do was take her seriously, and it would have saved him time and confusion. She knew all about time portals as they pertained to stone circles. In his skim-reading of her book, prior to her lecture, his cynicism had caused him to completely overlook this chapter.

"I don't know anything about physics, Dr. Lalonde, but I do know something about stone circles. The druids and the Wicca in this area have long believed that Stonehenge and Avebury had mysterious powers. If you were to ask me a week ago whether I believed this, I would have said, No. Today however, I would give you a different answer. I cannot seem to leave the Great Stones Way. As long as I remain on the road between these two great henges I am free to come and go, and to interact with the people in the towns and villages in, it seems, any time period in the future, but not the past. For some reason I can exist in their time, I can see them and what they are doing, but I can't speak to them. But here, in 2041 Figheldean I can buy a coffee at Starbucks."

"So what are you saying? That we're stuck in some kind of time corridor?"

"If that is what it's called, then yes. I can't go back to my museum in my own time."

Jake frowned. "Have you tried?"

"Of course, I've tried. Apparently I don't work there anymore."

"Well, who does work there?"

Maia paused for an instant. "Angeline Lisbon works there."

"Who?"

Maia's eyes widened. "Didn't you meet her? Angeline Lisbon was a graduate student at Cambridge studying sacred landscapes, especially stone monuments. She worked part time for the Heritage Trust and helped me out sometimes. Only her name is no longer Lisbon. She married. Apparently, she is the curator now. Oh, you should see it, Dr. Lalonde. You wouldn't recognize it. The place is three times as large. The place has become"— she slapped a hand to her mouth as though what she was about to say was shameful—"The place has become a theme park."

"Seriously?"

She nodded. "Quickly, let's get back on your bus and I will show you."

The driver was just getting ready to close the doors when they squeezed in and Maia paid her fare to Avebury. Jake's ticket was still valid and they sat down, she on the window side.

The trip did not take long by bus, not like it had taken on foot.

They soon got off at the roadside, and now Jake saw exactly what Maia was talking about.

CHAPTER THIRTY-FOUR

The hedgerows that undulated into the lush green fields of the chalky high country bordering the village were gone. No more was there merely a scattering of stone and thatched cottages at the bottom of the low hills. The indigenous vegetation and the twisted trees were torn up to make room for the expansion. The skyline was invisible from the town center, and the ancient barrows that once interred the Bronze Age dead and the unmistakable landmark of Silbury Hill sat obscured by encroaching development.

Past an old brick cottage with a half-rusted shed they entered a lane and encountered a familiar sign. A recognizable **No Parking** symbol stood near the church. They had entered the village proper. Correction—town proper. The quaint and formerly isolated community was no longer a small but charming village. It was a town in the midst of sprawling growth. The low stone buildings were crowded with new structures mostly made of glass, concrete and brick.

Jake Lalonde followed his guide along the flagstone pathway between some impressive topiary to the limestone and sarsen stone, ivy-covered walls of the former Avebury Manor's main house. The lead glazing in the windows was the original. One of the prominent features of the theme park was an Elizabethan waxworks. They went through the turnstiles just inside to pay for entry and were greeted by wenches in period costume.

Maia was silent and determined that he experience all without commentary. His was a thin knowledge of the historical town, and except for the megaliths for which it was famous, what he witnessed was appalling.

The manor itself had ecclesiastical roots dating from the 12th century Benedictine priory. There were wax statues of King Henry III who had granted the manor to William de Tankerville, the Chamberlain of Normandy (also represented in wax). Some of the wax figures had very dubious business practices, like Sir William Sharington, master of the Mint at Bristol, also a previous owner but who was stripped of the manor for 'clipping' the coinage.

Jake nearly leaped out of his shoes when a very convincing ghost, the 'White Lady,' (a holographic image) followed them around the house haunted by wax statues of prominent owners and noble people. She was apparently a young Civil War widow, though why she haunted the manor was unclear. He sniffed the air; a strong smell of roses rewarded him. Another apparition made an eerie appearance and his high-strung guide told him that it was the ghost of Sir John Stavell, who had died immediately after the English Civil War, when Oliver Cromwell excised the manor from him. And yes, there was a wax figure of him as well. Then there were the usual instruments of torture, screams coming out of the dark in the dungeon.

In various rooms there were craft workshops, a falconry center, and outside in the garages and stables were vintage carriages and horses. The cherry on top was the adventure playground that boasted rides weaving between the ancient megaliths. As he stared in horror at what was once a 4,000-year-old World Heritage site, and home of the largest open-air temple in Europe, a cart-wheeling band of medieval troubadours, beggars, jesters, stilt-walkers and fire-eaters wove their way throughout the village's narrow lanes.

Medieval minstrels, falconers and Tudor lords and ladies dressed in appropriate costume conversed with streams of visitors. Stands advertising authentic food and drink, and souvenirs cluttered the square, and clusters of customers drank cups of mead and consumed funnel cakes. Oh no, the funnel cakes weren't authentic Tudor fare, but then neither was the mead, which was some kind of modern beer, laced with honey.

An hour later they were ready to visit the refurbished museum. The place where Maia pointed was unrecognizable. The stone building with its small windows had an extension of glass and concrete, making the current museum twice as large as the original.

Inside, it was bustling with visitors, but when a gap came at the front desk Maia stepped up to request the whereabouts of the curator. The man behind the counter was not Nigel. If this were 2041, as Maia insisted, then Nigel would have long been dead. In their time he was already in his 70s.

"Is the curator here? We would like to speak with her if that is possible," Maia entreated. Jake's only contribution to the discourse was a faint nod. He felt as though he were a participant in a Twilight Zone episode. And he was certain no one here would understand his reference to the vintage TV series.

The bright young face in front of them broke into a huge smile. Twenty odd years ago, Brits, unlike Americans, did not sport flashy grins. Seems things had changed.

"She's outside with a group," the young man explained. "May I give her a message?" He tore off a sheet from a Post-it pad and poised a pen to write. "I'll send someone to fetch her."

Maia shook her head. The young man described the curator's appearance if they wished to look for her themselves, and then Jake and Maia exited the museum and ambled over to the nearest arc of standing stones.

Some things apparently remained the same. Fragments of the famous sarsens were built into almost every original cottage in this village, either in their foundations or in the supporting walls. Deliberately broken up into useable chunks the ancient megaliths served as standard building material. As they stood in the village lane he was reminded once again of the massiveness of the stone circle. How could the National Trust or the people of the village let this happen? The commercial development was an eyesore. But then he recalled, too, how economically destitute the village had been prior to the expansion.

He studied the crest of the ditch, all the way to the silhouettes of the standing stones. A woman gesticulated beside one of the far sarsens at the distant edge of the circle to a crowd of avid listeners. One would never know it to be the rim of the moat now, with all the buildings and rides and people swarming about and obscuring the landmark stones. Following the curve of the landscape, Jake and Maia made their way, pushing past the milling visitors, until they arrived at where, clad in a very becoming pale blue dress and yellow cardigan, the curator lectured to a group of tourists.

She was quite beautiful, even though she must be in her early fifties. They had caught her attention and from her quizzical expression she appeared ignorant of their identities. Their anxiety however must have been palpable, and Jake appealed to her with his eyes. The truth was not an option, and they had no plausible explanation for interrupting her, but she was their only hope.

For whatever reason, she seemed to understand their urgency. Blinking out the sun's glare from beneath windswept hair, she excused herself from the group and approached. "Can I help you? I'm the museum's director and curator, Angeline."

The familiar sarsen in front of them had withstood the sands of time. What was twenty-five years when it had survived for twenty-five thousand plus? He remembered it from his last visit. Even in *this* time it appeared the same. He exchanged looks with Maia. Lines of confusion passed across her face. Yes, he was searching for a face. *Her* face. But it failed to materialize.

He refocused his attention on the curator, all the while refraining from inhaling too deeply, because of frayed nerves. She was clearly busy and had no time for their questions—which had nothing to do with the theme park or the museum. To gain her confidence and to convince her to meet with them after work they must conjure up a probable reason. What would be a likely excuse that would compel her to accommodate them? A loud gasp caused him to pivot, and caught Maia gawping at the Barber Stone—the megalith he had just inspected. He focused on it, and almost choked himself. On its surface was the image of Thomas Chancellor, the Interpol agent.

They both turned to the curator who was perplexed by their reaction. "Is something wrong?" she asked.

Jake waved both hands at the stone.

"I'm sorry? Look if there's something you wished to discuss, please hurry. I have to get back to my tour group."

Jake repeated the action, indicating the stone. She stepped back to examine the megalith in fuller perspective. "I don't understand what is troubling you. Has the stone been vandalized? I don't see any graffiti. We're very vigilant about security around the original monuments."

She gestured to the security officers that were roaming everywhere. Jake wondered why they bothered with security. This was a theme park for God's sake, and they had taken no pains to cordon off the monuments from meandering tourists.

The curator sympathized with Jake's concern. "The park is still under construction, as you can see." She motioned to the cranes in the near distant horizon.

"You don't see a face in the stone?" he asked.

She shrugged; then tittered. "Oh that. Actually, I do see a face. Everyone does. It's a psychological phenomenon most people experience. We're actually planning to transition part of the stone works into an exhibit called 'Faces in the Stone'."

"But—"

Maia jerked on his shirtsleeve. She muttered under her breath something about *this* Angeline not recognizing the face because she had never met Thomas Chancellor.

"We need your help," Maia said. "We were wondering,

when it's convenient, if we could meet with you to discuss…" Her voice trailed off.

"The stone," Jake intervened. "The Barber Stone. We would like more information about it, and the skeleton that was found beneath it. You see… we are both archaeologists. I…" It was his turn to stutter. Why was the Barber-surgeon important? The possibilities were bewildering but he had a feeling it might give him a clue as how to get home. "I understand it is stored here, at the museum?"

"Of course," Angeline said. "Always pleased to help a colleague." She dug into the deep pockets of her cardigan and fished out a business card. "Call my office. My assistant will set up an appointment for you to see it."

"Thanks."

Maia smiled as they simultaneously reached for the card, and then turned to go as Angeline returned to her tourists.

Jake read the information on the card:

Alexander Keiller Museum
Avebury Town Theme Park
Avebury, North Wiltshire, England

Angeline Lisbon Radisson
Director and Curator of Historic Monuments, PhD

CHAPTER THIRTY-FIVE

Maia was baffled by his reaction. So was he. A sudden sensation of vertigo.

"What is the matter with you, Jake?" They had decided to address each other by first names, since it looked like they were stuck on this adventure together.

"I'm sorry, Maia. You never told me what Angeline's married name was in this particular iteration of the future."

"Excuse me? My apologies; I thought I had. But seriously, Dr. Lalonde, I mean Jake. What *is* the issue?"

"It's her *husband's* name," he spat. The name brought a foul taste to his mouth. It was difficult to bring himself to speak it.

"Radisson? I understand he is a very prominent international developer. American I believe."

"Damn right, he's American. And he should be dead!"

She was beginning to look scared. Had the stress of being sucked into a time warp made him lose it completely? That was the question that was reflected back at him in her alarmed eyes. "I thought you didn't know Angeline Lisbon? Why are you so upset that she married this Radisson fellow?"

How could he explain to her the complexity of the relationship? He would have to go back years (and in a different timeline for God's sake!) to explain how he and the developer had duked it out over a theme park. Yes, a *theme park*. And that was why this particular development had him so riled up. The idea of a tourist attraction, in an important archaeological site such as Avebury, was sacrilegious, but if the theme park had been built by *him*…. Well, what could be worse or more ironic? For Maia to appreciate the irony he would have to go back to the time of the Raven's Pool, a shaman's ceremonial pool, part of a sacred burial cave that the developer had destroyed in an attempt to turn some sacred native sites on the west coast into a theme park.

But what was the point? At the moment, who the curator had married was irrelevant.

Much as the answer to the question nagging in his mind frightened him, he *needed* to know. "Just tell me one thing. I don't even know if you'll have the answer. But I'll ask you anyway. Who is the developer responsible for this monstrosity?" He spread his arms wide to take in the entire site of the theme park.

"I think I know," she said. Her voice had trailed away and her gaze landed on a large sign by one of the standing stones. He recognized the logo instantly. Radisson Enterprises.

"Are you all right, Jake?" Maia asked.

He had gone silent and deathly pale. He could feel all of the blood drain from his face. "Yeah.... Yeah, I'm fine. Let's get out of here."

***

Jake was silent for the next little while. After arranging with the secretary at the museum for an appointment next morning, they decided to visit the Red Lion pub for a bite. At least the Red Lion Inn had survived the wave of development, and except for extensions in back for additional bedrooms, its thatched roofed facade remained pretty much as it had since it was first built in the 17th century.

Jake forced himself to forget about Radisson for the time being. For some reason—that truly puzzled him—the idea of Angeline and Radisson together made him gag. However, he was powerless to change things. His only hope was to focus on finding a way to escape this time continuum, which seemed to exist in a corridor between Avebury and

Stonehenge.

The whole idea of time slips and missing periods of time preyed on his mind, and as soon as he and Maia had settled into a booth with two pints of pale ale, and an order of Scotch eggs and fried potatoes, he asked to see Diana Lune's book again. The events of that night descended upon him like a landslide.

Jake realized now that he had skipped all of the most pertinent sections of the presenter's treatise the first time around when he stopped at an eye-catching chapter.

The Universe as an Endless Field of Potential

The Quantum Model of the universe can explain the mysterious phenomena of 'Missing time' and 'Time slip'. In this model, the universe is an endless field of potential where there is no set or fixed outcome or points in time.

Because subatomic particles are capable of moving between and interacting across all points in space and time, all possible outcomes in the past, present and future may exist in a vast, omnipresent field. And it is through this field that some lucky few have traveled.

The manner and means by which an individual can stumble into other periods of time or parallel dimensions are through specified portals. Certain people are more amenable to the phenomenon than others. In different regions of the world the veil between space and time and parallel dimensions is thinner, and the unsuspecting may accidentally pass between or into them. Through this model many supernatural and paranormal phenomena, including Missing Time and Time Slips, move into the realm of possibility.

"Does any of this make sense to you, Maia?" Jake asked. "Do you see any way out of this at all?"

"The only thing I've seen as a constant since I've been stuck in this strange corridor is that faces only appear in the stones at Avebury, and not at Stonehenge. So for whatever it's worth, now that I saw that face of Mr. Chancellor on the Barber Stone, I think we need to be here in Avebury. I think that he might be looking for us."

"I agree." He paused thoughtfully before asking, "Do you think the curator at the museum will know anything that can help us? Do you think she'll even believe us?"

"Now that I've had time to think about it? No. No I don't think she can help us much. It might be best not to involve her."

They did not have to call Angeline the next day to cancel the meeting. She called them. And it wasn't to cancel. In fact she wanted to move up the hour of their meeting. She sounded worried, anxious—almost desperate—and that made Jake determined to see her immediately.

"What's wrong?" he asked when they were invited into her office.

"I'm glad you could come so quickly," she said. "I need your help."

They had arrived before the theme park opened as Angeline had requested. They had booked rooms at the Red Lion Inn so it was just a matter of going down the street to the museum. In his distraction he had not noticed anything between the inn and the museum, not the air temperature or the weather or even the hour of the morning.

"Yesterday, you mentioned you were an expert on raven iconography," Angeline began.

Jake exchanged a quick glance with Maia and nodded.

Angeline glanced at her watch before returning her attention to them. He knew the theme park opened in less than an hour. "Maybe it's nothing. But do you remember our discussion yesterday about the 'faces in stone'?"

"Yes," Jake said.

"You saw a face in the Barber Stone."

"I did."

Maia bobbed her chin as well for she had seen it too. It had been the spitting image of Thomas Chancellor.

"I'm used to people seeing images in the stones, but what has me concerned…" She hesitated before continuing. "Well…perhaps it would be more meaningful if you saw it yourself."

The first thing Jake noticed as they left the museum and headed onto the grassy field was an infinite number of ravens perched on the monuments. His eyes widened and he turned to Maia who had recognized the spectacle too. Why had they not noted the ravens this morning when they left the inn? Well, it had still been dark and he had been preoccupied and possibly the birds were asleep. They were awake now, pinning their beady eyes on him, in clusters of hundreds. "Does this happen often?" he asked, nervously.

"Never," Angeline said. "It's very strange. Shortly after you left yesterday, around closing time, they descended on us like a plague. I have no idea where they came from. I'm hoping they'll leave when the park opens this morning and the visitors arrive. I've never seen this many ravens roost in one place. Apparently, on farms during lambing season this can happen. But there are no lambs on the property. I just hope a call to Animal Control can be avoided. I'm sceptical of what they could do. And a bunch of dead birds on the premises is the last thing we need. Though I'm sure killing them is not an option." Her slight shoulders heaved and she turned up one of the paths.

The theme park's employees were out and about setting up outdoor exhibits and opening food stands. Some were attempting to scare off the ravens with brooms and shovels. The birds took flight, and then returned to roost. Jake observed the ones that had returned. They were ignoring the food stands, which was unusual as the thing most ravens desired was food. Their eyes seemed to follow wherever

Angeline went. On a large megalith a group of fifty birds
gathered on its top. Jake did a double take. Two of the birds
were wearing coloured bands around their ankles. One of the
leg bands was blue and the other yellow.

Past this stone several sarsens sat in a familiar curve near
some westward facing elms. He recognized the level bank
and the barn sitting on it, and the slope of the ditch to the
other side where a house now stood instead of stones.

They wandered along the top of the bank following a
paved path. From here Jake could detect well-worn tracks
where visitors had crossed directly to the inner circles
following the traces of former hedgerows and rock walls to a
further grouping of megaliths. The development had left the
original position of the stones alone, although reconstructed
copies now replaced the markers. The remains of the two
inner circles had artificial stones to replace the original
sarsens. In the northeast quadrant two stupendous megaliths
posed at right angles to one another.

Angeline headed south to a clean arc of sarsens, the
replicas of the south inner ring. She stopped to send her gaze
to a towering megalith with a notch at the top. "Please tell me
that you see it."

He not only saw it—but it sent him into a reverie of déjà
vu.

"And that's not all." She pointed to the adjacent stone.
Then led them to a third megalith, again similarly shaped.
The next one they came to replicated the last. And so on until
they arrived at the sixth stone. There was no doubt in his
mind. He could tell from the look on Maia's face that she
was feeling it too. Double déjà vu. This was the exact
scenario that he and Maia had experienced the day they met.

"Am I seeing things?" Angeline asked.

Jake's jaw dropped. The arc of standing stones looked
exactly as they had in *his* time. Each of the stones projected
an image of a raven.

Then a disturbance overhead attracted his eye. Black
feathered masses huddled on all six of the megaliths, but four

individuals had colored bands around their ankles. As he rotated to seek the two that he had observed earlier with the blue and yellow bands, they came winging across the site to land on the arc of sarsens. Now each stone had one raven with a colored band on its leg.

CHAPTER THIRTY-SIX

The last time he had heard about banded ravens was at the Tower of London. Legend had it that if anything happened to them, if they flew away or were abducted or died, the great city would fall. Six were missing. The tour guide had told him the colors of the bands. They were identical to the bands on the Avebury ravens. He could only interpret this as some kind of omen.

But how were they going to get out of here? He still had a feeling that viewing the skeleton of the barber-surgeon might help them. He told Angeline that he had no idea what the appearance of the ravens meant. He insisted that he had further research to conduct before he could proffer any sort of an answer. It wasn't exactly the truth. She asked him if he was still interested in viewing the remains of the barber-surgeon. He nodded and she led them back to the museum and to the back stairs.

Once there, Angeline switched on the light to illuminate their descent, but it barely made a dint to the darkness. For some unfathomable reason Jake's heart was pounding. Blood rushed in his ears. He forced himself to ground his anxiety. True, he still felt as though he was moving about in a dream world, but if that were the case, then Maia Pickerton was part of his dream.

He plunged down the steps in the wake of the women.

Angeline paused at the bottom of the stone steps and switched on another light. The place was not only dark it was unsettling. How many years would it take before museums started to renovate their basements?

Jake saw that they were on a landing and their guide turned to give them safety instructions. She descended a few more steps and tossed a backwards glance to ascertain their compliance. He travelled blindly, thinking repeatedly that maybe they should turn back. What could some forgotten bones tell them about finding a way home?

This place did not look terribly organised. In the tangle of stairways and tunnels the remains could be anywhere.

The illumination from cobwebbed light bulbs stabbed feebly into the distance; the smell that invaded Jake's nostrils was musty, damp. After the comfort of upstairs the air felt strangely cold. The walls were silent. The uneven ground showed broken concrete in some sections. Another set of uneven steps appeared out of the gloom leading to a sub-basement.

He watched the two women ahead of him negotiate the crumbling stone stairs. After an interminable time they reached level ground and ducked under a low, arched ceiling to an empty corridor. A locked door appeared to their right at the end of the stone passageway, and he trampled on a peeling wooden boardwalk overtop an earth floor. Angeline unlocked the door.

Footprints marked the dust; sometimes this room was used. But the janitorial staff obviously never made it down here. She warned them to be cautious before attempting to locate the right box. Inside the vault were crates and boxes, stacked one atop the other, and some were opened with objects haphazardly scattered.

A large table reared out of the shadows in the center of the room. She advised that they wait while she retrieved the carton containing the skeleton.

When she returned, she held a cardboard box filled with paper bags, each labelled with the elements of the bones in black ink. "Are you acquainted with the legend?" she inquired.

Jake nodded. He removed the skull from a large paper bag while Maia sorted the remaining contents. What was he looking for? On that Jake was vague. But it seemed to him the answer lay among the secrets of the Barber Stone.

The popular folklore among the locals had not changed. The official story continued to assert that the thirteen-ton megalith had killed a man during the stone felling, and that in1938 Alexander Keiller's excavation had discovered remains beneath it. The accepted hypothesis was that while helping to topple the massive sarsen during the 14th century Christian frenzy, a support had given way and the stone had fallen, fracturing the victim's pelvis and snapping his neck. He was wedged so that it had been impossible to remove his corpse.

The skeleton's rotted satchel had held three silver coins dated to 1320, and had helped to determine the period of stone burying. Iron scissors and a lance or probe were among his possessions and led the experts to postulate that he was some kind of itinerant barber or surgeon. Alas, his journey to the county's market fairs with his knives and scissors was cut short when he had offered to help with the stone-felling, and ironically was crushed, his body buried in the back rubble.

But here was new evidence. Jake held the skull up to the hanging light bulb overhead. Apparently that was not how he died at all. Had the stone fallen on him, his head would have been crushed. There would at least have been signs of fractures in the skull and these were missing. Nor was his neck snapped, for there were no cracks in the cervical vertebrae. Maia passed him a magnifying glass that lay on the table, and he saw further reason to challenge the local story. A cut in the skull appeared to be that of a dagger wound. From this Jake could only conclude that the barber-surgeon was not crushed at all but died prior to the burial of the megalith and was interred beneath it. Alternatively, he was buried alive and had died of suffocation.

"Here are the artefacts that were buried with him," Angeline said.

Among the scissors, coins and lances was a bronze disk about the size of a dinner plate. "I never heard that this was among his possessions," Jake said, gingerly fingering the disk with gloved hands.

"It didn't match with the barber-surgeon identity—so, no, it's not mentioned in the official story."

Jake's eyes dilated as he realized the disk was engraved. Beneath the dirt and grime was an emblem. Three moons.

***

"Do you remember the last thing you were doing, before you ended up in this time corridor?" Jake prodded Maia.

"Not really," she answered, sipping her tea across from him where they were breakfasting at the Red Lion pub. "But if I were to venture a guess I would say that I was boarding a bus."

Jake recalled what *he* was doing. He was dancing in the middle of Stonehenge. And yet when he had returned to the famous stone circle nothing had changed. He was not transported back to his own time. Diana Lune's book espoused theory after theory of teleportation with the use of stone circles. She believed they were portals to alternate times and yet there were no simple instructions on how they worked. He had to struggle hard to crush his cynicism. Nothing about his and Maia's situation could be easily explained. And yet it had happened. He was here in some version of the future and so was she.

He mined his brain for some clue. The events in the days just before he found himself wandering down the motorway were coming back to him. What was that seminar he had attended? There was something about a government experiment in teleportation. Subjects used in the project's experiments claimed that researchers had succeeded in harnessing 'radiant energy'. And what was 'radiant energy'? From what he gathered at the seminar, it was a universal time-and-space-bending force, which allowed for 'real time' teleportation as well as time travel. Was any of it true? There was only one way to establish the facts. And if it *were* true, this was how he hoped to find their way home.

If he remembered correctly the project was purported to be a joint technological venture by U.S. and U.K. governments. It was highly classified and never proven legitimate. And yet rumors had persisted over the decades that such a project had existed, that experimentation initially took place in the 1960s, and that activity was revived at the turn of the millennium. Rumors persisted that the experiments were so secretive that they had taken place in unexpected locales, the outskirts of cities like Seattle Washington and Cambridge in England. Since he worked at the University of Washington in Seattle the rumors had abounded. No one however had ever exposed the location or the veracity of the experiments. So, if he were some government minion in England where would he situate such a project so as to avoid exposure?

Along the Great Stone's Way was a patch of land—several acres in fact—owned by the Ministry of Defense, ostensibly used as a firing range for training soldiers. Well, that would be enough to deter visitors from meandering where they were unwanted (after all who wished to be the victim of a stray bullet?) and he knew just the piece of land that it might be.

"Have you heard of this project?" Jake questioned Maia.

"Yes. It is one of those conspiracy theories that the public so loves."

"But there might be some truth to it. After all, how did *we* get here? We are clearly in the wrong time plane."

"Well, it's worth a try," she said. "Let's just say the project is real and that they have some sort of teleportation device that can move us from one place to another, or even one time period to another, what are we going to tell them? That we'd like to buy a ticket home? Or worse, what if they are responsible for our being out of our time. Do you really think they will help us? What's to stop them from sending us somewhere else in their filthy experiments?"

"Well then, we won't ask," Jake said. "But we certainly

need to learn if there is any truth to the rumors. We need to rent a car." He slapped down his last few pounds to pay for their meal.

"A car?" Maia said. "Do you think I haven't tried to drive out of here?"

They went to a local library to see what they could discover on the Internet. Like all conspiracy theories everything they could find was simply that—a conspiracy theory. There was very little fact. Much of it was attributed to the research of the infamous engineer/physicist Nikolas Tesla. But what they read deemed him a madman or an unfulfilled genius that died before he could invent ray guns, brain readers and time machines. But was it really so crazy? The discovery of electricity, gravity and sound waves had enabled miracles like the light bulb, airplanes, televisions and computers. Maybe a time machine wasn't so farfetched.

However, one thing was consistent in every article they read—Nikolas Tesla was a futurist and his research was highly regarded no matter how crazy it may have seemed, and after his death the U.S. federal government had seized all of his research and stamped it classified. There was only one tiny mention of a British secret laboratory somewhere on a Military base. Where better than the MOD (Military of Defense) lands between Avebury and Stonehenge? Besides, they didn't have much of a choice. They were restricted to the landscape along the Great Stone's Way.

"I suppose it's worth a try," Maia said. "What have we got to lose? The worse thing that could happen is that we will be captured by the military and thrown into some kind of jail for trespassing."

Jake chuckled. Think what you like about British humor, the people themselves really did have an admirable bulldog disposition.

CHAPTER THIRTY-SEVEN

Halfway between Avebury and Stonehenge was Casterley Camp, high on Salisbury Plain. It took a while to realize what puzzled him about the landscape. It was as wild and empty as any unpopulated backwoods in southern England with a large burial mound in the background. Perfect high grazing country, there was not a single sheep—and for good reason. They were on the grounds of the MOD.

Old signage showed the scheduled days for firing practice, and urgently warned visitors to avoid the grounds on any of these days "lest they be struck by a 'projectile.'" Apparently, however, the military had ceased this practice in 2041 because the sign was old and rubbed and had a 'Closed' sign slapped overtop of it.

There were some old concrete structures that were clearly abandoned.

"What do you think?" Maia asked. "Should we see if anybody's home?"

"I'm pretty sure not," Jake replied. "But no harm in checking."

Chains and locks sealed all of the fences and doors. He went around to the back where they would be out of sight of any traffic or pedestrians, and saw that it was the same there. Most of the buildings were windowless, and those that had windows were boarded up. One of the windows had its boards swinging by two rusty nails and Jake shoved his face up against the grimy glass pane. Darkness grazed his sight, but he could glimpse the outlines of what looked to be desks and computers. He jerked sideways to locate Maia. She stood four paces away. "Step back," he said. "I'm going to see if we can't get in through here."

He twisted the board away, rusted nails and all. Then he pried the remaining boards off with the first one. The nails were so rusted, and the wood so badly decayed that it was hardly a problem. One more time he scanned the bleak surroundings to see if anyone was about. The road where the car was parked was empty, and so was the encompassing field. He smashed away the glass with a cobble he found on the ground. The window was small, but wide enough to squeeze through after he had chipped away the remaining sharp edges to allow him and Maia safe passage.

The room was dim and only the daylight from outside illuminated the interior. Jake approached one of the computers and switched it on. It failed to respond. Gauzy spider webs and dust coated everything. The inert equipment had been abandoned, unused in years.

"This can't be the place," Maia said.

Jake approached a file cabinet and yanked at a drawer fully expecting it to be locked. It wasn't. But neither was there much inside the drawer. A few paperclips and thumbtacks and yellowed file folder labels lay scattered at the bottom, but no files.

He opened the drawer beneath it and the one under that. They were all the same—empty of documents.

He slammed the last drawer shut and straightened his back.

"Look, Jake," Maia said. "See the label on this drawer?"

Jake turned his eyes downward and caught the words typed in upper case:

PROJECT PEGASUS

But the drawer was empty.

He glanced at the office door. It was ajar. He gestured to Maia to follow him. He went through the door into a corridor. On either side of the straight hallway were more doors, all closed. Daylight flowed in regular squares from intermittent skylights overhead. He tried the lever of one of the shut doors; it opened. Inside were more desks and file cabinets and computers covered in dust and cobwebs. A thin stream of light shot through a gap between two boards covering a window. It was not much illumination, but enough for him to make out the furnishings of the office. He was pretty certain these computers were off-limits too. He was correct. There was no electricity. That meant the elevator he had detected at the end of the corridor was useless.

There was a stairwell. It was unlikely the stairwell would be lit if nowhere else in the building was. He was wrong. A thin line of glass bricks running from floor to ceiling gloomily illumined the way with daylight, at each level.

They plunged three flights into a sub basement. The doors were unlocked. Jake led Maia out onto the lowest floor where they were met with complete blackness.

"Any ideas?" Jake whispered. He had no reason to whisper. Clearly this place was long abandoned. Not a single sign of life other than a few rodent droppings and spider webs.

A narrow strip of light suddenly shot forward. "I was saving this until we really needed it," Maia said. 'It' was a pencil-thin flashlight. Its beam was weak, but bright enough to reveal their surroundings.

Fewer doors appeared here, and many more long, unadorned, stretches of wall. Each door had a label. Storage units? At the far end was a set of double doors. A sign on the adjacent wall said:

JUMP ROOM

No windows.
"What's wrong, Jake?" Maia asked.
"I think we found it."
"The teleportation device?"
"The remains of it."

"Is the door locked?"

"Yes."

"Then what makes you think this is it?"

"The term 'Jump Room.' I've heard the term used before. I think it was in some lecture I attended. It's a moniker for 'Time Machine'."

She was silent. How could he blame her? He shook the door levers but they were stiff and cold. If this door was digital and there was no electricity to operate the locks, why was it stuck? He shook the levers again and this time the doors swung loose.

The doors were heavy, and when he pulled the right one wide it revealed an empty room. Too dark, and their tiny flashlight useless. But then the tentacle of light struck a sign over a door:

PLASMA CONFINEMENT CHAMBER

Now Jake had absolutely no doubt that they had found *Project Pegasus*, but it was of no earthly use to them. The facility was defunct.

The flashlight winked and the yellow light turned to amber. "We better get out of here. That flashlight's going to die any minute."

Maia agreed and they fumbled their way out of the scary lab and down the empty corridor to the stairwell.

Once outside again, they had a decision to make. They had no way of knowing if Project Pegasus had actually invented teleportation or if it was just a failed experiment. Whatever, it didn't matter. The lab had long since been deserted.

"So, now what?"

Jake was ready to pack it in and admit defeat. But what would be the point in that? Something had brought them to the year 2041 and trapped them in the Great Stone's Way. That same something should get them out. He racked his brains to recall everything he had ever read about hypothetical time travel.

A common denominator was radiant energy.

He led them back to the car where he retrieved a parcel from the trunk. He brought it with him to the front seat. Maia got in beside him. He was silent for a few seconds while she watched him. They had to locate a natural source of radiant energy and that meant following the druids' path.

He attempted to explain what he meant to do, how sacred sites were believed by the ancient druids to possess special powers. His fingers worked nervously in front of him and the sound of crackling paper resounded sharply. Maia looked over, frowned. He avoided her gaze and glanced down guiltily, forcing his fingers to cease their fidgeting. She narrowed her brows further, but when he failed to reveal the contents of the paper bag on his lap, she lifted her eyes to his face.

"You accept these primitive beliefs?" she asked him.

"At this point. I'll believe anything. Just tell me. How do the druids locate nature's energy sources?"

She replied unhesitatingly. "With dowsing rods."

"Do you know how to make one?"

"It doesn't require much skill. All we need is a Y-shaped branch."

Behind the abandoned military base some trees grew. Jake broke off a branch from a nearby hazelnut tree. It was about two inches in diameter and the bark flaked off at the broken end. "How will we know when we've located the energy source?"

"Oh, we'll know," Maia said. "Apparently, the signs are obvious."

Avebury circle with all of its exhibits and displays was swarming with tourists, and as a result, Jake was pretty certain that any radiant energy the stones might possess had long since departed.

They boarded their hired car and backtracked to the Sanctuary, the former site of a small stone circle called Overton Hill. The stones had long since vanished having been used as building material or simply removed by farmers. What remained was a ring of concrete markers. The site had not yet been developed for tourism and the reason was obvious. What could possibly be of interest here?

Jake had never used a dowsing rod before, but according to Maia it was simple. He had only to hold the rod by the top of the Y in mimicry of handles and allow the rod to do the rest. He wandered in and out, his footsteps creating a path of concentric circles. He wasn't sure what he was supposed to feel. Eventually he came to a spot where instinct caused him to pause. A creeping sensation. The sky chose this moment to break open and Jake dragged his hood over his head, a garment Maia had wisely advised him to buy. If they were going to be wandering up and down the Great Stones Way, they had better be prepared for inclement weather. Maia also wore a hooded rain jacket but it wasn't doing much to keep out the rain. Cold raindrops bit into the exposed skin of his hands and face as he followed the twitching rod.

Then the squall stopped as suddenly as it began. A rainbow arched over the sky, and as Jake traced its luminous curve into the distant horizon, it ended over the mound of Silbury Hill. He felt a strong stirring in the dowsing rod, and understood. It wanted him to follow the rainbow.

Jake urged Maia to return to the car with him, and they headed onto the A4 motorway that would take them to Silbury Hill.

They parked by the side of the road and got out. In the shadow of the enormous mound was the West Kennet Long Barrow, an ancient tomb built by the Neolithic inhabitants of Salisbury Plain. Jake stood in awe of the sacred landscape that spilled across his vision. Silbury Hill was the largest man-made mound in Europe and compared in height to the Egyptian pyramids. The adjacent barrow overlooked what was once an avenue of stones raised to form a winding one-and-a-half mile ritual link between the monuments of the Sanctuary on Overton Hill and Avebury.

Ten minutes passed before they reached the long barrow.

The elongated mound stretched east-west for a hundred meters. The earth used for its construction had been dug from two trenches on either side and was backfilled over the millennia by natural erosion. Jake had the dowsing rod in his possession and stood in the grass at the entrance to the tomb. The sky had cleared and all of the rainclouds had dissipated. A fine breeze washed the plain and the short hike up the sloping land had quickly dried their clothing and their hair. Oddly, no tourists were visible. The development of the Avebury theme park had not quite reached these remoter monuments. In fact, no one was here. Any stray wanderer had quickly departed to find shelter when the clouds broke.

Inside the chamber, the smell of wet stone invaded their senses, and they ventured well into the barrow for ten meters. Separate chambers appeared, two on either side of a narrow passageway. This yawned into a further chamber at the far end. The entrance was flanked by a semi circular forecourt, which framed the dark opening and was partially obscured by massive stones once used to seal the tomb.

Jake felt the hazel branch in his hands convulse. He almost lost it, and then gripped its Y branches firmly with fingers clenched. A deliberate pull drew him deeper into the chamber where he experienced a true surge of energy.

Maia turned to him. "Jake," she said. "Is something wrong? You look pale as a ghost."

Any attempt to answer her failed. No sound emerged from his mouth. Light-headed, breathless, his vision seemed to narrow into a kind of tunnel vision and his hearing muffled. And then he descended into a trance.

It was as though his soul had left his body and he was viewing it from somewhere above. His eyes darted to the daylight flooding the mouth of the barrow. His focus moved to trace the light and then—the view was outdoors. His vision was frozen, no longer a matter of will. Green velvety downs rolled out before him and he espied it all as though a bird in the sky. And then a double track of electric blue, like lightning bolts, shot across the landscape over the hillside to

nearby Avebury. The bolts ended in the stone circle at one of
the megaliths—one he recognized. It was called the Devil's
Chair, and actually possessed a ledge upon which one could
sit. The vision zoomed onto the stone to a circular
depression, about the size of a dinner plate, just behind the
seat. Inside the depression was a familiar symbol. Triple
moons.

How to access it with all of the tourists milling about?
Then it occurred to him that the hour must be late as the sun
was low in the sky. They had spent the entire day wandering
from sacred site to sacred site, and nightfall was nearing. By
the time he and Maia arrived at the stone the theme park
would be closed, all of the visitors would have gone home,
and they would have the place to themselves.

Where had the vision come from and why that megalith?

Every sign led in that direction.

The Devil's Chair stood at the southern entrance where
the West Kennet Avenue joined the Great Circle of Avebury.
Legend said that on the night of the full moon, when the
clock struck midnight, the stone crossed to the other side of
the road by some mysterious force. That would be quite a
feat. The stone must weigh nearly one hundred tons.

What if 'crossing the road' had a deeper meaning? What
if by 'crossing the road' people had meant that anyone seated
in the Devil's Chair (at the appropriate time) crossed into an
alternate universe?

Now, he was thinking exactly like Diana Lune.

CHAPTER THIRTY-EIGHT

They returned to the car. He asked to see Maia's copy of the book, *Sacred Stones of Raven*. There was a chapter on druids and the stones of power. Jake came to the section he was seeking, the part describing the Barber Stone. At the top of the page was the chapter heading: ***The Ghost of the Barber-Surgeon***.

"What has he to do with any of this?" she asked.

"I believe he was a druid, and not a barber or surgeon at all."

"But he carried the tools of the trade. And coins."

"Druids need money to live on too. They also need to cut things—like anybody else." He paused. "I think he may have found a way to use the stones' power."

She frowned. "But he was crushed, killed."

Jake shook his head. "No, not crushed, remember? His neck was not snapped. He wasn't dead when he went under the stone."

"But he *is* dead. The skeleton—it is evidence of his death."

Was it? Was it possible that he was just trapped, the way Chancellor was trapped, but in a different time plane? Jake paused. He did not attempt to convince Maia of this theory, although he had little doubt that she would not oppose it. Nothing that had happened to them made sense, so why shouldn't his postulation be true?

"Maia, I'm going to tell you something that sounds really bizarre, but I think I've seen this barber/surgeon/druid. I need to find him again."

"You've *seen* him? Where?"

Her voice was excited, amenable. He answered, "When I was trapped between Figheldean and Stonehenge I saw a man dressed like a 14th century barber. His clothing was unmistakably Medieval." He suddenly stopped speaking. It occurred to him that that wasn't the first time he had seen the strange man. The day he went to meet Maia Pickerton in Avebury he had seen the very same man in the very same clothes, carrying that same pouch-like satchel as he wandered along the downs into the fog. He had also seen him at Stonehenge. Yes! That was the movement he had caught beneath the lintel to his right. It was the figure of the same man—the barber-surgeon. Only now Jake was certain he was neither barber nor surgeon. He was a druid who knew how to teleport using the power of the standing stones.

"He moves between the two stone circles. In fact, he may travel between any number of stone circles. I don't know for certain."

Maia, to her credit, remained encouraging. After all, she was the one who had pointed out the time-travel theory in the book. Moreover, something had brought them here. And Jake was determined that that same something would take them back.

"He's our ticket home!"

Jake shrugged. "Well, if not our ticket, he will certainly be our guide. Either way it's time we found out. Let's go."

They re-entered the car and backtracked to Avebury.

When they pulled into the parking lot, it was almost empty. The sun sloped steeply and the theme park was closed.

Soon it would be sundown and the landscape would be cast in shade. Already long shadows from the standing stones stretched across the trampled grass.

Jake remained in the car thinking, Maia beside him quiet. He stared toward the West Kennet entrance in the direction of the South Circle. The Devil's Chair sat amidst the arc of stones near the roadway. He restarted the car and

drove a short distance, to park on the roadside just short of
the southwest curve of the South Circle. He exited the car
and reached into the trunk to remove the brown paper bag he
had stashed there. Maia allowed him this eccentricity, and
continued with silence even after he returned with the
mysterious bag.

Were his eyes playing tricks on him? He jerked a thumb
towards their destination. He was uncertain because of the
angle of the light and the deepening shadows, but it appeared
that someone was sitting there, probably some tourist waiting
for his friend to snap a final photograph before the sun
dropped below the horizon. But when Jake moved his head to
search, he saw no friend with a camera, only shadows. The
huge megaliths stood like giant soldiers waiting… The man
was alone.

Was someone seated there or not? Jake moved forward,
before he stopped in his tracks. Then as he took another step
forward, the man faded out of his vision and was gone.

"Did you see that? Somebody was sitting there, on the
ledge, on the seat of the Devil's Chair!"

Maia squinted, shook her head. "I don't see anyone."

"But I could swear I saw him. He was wearing the same
grubby outfit."

"Well, he's gone now."

Jake hurried up to the megalith. The seat was empty. But
behind it was a shallow hole. This was the indentation he had
seen in his vision inside the West Kennet Long Barrow. He
suddenly felt a tug on his sleeve.

"Look. You're right. There he is."

The light was falling fast and the shadows mingled. Jake
turned to fasten his gaze in the direction of Maia's pointing
finger and saw the shape of the barber-surgeon on the
opposite side of the street walking swiftly. A stiff wind rose
and whipped Jake's hair across his eyes momentarily
blinding him. He snapped his eyes wide and stared at the
fleeing figure. "What's he doing?" Maia whispered.

He wasn't doing anything. He slowed his pace, sent one

backward glance over his shoulder and walked into the megalith and vanished. It was as though he had simply passed through solid stone.

With cold fingers, Jake gripped the brown paper bag containing the precious contents and raced across the street. He stopped ten paces from the Barber Stone and choked on a breath. Maia came hurrying up behind him and she too, stopped, astonished.

"Where did he go?"

The last time they were here he had caught a glimpse of Chancellor's face in its surface. He studied the texture of the Barber Stone. Chancellor's image was no longer there. In its place was the spitting image of Diana Lune.

"Jake."

He turned to look at her.

"It's getting dark. Maybe we should go. We can finish this tomorrow."

The last piece of his memory had fallen into place; he had a feeling there would be no tomorrow if they didn't finish this tonight.

Across the street a dark, solid mass towered stark against the twilight sky. Opaque clouds hurried overhead, rimmed with pink.

But it wasn't the sunset that had caught his attention. His eyes narrowed as his vision landed on something past Maia's head. She turned to see what he was staring at. Across the broad peak of the Devil's Chair perched six black ravens. As Jake squinted at their ankles, he knew what he would see even before he saw it. He motioned for Maia to follow him as he rushed across the street.

"Where are we going?"

The ravens were his guides and they were leading him to his way back home. He stopped, loosened his hold on the brown paper bag and studied the circular indentation in the stone just above the ledge where one could sit. He glanced down at his precious parcel, and then, gently, removed it from its wrappings.

"How did you get that?"

"I borrowed it after you and Angeline left the storage vault."

"And you've been carrying it around with us all this time? Why?"

Jake fell silent. He lifted the bronze engraved disk and his eye landed on the symbol—three moons.

"I saw this here. In a vision." He fit the disk into the hollow behind the seat and it snapped into place. In the falling darkness the bronze glowed faintly as though a candle had been lit behind it. The outlines of the triple moons grew prominent.

He seized Maia by the hand. "Sit down!"

They both dropped down onto the thin ledge, she practically in his lap, and the Devil's Chair began to spin.

PART 3: THE SERPENT TEMPLE

CHAPTER THIRTY-NINE

Searchlights filled the open fields with light. The moonlit sky widened Superintendent Pettigrew's scope of vision, and cast deep specter-like shadows. Three human forms scurried out of his binocular's range.

What were people doing in the middle of the downs among the standing stones in the dark? The superintendent signaled the pilot to cut the lights as he adjusted his infrared glasses and set them to zoom. He tried to locate the interlopers again, but they were hidden. It was suspicious behavior if they had nothing to hide.

Although he was unable to pinpoint the intruders, strange grooves materialized on the ground. They seemed to form a pattern, a pattern he had seen before. He shifted his attention to a sheet of paper that he had taken from Chancellor's hotel room and compared the rough sketch with the scene below. They were identical to the minutest detail.

Toward the north, in the center of one of the inner rings were the remaining stones of the Cove. A circular depression appeared where the stones previously stood. This feature was barely visible but with the slanting light, shadows sharpened to delineate its shape. To the left and right more features, in the form of deep grooves, flowed from east to west.

Superintendent Pettigrew of New Scotland Yard now realized that the stone circle of Avebury was more than what it appeared when seen from above. The angle from which the helicopter approached made it strangely elongated, and Serena Dunnel's earlier words lingered in his mind. She accompanied him and his team, and now sat behind the pilot, silent, the thunder of the rotors drowning any chance at conversation.

What did the pseudo Interpol agent have to do with ancient folktales? And how did it have anything to do with the disappearances of the museum curator and the American archaeologist, as the fiancée seemed to think?

He bent his head to consult the diagrams. Then cast a glance at the briefcase by his feet. The raven mask was inside it. What it had to do with this serpent's temple mystified him. But instinct had warned him to bring it. As he observed the outline below he found himself asking: what possible connection could Haida culture have with a Neolithic temple? After apprehending this find he had done a quick search of Haida art and found a remarkable similarity. The two animal figures represented in the configuration of the stones were knotted together, as animal figures often were in Haida art. And then he recalled the Celtic folktale he had discovered among Chancellor's papers.

The myth was simple, moralistic. The Snake and the Raven. The sheet of paper rustled in his hands. The phrase *'returned from the dead'* was underlined in red ink. Why on earth was that important?

Pettigrew motioned the pilot to flood the field. He glanced down and saw three figures emerge from concealment to stand in the open, in full view of the helicopter's searchlights.

So, they had decided to cooperate. He gave the pilot the signal to descend.

After landing, he, three of his men, and Ms. Dunnel debarked in a clear space, in the heart of the freshly clipped meadow. The pilot was instructed to stand by. Pettigrew and his team approached the waiting figures where they stood in front of a massive stone.

"Where is he?" Serena demanded. "It's obvious you three know something."

What a motley crew, Pettigrew thought. He studied the trio. Who would have thought these three individuals had anything in common? The attractive dark-haired graduate student looked frightened. The perky redheaded cryptozoologist exhibited defiance. The ex Interpol agent wore a cool noncommittal expression, and yet he flattened a protective hand toward the lovely Angeline Lisbon who stood slightly behind him. The backgrounds of the women checked out, but the man's profile was a different matter.

"Jake," Serena repeated. "Where is he?"

"Now, Ms. Dunnel, please let the police handle this."

"Ask them where my fiancé is."

"In due time." Pettigrew turned to Chancellor. "Who are you? What is your purpose here? And don't give me that rubbish about being an Interpol agent. I know you were sacked."

"I'm the only one here who can stop a crime that's about to be committed."

Oh? Is that so. He kept his words short and clipped. "To what are you referring?"

"I'm talking about Lalonde. You want to find him, don't you?"

Pettigrew nodded. "I'm listening."

Angeline Lisbon and Drey McFee traded anxious glances. Just what was going on? There was only one way to deal with this type of situation. He said, "I'm going to have to take you three in for questioning."

"Take us where?" Chancellor demanded. "There is no police station for miles around. And we don't have time for that anyway if we're to save him."

"Then we will have to conduct the interrogation on site."

"And *I* said we have no time for that! Two lives are in danger."

Pettigrew's brows rose. The tenor of this man's voice was inappropriate. If anyone was about to give orders, it was not some quack paranormal specialist. "I am well aware of that. Perhaps you should tell me what you know."

All the while Chancellor was talking his eyes flickered back to the fiancée. The pretty grad student shot questioning glances his way but he seemed not to notice. "I think you three have much to explain." He glanced over at the Red Lion Pub. "We will have to appropriate a space at the inn."

The proprietor was more than gracious and gave them a private room at the back of the bar. There were four tables with chairs. Pettigrew sent his three men to the other tables to guard each individual to thwart any consultation with the others. He did not want them to synchronize their stories. It was clear that Chancellor was going to be the most difficult of the three. Which was why he would interview Angeline Lisbon first.

He waited while the others settled at their designated tables. The fiancée objected to being included in the interrogation. Something flashed at her throat as she thrust out her chest in defiance, opening the collar to her coat. He stared at the chunky gold necklace but it slipped under her lapel as she relaxed. No one else noticed as no one else was facing her. He motioned to his man to have her seated at the farthest table.

"Have a seat, miss," he said returning his attention to Angeline.

She sat down and nervously twisted a diamond ring on her finger.

His cellphone chimed and he glanced at the caller ID. *Shit.* Them again. He would have to take this. "Please wait here," he instructed her. Then he addressed his officers. "Keep everyone here. No loo or refreshment breaks until I return."

He left to retrace his steps outdoors, and into the privacy of the dark and the standing stones.

"Pettigrew," he said into the cellphone.

"Superintendent." The voice at the other end of the line was terse. "You are under orders to hand over the three suspects in your custody."

"I am conducting a missing person's case. These individuals are persons of interest, not suspects. As yet they have been connected to no crime. I think I am entitled to a little more information. Just what is it you think they're involved in?"

"I am not at liberty to elaborate. Suffice it to say they may have stumbled onto something that is top secret and classified. We need to learn just how much they know. In fact we have reason to suspect they are in possession of knowledge that is pertinent to the security of the western world."

You would think the motley group he had in custody at the Red Lion Inn possessed the secret to time travel. These government officials were always so over-the-top melodramatic. He snorted before he scoffed. "A woman disappeared. And now it looks like a man, an archaeologist by profession, who happens to be an American, has disappeared as well. My job is to find them and I need these witnesses to provide me with some leads. I will cooperate with the department as long as it doesn't interfere with my investigation." He paused. "You can have them when I have concluded my interrogations."

"We want these three in our custody," the voice snapped. "Either you bring them to us or we come for them." The line went dead.

Who the devil did that uppity bastard think he was? Pettigrew scowled. If they wanted these three so badly they could come for them themselves. Meanwhile he had a job to do.

He returned to the inn where his officers were waiting with the witnesses. He sat down at the table where Angeline Lisbon fidgeted with her diamond ring. He activated his notebook computer and reviewed her file.

"I see you're engaged," he said, blinking at the ring. "Who's the lucky fellow?"

She swiftly withdrew her hands and shoved them beneath the table out of view. "Jake Lalonde."

His eyes widened at that. "I thought Ms. Dunnel was his fiancée."

"She is."

Was she being facetious on purpose? "I don't understand." He frowned. "Are you telling me that Lalonde is a polygamist?"

"No."

"Then…?"

"You asked. I told you the truth."

Was the other one aware of this turn of events? He glanced at Serena Dunnel, who perched restlessly on a chair at the far wall. "Do you know where he is?"

"Yes. But you'll never believe me."

He flipped back and forth through the uploaded files on the three suspects (Lord, now *he* was calling them suspects). He scrolled through the notes on the young woman he was currently interrogating, and saw no reference to a fiancé or any relationship with the archaeologist mentioned at all. Was this a recent event? Was Jake Lalonde involved with two women? This was not the line of questioning he had intended to follow.

"Where is he?"

"Trapped between times, inside a portal."

Something triggered in his memory. An image flashed of a young woman standing in the center of Stonehenge defacing one of the sarsens. His head reared to study Angeline Lisbon's face. The swiftness with which she had responded to his question was disturbing. She had not paused to invent a lie or concoct a credible story, and now she rewarded his asperity with bluntness; all fear vanished for having spoken her mind.

No. This was not the same woman. This woman was slender and beautiful in an exotic and ethereal way—and much too young. The other woman had been bolder, larger-featured, more obviously of European descent, although also attractive—and several years older. But the comment that had triggered this memory was something he recalled from his rookie days. The deranged woman at Stonehenge had declared unmistakably: "*I can time travel.*"

Was she jerking him around or was she mentally

deficient? Did she know what it meant to perjure herself during a police investigation? Her gaze held steady and he looked down. The best thing he decided was to act nonchalant. He was used to dealing with lunatics... Had this young woman ever visited a psychiatrist? He scrolled through her file as she watched him with catlike toffee-green eyes... No one-on-one visit with a psychiatrist, but she had joined group therapy a month or so ago at Cambridge University's mental health department, to conquer a fear of the dark. Seeking treatment for a common fear did not make her a lunatic.

"Would you mind repeating what you just said?" he asked.

"I told you you wouldn't believe me."

"You know, Ms. Lisbon... I *do* believe you."

A few seconds of silence followed. He watched her, and when she declined to elaborate he dismissed her, and directed her to wait outside in the pub with the police officer he had assigned to her.

He gestured for the next interviewee to approach. This one was Drey McFee, the cryptozoologist.

"You're wasting your time interrogating us, superintendent."

"I think I will be the judge of that," Pettigrew answered.

"We think we know where Lalonde is. We just aren't sure how to get him back."

"Where is he?"

"Trapped somewhere between timelines."

So they had coordinated their stories before the helicopter had landed. They meant to repeat the identical tale. Pettigrew exhaled. What kind of an idiot did they take him for? "I see here in your records that you've been treated for delusions."

"You will also see in my records that I was eight years old."

"You thought your mother turned into a swan and flew away, thereby abandoning you."

Her shoulders lifted. "I was a child."

It was true that there were no recent records of her having been treated for further mental illness.

"All right, Ms. McFee. Go outside and wait with your friend. This nice police officer will accompany you."

It was time to get to the bottom of this. He called Chancellor over. The pseudo Interpol agent sat down in the seat just vacated by the cryptozoologist, and faced him, drumming his fingertips on the tabletop.

"I suppose you are also going to tell me that you know where Jake Lalonde is?"

"No. I don't know where he is. Not exactly."

"Exactly, what *do* you know?" This was the most bizarre case he had ever handled. All of the suspects or witnesses seemed to be insane. Or at least mentally unbalanced. His patience was wearing thin, and the sound of drumming fingertips was wearing it thinner.

"I can't tell you where he is," Chancellor said, slapping his hands down. "But maybe I can show you."

What did he have to lose? He had leafed through Chancellor's file and saw that he too had been institutionalized for mental illness. Strangely, he did not appear mentally unstable. In fact, of the three individuals interviewed, he seemed the *most* stable. "Fine," he said. Pettigrew got to his feet. "Show me."

He waved the remaining policeman to follow, and to keep an eye on Chancellor in case he tried any funny business. He told the others who were waiting in the main area of the pub to come also. The more the merrier.

The standing stones held stories from ages past. Once outside, Pettigrew felt again the mystery of the place. Some of the stories were not even particularly old. Like its more famous sister circle, Stonehenge, it had secrets.

The image of the deranged woman from his rookie days intruded once more into his thoughts. She had been scoring something onto one of the sarsens. But memory failed him as to what it was. He recalled his partner suggesting that it was some sort of Wiccan symbol. If he returned to Stonehenge would it still be there?

Preoccupied with his thoughts he wandered off-track. Chancellor cleared his throat to get Pettigrew's attention. He angled a thumb to his right and guided Pettigrew back to the Barber Stone.

This time it wasn't the curator's image that appeared on the rock. He remembered this megalith from his initial visit to Avebury when the missing curator's face had shown up on its surface.

He glared at Chancellor, incredulous—because, clear as day, the face of the American archaeologist gazed back from the stone. "Now I know you three are up to something. Who carved this image into the stone?"

"No one."

Chancellor fished a flashlight out of his pocket to prove there were no chisel marks or any sort of human tampering. "Step forward, and you'll see that the image vanishes."

It did. It *had*. This was one of those simulacra that Angeline Lisbon and Drey McFee had mentioned during their first meeting. If it was just a trick of light and shadow how could the image have transformed from a likeness of the curator to a likeness of the archaeologist without a person modifying it?

The night had turned cold, misty. A swirling fog drifted along the ground in lacy tendrils. It was the perfect setting for a ghost movie.

Thousands of ravens flocked in the sky, blacking out the last gleam of dusk like a massive dark cloud. The sound of their approach resembled that of a helicopter. They descended to huddle on the stones of Avebury. They rattled their wings, shivered. Then went quiet—watching—waiting.

What were they waiting for?

Pettigrew narrowed his eyes. "What's going on with the birds?"

Chancellor did likewise.

The women were silent.

"I don't know," Chancellor said.

But the ravens, like everyone assembled, felt the chill in the air, the anticipation of something about to happen.

CHAPTER FORTY

"All the earth is sacred. We love the land and revere the spirit of *Place*."

A voice was coming from the circle of stones, from beyond one of the megaliths. Which one? Superintendent Pettigrew spun around, as did everyone else in his party. The acoustics were stupendous and the oration reverberated from stone to stone.

"Kneel…all who are believers. Those who do not believe…will take their chances. These are the mysteries of the land…of the ancient sites. Here lie the powers of stone and mounded earth, of sacred well and healing spring. Channel thy energy from within the land and from the sun, moon and stars that we may attune ourselves to the rhythm of the Earth and the energy that flows like serpent-lines of force—from sacred site to sacred site!"

Superintendent Pettigrew signalled his men to find strategic locations in order to track down the orator. The officers in bulletproof vests and standard issue revolvers moved into position. "Do not engage," he said. "Do not shoot. I want to see who this person is."

He turned to take a head count: the grad student Angeline Lisbon, the cryptozoologist Drey Mcfee, and the morbid ex Interpol cop Thomas Chancellor.

Where was Serena Dunnel?

He ordered one of his men to return to the inn to search for her. "And while you're at it, I think I left a black briefcase in there. Bring it back with you when you find the woman."

"Your man won't find her in there," Chancellor said.

Pettigrew frowned. "How do you know? You know where she is? Tell me."

"That was *her* voice we heard."

"You're certain?"

"Pretty sure. And if Serena Dunnel is who I think she is, you won't find that briefcase either. At least you won't find what use to be inside it."

Pettigrew sent him an appraising, sidelong glance. "Tell me Mister Chancellor, how do you know so much? How can you know so much unless you are part of the plot?"

If they each believed this story about an individual who had the power to alter their reality and who could make them all believe that they were living a different reality, then what Angeline Lisbon had told him must be the truth—at least a version of it. She and Lalonde were engaged. And because Chancellor was obviously very protective of her it begged the question: Was this a lover's triangle, and had the man murdered his rival so that he could get the girl? He had suspected the ex Interpol agent from the beginning, but could find no motive. Was this it? But that did not explain the curator's disappearance. Unless she had witnessed something she wasn't supposed to see.

He decided to try out his hypothesis on the suspect, and got only an impatient snort for his efforts. Neither Chancellor nor Angeline took him seriously.

"That is a completely unsubstantiated insinuation. There is nothing between me and the girl—other than a mutual desire to rescue the man she loves."

A look of pitying scorn came from Angeline Lisbon. "You aren't listening to us. You saw the image of Jake in the stone. It means he is trying to find his way back to us."

"Branwen is calling him," Chancellor said. "You heard her voice. Tonight is the night of the summer solstice. We have to stop her."

Deep breaths, Prettigrew reminded himself, before he imploded. "You expect me to believe that this woman is actually a goddess? How gullible do you think I am?"

"I don't care what you think. It only matters what *she* thinks. And what she thinks… well, you don't know the half of it."

"Then try me."

Chancellor stared in the direction of the inner circles. "We don't have time."

Pettigrew exhaled, exasperated. "Where is he?"

"He is trapped inside the Great Stone's Way."

"Beg pardon?"

The Great Stone's Way was a walking path, a tourist trail administered by the National Trust between the two most famous stone circles in Britain. It consisted of open fields. How could Lalonde be trapped in it?

He was totally flabbergasted. Pettigrew's man returned a few minutes later, empty-handed. No Serena Dunnel and no briefcase with the mask.

Chancellor could not resist an 'I told you so.' "I informed you quite clearly that you wouldn't locate her—or the mask."

"How do you know about the mask?"

"You found my briefcase, didn't you? I put it there."

Pettigrew decided not to ask why. He would only get gibberish for an answer.

Chancellor's impatience was beginning to show. "You heard the voice," he said. "'*Here lie the powers of stone and mounded earth, of sacred well and healing spring. Channel thy energy from within the land and from the sun, moon and stars that we may attune ourselves to the rhythm of the Earth and the energy that flows like serpent-lines of force—from sacred site to sacred site!*'" He paused to allow the words to sink in. "Don't you get it? 'Sacred site to sacred site.' Avebury to Stonehenge. The path between those two sacred sites is called the Great Stone's Way. That is where Lalonde is trapped."

It was clear to him that his silence was causing Chancellor great aggravation. He maintained his silence until

Chancellor threw him a look of sheer desperation.

"She had to contain him until tonight. To make certain he didn't escape her again. She needed to keep him in her power until the night of the Summer Solstice... Don't you get it? We're wasting time. We have to get to him before she does."

Nothing the Interpol agent spoke made sense, and Pettigrew was leaning more and more towards his theory that all three of these people were delusional and seriously in need of psychiatric aid. "What does the solstice have to do with anything? And exactly what is it that you three believe is going to happen tonight?"

The Summer Solstice was the time of maximum light, Chancellor told him, when the countryside revelled in colorful, fragrant splendour. The year had expanded to its widest point and now the hours of light were as long as they would ever be. By tomorrow the sun's power would start to wane and the days grow shorter. The sun had touched the northernmost point along the horizon and was about to embark on the long, return journey south. It was on this night that Branwen and her mate performed the Handfast. But what she had in mind was much greater than simply a bonding. She meant to force Lalonde to undergo the 'change.' He would become The Raven, and after that there was no turning back.

Needless to say Pettigrew was incredulous, but when he saw the same expression of apprehension and desperation on all three of his suspects he had no choice but to accept that, no matter his cynicism, this was what *they*—Thomas Chancellor, Drey McFee, and Angeline Lisbon—believed.

Over the banks of the massive circular ditch points of light rose into the air. He was not given much time to muse on the subject. The lights flickered and Pettigrew soon acknowledged that these were firebrands, and that the conveyors of the dancing flames were headed to the clusters of stacked wood and kindling to set the bonfires aglow. He had only three officers with him, not enough to round up the growing numbers of individuals who were climbing onto the mounded ridge garlanded in flowers and now dancing and spinning towards the great fires.

Who had authorized this extravaganza? Ordinarily a massive amount of security would have been implemented for a festival involving fire displays. And then he realized it was likely no one had granted these villagers permission. What permission was required when the curator of the historic site was missing? Was this the motive for her abduction? Because he was fairly certain that this behaviour and the lighting of the multiple fires not only endangered the wildly cavorting young people and the prehistoric monuments, but a single stray spark was all that was needed to set the steeply sloped thatched roof cottages aflame, and burn the entire village to ash.

But he had to stop them. "Arrest those people!" he shouted to his men.

Not a single person took notice of the firearms. The officers had pulled their guns on the villagers, but failed to deter them from their dancing. They continued their lunatic festivities. He couldn't exactly have his men fire on these innocents. Many of them were adolescents, barely having reached puberty. He ordered his men to put away their weapons. They would have to find another way.

Meanwhile, young women and girls in flimsy muslin and gauzy white lace twirled around the policemen, arms filled to the brim with daisies and freesia, peonies and branches of fragrant apple blossoms. "Who is in charge of this festival!" Pettigrew shouted.

No one paid him any mind. The situation reminded him of that day in Stonehenge when the lunatic woman spun, arms akimbo, in the heart of Stonehenge, oblivious to the authorities trying to stop her. But this time there wasn't just a single woman. This time there were dozens of dancers, chanters and torchbearers. Most of the latter were young men in loosely belted tunics and leggings, whirling flaming firebrands over their heads to form sun-wheels. Other folk balanced blazing barrels stuffed with oil-soaked straw on top of poles and performed feats of daring by jumping through the tall flames of the bonfires. "Are you daft, people?" Pettigrew heard one of his men holler to one such daredevil. The fire-jumper's skimpy clothing had nearly caught fire, and the officer was pounding out his smoking sleeve with his jacket.

And then the commanding female voice was heard again. "Lay down your earthly weapons and join the festival. The moment has come!"

Across the road to the field containing the ominous standing stones of the South Circle, movement caught Pettigrew's eye. A forked bolt of light plunged from the sky and struck one of the megaliths, ricocheting blue lightning (if he wasn't mistaken or crazy) into their midst. The ravens that were hunched upon it scattered. And seated on the shallow ledge were a man and a woman.

Superintendent Pettigrew struggled out of his bedazzled inertia, and motioned his men to cross the road.

CHAPTER FORTY-ONE

The dancers had gone quiet at the startling appearance of the newcomers. Superintendent Pettigrew and his men assembled in front of the ill-starred megalith.

"Get off that rock!" Chancellor hollered before Pettigrew could bark the order. "No one else touch it."

The woman left her perch, followed by the tall, imposing youngish man. Angeline ran up to the woman and they clasped hands. The latter stared wildly about, but other than that she appeared more or less composed. Where had she been and how had she suddenly appeared on the seat of that stone?

"Mrs. Pickerton, I presume? Maia Pickerton? Curator of the Alexander Keiller Museum?"

"Yes, that's me," she answered.

He turned to the man who had followed. "And you are Dr. Jake Lalonde, our missing American archaeologist."

"I am."

It was taking all of Pettigrew's training to keep from exploding with questions. His eyes roamed past the newly returned victims to the megalith they called the Devil's Chair. "I am Superintendent Simon Pettigrew of New Scotland Yard." He paused, and then asked, "Where the blazes did you come from?"

"You're looking at it," the archaeologist said, pointing at the stone.

Was it possible that these two missing persons, newly found, were never missing in the first place? If that was the case: why? Why would this group of people: an ex Interpol

Agent, a Canadian graduate student, a cryptozoologist, a British museum curator and an American archaeologist wish to play such a ruse with him? And this Serena Dunnel—who had made herself scarce—was she really Jake Lalonde's fiancée or did the other girl, the raven-haired beauty actually hold his heart?

Pettigrew glanced away from the stone. He was no fool. He was beginning to suspect he was being played.

His eye followed the archaeologist's whose gaze now fell limpid at Angeline's heart-achingly tender smile. It was as though she symbolized water, the life-giving element without which no living being could exist. Her gaze mimicked his, but they did not reach out to each other physically. It was odd to say the least. Angeline clearly knew who the archaeologist was, but it was as though the archaeologist was smitten for the first time. Pettigrew quelled a smirk. Just what would the fiancée have to say about this?

"Lalonde," Chancellor said. "We have to get you out of here."

Pettigrew took a step forward. "No one is going anywhere until I get an explanation."

"Later. You have no idea what is about to happen if we don't remove him from the vicinity fast."

The superintendent stood his ground, confronting Chancellor. "Fine. Then tell me. I am tired of your mind games. *Tell* me. What is going to happen?"

The three police officers under Pettigrew drew their revolvers on Chancellor.

"Nothing those three can do anything about—with guns," Chancellor said.

"Arrest him," Pettigrew ordered.

An officer grabbed both of Chancellor's arms and cuffed him. "A fat lot of good that's going to do... Angeline, tell him what you told me."

No hesitation. "Branwen has come for Jake. That is what she calls herself now. She wants to transform him into the physical incarnation of her mate. The Raven."

Pettigrew's hands rose to the sides of his head in frustration. He was torn between mind-numbing frustration and hysterical laughter. His fellow officers chuckled, and he sent the excited graduate student a mocking smile.

She scowled. "I'm serious."

"She is," the cryptozoologist broke in. "I saw it myself. With my own eyes. I saw what was going to happen to him."

"Right, Dr. Lalonde is going to turn into a bird and fly away, just like your mother did."

The look on Angeline Lisbon's face branded him a monster for the cruel jibe. But it was only the truth. According to McFee's health records, she had been institutionalized for having such thoughts.

No one was laughing. Drey McFree was angrily silent. They were all in it together, including the newcomers. He no longer understood what purpose he served for this case. There were no missing persons for one thing, and no obvious crime committed. As far as he was concerned whatever the MOD wanted these people for they were welcome to them. See if *they* could get any sensible answers out of this lot.

This motley group owed him an explanation. And he'd be damned if he was going to leave the scene with so many loose ends.

How could it be that they were all caught up in the same crazy fantasy? He knew cults existed that brainwashed people and made them believe insane things. Was this possible? Had this happened to all of them? And if so, who was the brainwasher? The MOD? He gathered his composure. These people were serious. He turned to Maia Pickerton. "Do you also accept this story?"

From the look on her face he already knew her answer. This only made his suspicions grow. "No, don't answer that. Tell me instead, where have you been for the past seventy-two hours?"

"Oh, superintendent," she wailed. "I only wish that it *wasn't* true."

"Where did you meet up with *him*?"

The same helpless look came over her face that was on the other three accomplices as he shot a hard stare and an accusing finger at Jake Lalonde.

"We were trapped in a time corridor," the archaeologist said.

And I'm the Queen of England, Pettigrew muttered. Fuck. He was getting nowhere with this line of questioning. Where was the fiancée? The *original* fiancée—Serena Dunnel. She was the only sane one among the lot.

"We have to get out of here," Chancellor said. "We're wasting time."

A pale gleam could be seen on the horizon. They had been here all night. Soon the sun would rise. It would be the dawn of Summer Solstice. He knew that was what the dancing and fire throwing was about. The bonfires were already dwindling to coals; the fire-wheels hoisted by the young men were beginning to burn out. The revellers were unusually quiet. That suited him fine. He needed silence to think, to determine his next course of action.

Minutes ticked by and as they passed, things stirred. The villagers had begun to be active again. In the quiet of his peripheral vision, he saw the girls taking up their dancing and the men once again twirling firebrands. Music came from dark corners and the now engorged number of people swelled over the landscape. It seemed the entire village had come out to join in the festivities.

"Listen to me," Chancellor said. "You have to let us go. At the very least you have to let Lalonde go."

Pettigrew dragged his eyes toward the archaeologist. Jake Lalonde appeared to be in a trance, his eyes fixed on the dancers whose random dancing now formed a logical pattern.

A voice trilled out of the shadows: "*Raven...* Follow the pathway of the serpent to the temple of the sun. The circle is symbolic, the principle in the creative process. Once you have passed through the sun circle you will be recharged with new life!"

The words coming from out of the night had at first

seemed like gibberish, but now they were starting to make sense. As he watched, the young women and men began to walk—swaying from side to side as though in tune to some silent music—outside the pathway of the serpent, leaving the inner pathway free. It was the ritualistic route of the serpent worshipper towards new life.

"Hey, come back!" Chancellor yelled. But no amount of hollering seemed to pierce through to the mesmerized archaeologist. "Angeline, call him back!"

"Jake!" she shouted. "Please, don't leave me again."

The man's head twitched at the sound of her voice, but then he straightened and began to follow the dancers up the imaginary serpent's path.

"Blast," Chancellor cursed. "He doesn't remember you—after all my efforts to restore his memory. Trapping him in the Great Stone's Way must have eradicated his knowledge of you."

The dancers now linked hands and as they reached each dying bonfire, they passed over the orange coals without flinching or burning their feet.

Chancellor lunged after the archaeologist and Pettigrew signalled his men to follow. Even with his wrists handcuffed, Chancellor managed to tackle Lalonde with brute force; the man only threw him off with almost supernatural strength.

"Where is he going?" Angeline asked in a breathless whisper, as she caught up.

Chancellor crawled to his knees. "To *her*."

Their eyes followed as Lalonde traversed the path leading to the North Circle and the site of the Cove.

"He must not reach the Cove," Chancellor said. "If he does we will lose him."

"All right," Pettigrew snapped. "That's enough. Who's responsible for these theatrics? I want this show shut down. *Now!*"

"If only it was that easy."

"Mrs. Pickerton. Did you authorise this event?"

"No, Superintendent. The County Council furnished the

permits for the druids and Wicca to use the site for Summer Solstice."

"Is this normal?"

"No. I've never seen the festival conducted in this manner before. The bonfires are illegal inside the circle."

Pettigrew gave the order for his men to round up the villagers. "Don't use any rough stuff. Just send them home." But the villagers refused to go home. They refused to speak to the officers and acted as though they weren't even there. When one of the policemen seized a young man by the arm, the boy simply sat down cross-legged on the ground.

"And what the blazes are you three up to?" Pettigrew demanded as Chancellor, and his young female conspirators joined heads in rapid whispering.

Chancellor looked up. "You can't stop this by any physical means. We are going to have to perform a banishing ritual."

What was wrong with these people? Did they have absolutely no regard for authority? And then Pettigrew realized he was not dealing with ordinary people. Something was terribly wrong with all five of them, or else it was he who was going completely bonkers.

Superintendent Pettigrew snorted. He very seldom snorted, but then he very seldom felt such complete contempt for his fellow man. He ordered his officers to arrest Jake Lalonde. He had no idea what was going on with the man, but at the very least he could charge him with assault. He had practically thrown Thomas Chancellor across the field. He would take the rest of the witnesses down to London for questioning in the morning. They were creating a disturbance. They were all creating a head-pounding disturbance.

He heard a thud and a groan, as the archaeologist cast the police officers aside. He was fixated with his trek toward the Cove. One of the policemen raised his standard issue revolver. "No," Pettigrew shouted. "Stand down." It would not do to shoot a tourist.

"Lalonde!" he bellowed.

"It won't do any good," Chancellor said. "There is only one way to save him. We must perform a banishing ritual."

Hands tossed to the wind, Pettigrew surrendered. "All right. I give up. How?"

"We need something to represent an altar. We need a ritual robe, and we need a dagger."

"Where the hell are we going to get a dagger?"

"The museum has one," Maia said.

CHAPTER FORTY-TWO

The Greater Banishing Ritual of the Three Moons was ceremonial magic. The wide-eyed, incredulous superintendent of New Scotland Yard struggled to keep his jaw from dropping. At this point he was out of options. The Ministry of Defense was sending someone to fetch these lunatics, and his job for the time being was to keep them from running away. It seemed, however, that they had no intention of escaping. All of their efforts were focused on breaking whatever hypnotic trance had captured Jake Lalonde.

Pettigrew ordered the removal of Chancellor's handcuffs.

Maia Pickerton and one of the officers returned to the museum to dig up the dagger. Chancellor wildly searched the grounds for something to represent as an altar. Pettigrew had no idea what these people intended to do. For some reason the ex Interpol agent chose the megalith called the Devil's Chair. When the curator returned with the stone dagger, and a garment of doeskin Pettigrew finally acknowledged that these people were serious. They meant to perform some sort of ritual.

Angeline donned the white doeskin overtop her own clothes. She was given the dagger, which he recognized was made of razor sharp flint. The blade was so fine it sounded like glass when she temporarily laid it down on the ledge of the megalith.

The four of them, with the dark-haired one standing on the altar began the ritual, she now holding the dagger to her breast. Chancellor in the center of the remaining trio and Maia Pickerton to his left and Drey McFee to the right of him, simultaneously began tracing in the air what looked to be the symbol of the Triple Moon. Chancellor formed the full moon circle repeatedly with his arms, while the two women on either side of him traced the opposing crescent moons in slow repetitions, the one with her right hand, the other with her left. The purpose was to banish any chaotic and impure elements in the Great Stone Circle by invoking the spiritual forces. They called upon the earth's elements: fire, water, earth and air. Then the fertility goddesses of the West and East: Astarte, Asherah, Damara, Arianrhaod, Ceridwen, Rhiannon, and finally Branwen, the Blessed Raven and goddess of love.

The chants were repeated over and over, but Lalonde ignored the summons to the goddesses. What did they expect?

Astarte, Asherah, Damara, Arianrhaod, Ceridwen, Rhiannon. Branwen, the Blessed Raven and goddess of love.

"Chancellor," Angeline cried out. "It's not working. We're going to lose him!" Already Lalonde was near the Cove.

Where was this goddess person? Pettigrew wanted to get a solid look, and then arrest her for disturbing the peace. As far as he could see there was no one standing amongst the markers in the Cove. A heavy mist rose from the darkness and obscured the firebrands that had been relit. The bonfires were now glowing in startling orange and black embers.

Suddenly he saw a figure in the rising fog—a lovely feminine figure. She seemed to be dressed in white, but what sort of material her garments were made of he could not tell. Pettigrew left the group at the Devil's Chair to their voodoo, and started toward the North Circle.

Sirens screamed in the distance. Truthfully, had the MOD deemed that necessary? He wanted to get to the bottom of this before they arrived. He broke into a run and crossed the field toward the ethereal figure waiting in the Cove. He could see the strong, masculine form of Jake Lalonde headed towards her.

"Angeline!" he heard Chancellor shout, his body shrouded in fog. "You're the only one who can save him."

***

What was she supposed to do? All she knew was that he was her life. He was the voice that had accompanied her in this fog of a world that was only now becoming clear.

"Jake!" She stepped off the altar, the seat of the Devil's Chair and broke through the human fence of her friends. "Jake, stop. Please stop!"

She ran towards the North Circle in the wake of the superintendent. Behind her she could hear the multiple footfalls of Chancellor, Maia and Drey. No amount of magic could help them now. The only magic that would work was the magic of her heart.

Jake. I love you.

The words were spoken for only him to hear. And he heard them. She saw him pause. Turn.

The white figure in the cove froze. A deep, feminine voice came from out of the mist: "*Raven*...become your true self."

No. NO! Stay with me.
I've worked too hard to find you.
Please don't leave me.

"Manifest yourself to me, to the world. Embrace your destiny."

Angeline was fed up with this crazy person who was trying to steal Jake from her. What exactly was she? The enemy. Goddess, lunatic, witch. Whatever she was, whatever power she possessed, Angeline needed to expose her to the world, and in exposing her, diminish her strength.

All at once she found her fear evaporating. Her heartbeats began to slow. Her pulse gentled and her breathing came more easily. She walked up to Jake and took his hand. She jerked it to her breast and sent her eyes to capture his. He responded, to her relief, and sudden recognition burned in his gaze.

Angeline

He had spoken her name. And in a manner that only she could hear. His face came down on hers and their lips touched. That touch held the magic and the wonder of the first time. Nothing in her life had ever felt more real than this.

The whine of the wind. The warning *quork* of a solitary raven. The sudden movement in the Cove. She was uncertain which of these had alerted her. But they raised their eyes from each other as one, breaking the kiss, and turned to face the enemy. Together.

Behind them sirens squealed to a halt. An ambulance and a black SUV parked by the side of the road.

***

Superintendent Pettigrew ordered his men to seize the woman in white standing in the Cove. "Detain her for questioning."

He searched around to see if anyone had located Serena Dunnel but in the lifting fog it was unclear. "You three," he called to Chancellor and the two women accompanying him "don't move. There are some people here to see you."

His eyes scanned the night for the two young lovers. They stood in the heart of the field surrounded by the ancient megaliths, the moon whitewashing the rock to a ghostly pallor. They were in each other's arms like woodland sprites in the mists of time, with no plan to make a break for it anytime soon.

They had eyes only for each other, and no one else.

Tomorrow, he fully intended to question each and every one of them. Right now all he wanted was to get the MOD off his back. He ordered his officers to herd the villagers back to their homes, and then went to meet the approaching black-suited men.

* * *

The dawn rose bright the morning after. Jake and Angeline had spent the entire night talking. All of the others had gone to their rooms to catch what sleep they could. Jake felt raw, his nerves seared, but his mind clearer than he had ever known it to be. He could not stop watching her, her incredible beauty making a puddle of his heart. She was asleep right on the sofa, the sun streaming in through the partially opened drapes. He had no explanation for what had happened last night; no reason for why he felt the way he did. But now that they were together, he had no intention of spending one more second away from her.

He heard footsteps behind him where he sat in a Victorian style clawfoot chair. It was Chancellor with Superintendent Pettigrew and a man in a dark suit.

"Good morning, Dr. Lalonde," Pettigrew said.

Jake nodded. The presence of the dark-suited man made him nervous. Last night the agent from the Ministry of Defense had interrogated each of them. Jake and Maia had silently agreed through mutual looks to keep silent on their experiences trapped in the Great Stones Way.

Honestly, who would believe them? Other than Chancellor, Angeline and Drey—each of who had also experienced a similar teleportation event—not a single authority would have hesitated to provide them with a one-way ticket to the loony bin.

The person who puzzled him the most, however, was the superintendent from New Scotland Yard. Angeline had told him that Pettigrew was aware of Chancellor's theory concerning the standing stones. He just didn't believe him. To keep from being detained for psychiatric tests, Chancellor had suggested they go along with Pettigrew's theory. Whoever that woman in white was last night, goddess, lunatic, or witch, Pettigrew was certain she was also some kind of cult leader with expertise in manipulating gullible minds. She was responsible for hypnotizing them, and causing them to believe that they had been sucked into an alternate time.

Pettigrew wanted them to admit to this explanation so that he could chock it all up to a collective hallucination. If nothing else, admitting to being suckered was the quickest way to their freedom. So Jake and Maia had joined Chancellor, Angeline and Drey in reiterating the same story—that everything they had experienced was a figment of their imaginations.

That explanation was as good as any. And the truth was every one of them understood exactly what had happened. No amount of talking would convince a non-believer. Jake would much rather spend the rest of his life being thought of as a sucker than a mental patient.

A team was out searching for both Serena and Diana Lune. Evidence suggested that the women were one and the same. And that she was one of the most mysterious and notorious cult leaders in history.

But the man in the suit was not convinced. He refused to leave. He still wanted to interrogate Jake and Maia one more time. Ha, Jake thought. If they only knew the truth.

"You mean you can't remember a single thing that happened to you? You were missing for days," the man in the suit persisted.

"I'm sorry, I can't," Jake replied.

"I've just been to see Maia Pickerton and she claims the same thing. She was missing first. She was missing longer than you were. The superintendent says that you two just suddenly appeared out of the darkness, seated on that rock they call the Devil's Chair."

"So, I've been told," Jake said equably.

By this time the voices had awakened Angeline, and she rose from her reclining position on the sofa. Chancellor went to fetch a glass of water for her, as she wiped a lock of black hair from her sleepy gold-green eyes. "Good morning, beautiful," Jake said.

He spurned whoever heard him. In fact, he was hoping they would feel uncomfortable and leave. No such luck. Chancellor returned with the water and Angeline took a sip. "What's going on?" she asked.

"Miss Lisbon, I'm from the MOD. You may remember me from last night. I'd like to confirm what you told me."

"She just woke up," Jake objected. "She deserves a little consideration."

"I apologize, Miss Lisbon, but this can't wait."

Why couldn't it wait? Jake wondered. What the devil were these people up to? Hadn't the lot of them just been through hell and back?

"Before you answer," the MOD agent said. "I want you to know that Superintendent Pettigrew has a written statement from you regarding last night's events."

"What did I say?" Angeline asked, questing eyes searching the superintendent's.

"Don't answer that," the agent said to Pettigrew. "I want you, Miss Lisbon, to answer the question. Where did you tell New Scotland Yard that Dr. Lalonde and Mrs. Pickerton disappeared to...the truth now, we have your statement."

"We were hypnotised," she said. "At that seminar about poltergeists and time-travelling ghosts."

The agent grunted, exasperated. "By whom."

"By Diana Lune. Find her, and you'll find the truth."

"And you're sticking to that story as well?" The MOD agent had turned to Jake, who nodded. "And you, Mr. Chancellor?" He nodded as well. "I see." His narrow eyes bounced off each of them in turn. "Have any of you ever heard of Project Pegasus?"

Jake looked at Angeline. Had she recognised those words? Her face was as inscrutable as his own.

The agent made a slight clucking sound. He could not hold them any longer. Collective amnesia and forced hypnotism made them the victims not the perpetrators. They had committed no crime.

"If you change your mind," he said, "here's my card. Contact me to report any further peculiar incidences of 'faces' in the standing stones."

"Of course," Angeline said.

Jake was silent. He glanced down at the card and noted there were two cards: one with the contact information of the British Ministry of Defense and another with that of an American organization called DARPA. On this card was another word that caught his eye:

Ravenfall

"Once you return home, you will be out of our jurisdiction. If you recall anything or just wish to speak to anyone concerning your recent experiences, call that number in the U.S. and they will liaise with us."

Jake had no intention of contacting any of these people, ever. But he nodded graciously just to get rid of him.

When the MOD man departed, the superintendent observed him suspiciously. "I could charge you with assaulting my men last night and throw you into the clink, but I suspect it will do no good. Either you really remember nothing or you and your colleagues are the biggest practical jokers I've ever met."

Jake continued with his silence. What point was there to the truth? The policeman had already asserted his ridicule of the truth.

"You saw what you saw," Angeline reminded Pettigrew. "You will have to decide if you believe what you saw."

Pettigrew snorted. He rose and said his goodbyes and reiterated that he'd be in touch if ever he caught up with

Diana Lune. After he was gone and they were finally alone, Jake asked Angeline just exactly what had happened to her. She told him a frightening and totally incredulous story of being transported into the future with Drey McFee, a cryptozoologist. But how they returned was even more frightening and doubly incredulous.

"It's interesting," Chancellor said. "But I suspect the British Ministry of Defense and America's Defence Advanced Research Projects Agency are in cahoots."

Jake shrugged. The main thing was, it was over. "Do you mind, Chancellor," he said. "I'd like a little alone time with my lady."

The other grinned. "Not at all. I'd better go upstairs and see if McFee's awake yet."

Jake and Angeline exited the Red Lion Inn through the main doors. They walked out into the sunshine and stared across the street at the massive ring of standing stones. The air was fresh and clean, the wind mild and buffeting, the sky a watercolor blue. The smell of guano was gone and most of it had been washed away by rain, and new grass was springing up in clumps everywhere.

"Paper, sir?" the bellhop returning to the inn said as he passed by with a bundle under his arm.

Jake dug into his pocket for some coinage to pay for the morning rag.

"It's on the house." He smiled and tossed a rolled up newspaper at Jake who caught it with his left hand.

"What did we miss?" Angeline asked.

He squinted at the front page. The ravens had vanished from the Great Circle at Avebury. In the capital a story accompanied by a photograph reported that George and Grog and the other banded birds had returned to roost at the Tower of London, clipped wings and all. Superintendent Pettigrew had sent out an All Ports Warning on the suspect Diana Lune. The mystery of the missing local curator had been solved. The lost American archaeologist was also solved.

It was suspected that Diana Lune was a mental health

patient, and possible cult leader, who was on the loose and hypnotising people into believing they could time-travel. New Scotland Yard had interviewed five 'persons of interest' but decided not to recommend commitment of any of them to a mental health facility. They were all foreigners, except for Maia Pickerton, who was free to return to her post as curator of the Alexander Keiller Museum.

Jake turned the page and saw an announcement that Drey McFee an upcoming graduate of the Institute for Metaphysical and Humanistic Studies in Cambridge and ex Interpol agent Thomas Chancellor planned to joined forces as cryptid hunters on their return to Canada.

"Well, that got into the news pretty quick," he said.

"What do you mean? Drey and Chancellor's business venture?"

"I do, indeed."

He tucked the paper under one arm and took Angeline's hand. The engagement ring on her finger flashed in the bright morning sunshine.

Together they faced the wide-open vista, the wind whining in their ears and beating on their skin. It felt great to be alive.

The swelling hill and plain of the high chalk downs sloped west, the great earthwork and the interlocking stone circles shaping the landscape. The arc of the outer pillars hemmed in part of the village, and the houses and roads obscured its original plan. At the town core a winding lane led from the car park to the charming thatch-roofed façade of the Red Lion Inn. As Jake's eyes revolved to take in the vastness of this ancient and mysterious countryside, he followed the enormous moat with the bank at its rim. Here was the greatest ring of standing stones known to humankind—originally one hundred in total. That was why Diana Lune had chosen this ancient temple.

And there—there was the Cove. In this spot he had almost given his life to the goddess.

He inhaled the view and as he met the eyes of the

woman he loved, fear gave way to relief and then to excitement. It rippled throughout his body.

"Look," he said. "The Barber Stone."

They approached and stood studying it. No face materialised on the surface. Not even that of a raven.

"I feel impossibly light," Angeline said.

Jake was struggling to find the words to describe the same thing.

"Let's get married. Right here in Avebury. It just seems right."

Jake grinned. Her smile literally lit up his world. "Yes." A fitting end to what could have been a nightmare. "Let's do that."

To the north was the first of four entrances to the Great Circle. From the south and west, avenues of megaliths coursed for miles. He could envision himself and his white-garlanded bride approaching by one of these avenues on horseback to the flowered wedding arbor, amidst the stones. But wait. Wasn't one of these the entrance to the Great Stones Way?

Jake tugged Angeline's curled fingers to his lips. Kissed her ring. So what? They were finally getting married. He would put the Great Stones Way behind him.

Acknowledgements

The Raven Chronicles has evolved into a mega novel over the years, thanks to the fascinating myths and legends of Native American cultures. It is these traditional stories and their mythological figures from which my stories spring. I wish to thank Peter Goodchild for writing the comprehensive book *Raven Tales* from which I derived the idea of a global migration of the Raven icon. Thanks go to Karina Casines of Archaeology Magazine, who has provided me many opportunities to publicize my books including the Summer Reading List and the Holiday Gift Guide and have helped to build my audience. Thank you also to John Cullen at Far Sector SFFH and Clocktower Books, my first publisher, for publishing the short story which gave rise to an award winning short story and the Twilight Glyph Trilogy. To the followers of Jake Lalonde's quest and the diverse reviewers of the series, a huge thanks for giving me a reason to keep going. To my husband, my first reader and fan, thank you for sticking by my side through thick and thicker.

About the Author:

Deborah Cannon was born in Vancouver, British Columbia. She is a winner of The Canadian Tales of the Fantastic annual short story contest for her entry *Twilight Glyph* (2013), and is the author of novels and short stories, most of which were inspired by myths and legends. She is best known for The Raven Chronicles, a series of paranormal archaeological thrillers, which to date include *Raven Dawn* (prequel), *The Raven's Pool*, *White Raven*, *Ravenstone*, and *Raven's Blood*. Her best-known work of fantasy is *The Pirate Empress*, a Chinese historical epic.

When not writing fantasies and thrillers, she is a contributor to the popular franchise, *Chicken Soup for the Soul*. She also writes Christmas romances for pet lovers under the pen name of Daphne Lynn Stewart. She lives in Hamilton, Ontario with her archaeologist husband.

THE RAVEN CHRONICLES:

Raven Dawn (Prequel) Archaeologist Jake Lalonde gets the first clues to his cryptic Haida heritage when the abduction of children from a small Vancouver Island town brings the myth of an ancient cannibal demon to life. So begins Jake's spirit quest as he sets out to search for the origins of his totem crest.

The Raven's Pool (Book 1)
The serenity of the San Juan Islands is disrupted when a developer threatens to build a theme park atop a sacred Native burial, turning archaeologists Jake Lalonde and Angeline Lisbon into the targets of a 10,000-year-old feud between a Haida shaman and his chief.

White Raven (Book 2)
When Jake Lalonde and Angeline Lisbon visit a remote logging community of the Queen Charlotte islands, the alleged home of his birth parents, they find people mysteriously missing, wildlife brutally butchered, and a village with something to hide.

Ravenstone (Book 3)
On the island Kingdom of Tonga, a carving of a Raven replicated on Canada's west coast leads Jake Lalonde and Angeline Lisbon to his daughter, a pawn used to exact revenge for an insult committed by his ancestors.

Raven's Blood (Book 4)
When a colleague of Jake Lalonde and Angeline Lisbon is found dead amidst ghostly sightings and murderous cult activity, the clues lead to a Raven-worshipping goddess cult in the subterranean Mithraic temples of Rome.

Follow the adventures of Drey McFee in the ebook series **CLOSE ENCOUNTERS OF THE CRYPTID KIND** (available on Amazon)

Up Next:

New Series: Twilight Glyph Novellas

Inspired by ancient Native rock art. The Twilight Glyphs are prehistoric fables, an imaginary history to The Raven Chronicles. The adventures of archaeologist Jake Lalonde's Haida ancestors gave rise to the 10,000-year-old shaman of the Raven myths, Jake's forefather. In the title story *Twilight Glyph*, a Haida princess falls in love with a skin-changing Bear man whose people want her dead.

Ravenfall (Book 6)

The final installment of The Raven Chronicles. Archaeologist Jake Lalonde wakes up one morning to find his world completely changed. The U.S. government is blocking his research. They suspect he is capable of telepathy and teleportation. A militant First Nations minister believes he is the conduit to the original Raven. And a 10,000 year-old shaman is reaching out to him in his dreams. All Jake knows is that he is cursed with inherited memories. They allow him to commune with his ancestors. He has two choices. To serve DARPA or to embrace his Native destiny.

The Raven Chronicles series is available at Amazon and other locations in print and ebook versions. Also ask for the book titles at your local library

Manufactured by Amazon.ca
Bolton, ON

15806668R00160